DANGEROUS

BOOK FOUR

Beauty

O'CONNOR
BROTHERS

RHONDA BREWER

Dedication

This book is dedicated to my wonderful aunt, Gertrude Holwell. You are more to me than merely my aunt. You are one of my best friends and a big sister. Thanks for always having my back and encouraging me in my writing. I love you with all my heart

Acknowledgements

So many people made publishing this book possible. Thank you to Author Candace Osmond and her husband Cory Majeau of Majeau Designs, for the incredible cover design. Huge thanks to the amazing FuriousFotog himself, Golden Czermak and model Caylan Hughes.

I want to thank the many authors who helped me along the way with advice, experiences and the pep talks to make this possible. Not only with this book but the others as well. Abbie Zanders , Susan Stoker, Kathleen Brooks, Rhonda Carver, Cynthia D'Alba, Amabel Daniels, Victoria Barbour, Kate Robbins, Eve Jagger, and Lynn Raye Harris. They are amazing authors and fabulous ladies.

Special thanks to the best P.A.s anyone could have Nicole Kuhn and Karie Deegan. To my beta readers, thank you for your time and input. Especially, Michelle Eriksen, Jackie Dawe, Nancy Arnold-Holloway and Mayas Sanders. You are great friends and give incredible advice.

As always to my family, you are the rock that keeps me grounded. You helped me to follow my dream. I love you all.

Chapter 1

Emily Bradshaw pulled her knees up to her chest as she settled on the window seat. Staring through her childhood bedroom window not really focusing on anything in particular. The room was one of the highest points of the large mansion. On a clear day, the entire town could be seen, but Emily hadn't been in SummerBrook for months and didn't miss it one bit.

The town was a place full of people who snubbed their noses at anyone who didn't have money. Of course, that wasn't Emily's issue. The Bradshaw's were very wealthy. The problem was the spoiled brats who turned their noses up at the career she'd chosen for herself. Emily didn't care. There was only one reason she was back in SummerBrook.

She rested her chin on top of her knees and wrapped her arms around her legs. It was the first time in her twenty-nine years, she'd seen police cruisers parked all over the Bradshaw Estate. She'd counted at least six as well as some vehicles that were most definitely unmarked cars. The reason they were there brought a lump to her throat, and she had to blink back the tears before they fell.

Emily turned her gaze away from the scene outside and scanned the room. It had been left behind when she was twenty, but it didn't look any different. *The Purple Princess Room* was what her father named it. Her sister had a similar room on the opposite side of the large house known as *The Pink Princess Room*. There was a Yellow one too, but that had been sealed off a long time ago, and it was something she didn't want to think about considering what had brought her back.

The room was every little girl's dream. In the center of the room was a white canopy bed draped with a sheer purple mesh. A white vanity with purple trim sat in the brightest part of the room still had pictures stuck around the edge of the mirror. Next to the bed was a matching nightstand and the dresser on the far side of the room. The dark purple comforter and throw pillows with crowns on them brought the whole room together.

As beautiful as it was, she had to leave it behind. Not that she wanted to go, but a huge argument with her father had her packing bags and moving into a small basement apartment just outside St. John's. If Emily was being honest with herself, he had every reason to be so furious with her. She'd turned down a full scholarship to Dalhousie University without even discussing it with him or anyone.

2

Her father's dream was for her to become a doctor, not hers. So when she put her foot down and told him, she'd follow her own dreams and open a beauty salon, he was more than a little pissed. It was actually where she got the name of the salon because he kept telling her not to be 'snippy.' Hence the name, *Snippy Gals*.

"Are you okay, Em?" the deep timbre of her brother's voice brought her back to the current nightmare. Edward was eleven months younger than her and had been one of the good children. He went to law school like Nelson Bradshaw had wanted.

"I don't know how I feel. Numb mostly." Emily dropped her feet to the floor.

"I know the feeling." He joined her on the window seat, and she rested her head on his shoulder.

"It's not like her to disappear." Emily choked out.

"I heard one of the cops tell dad her phone was off. No way to track it." Edward wrapped his arm around her and gave her a little squeeze.

"She's been gone for almost thirty-six hours." Emily blinked back the tears she tried to hold in for the last day and a half.

"Any room there for me?" Elaine's soft voice came from the doorway.

"Always room for my baby sis." Emily forced a smile as she scooted over for Elaine to join them.

3

Elaine was a little less than three years younger than Emily and just finished a business degree. Now she was working with their father. According to her dad, Elaine was going places, but Emily knew it wasn't what her sister wanted to do. Elaine loved to design clothes, and she was good at it, but dear old dad convinced her that it wasn't a viable career.

For a few minutes, Emily sat with her siblings as they silently comforted each other. The only sound was the muffled voices from downstairs. The house had been invaded by police since Lynn Ann Bradshaw disappeared.

"Do you think she's okay?" Elaine sighed.

"Mom's a tough cookie." Edward always a cup half full kind of guy.

"But…" Elaine began to sob.

"We've got to think positive, El." Emily hated to see her sister so shaken, so she followed her brother's lead. "Mom's gonna be okay." Emily reached across Edward and grabbed Elaine's hand. "You'll see. Mom will be home soon."

Elaine nodded, but from the tears running down her cheeks, Her sister seemed to have trouble believing their mother would ever come back. Emily had to force herself from those thoughts more often than she liked.

"Excuse me." Emily glanced towards the bedroom door. A very dreamy police officer filled the doorway.

4

"Did you find her?" Elaine jumped to her feet.

"There's been a new development." Emily glanced at the officer's name tag. O'Connor was printed in thick white letters. Apparently, the police from Hopedale had to be all related because she'd seen at least three with the same name. "Your father asked me to come get you."

"Thanks, Constable O'Connor," Emily didn't know how she actually got the words out.

"It's probably a good idea to call us by our first names. There's three of us O'Connors here now, but counting Uncle Kurt, there are five. You can call me Nick."

"We appreciate everything you guys have done for us." Edward shook Nick's hand.

"No need to thank us. It's our job to help people." Nick turned and disappeared from the doorway.

Emily descended the stairs behind her brother. With each step, her stomach seemed to flip flop more. There was just one thought swirling around her brain. What was this new development? Was it good news or bad?

"I'm telling you I don't know what the hell Lynn would be doing in Gander."

Emily gasped when her father's voice echoed through the living room. When he was stressed his voice could probably be heard from one end of SummerBrook to the other.

"Does she know anyone who lives in that area?" Kurt O'Connor stood in front of her father.

"How many times do I have to tell you? I don't know." Her dad's face was flushed as he leaned forward. "Kurt, you need to find her."

"Nel, we're doing everything we can." Kurt placed a hand on her father's shoulder.

Kurt was a friend of her father's and had been the first one to come when her mom went missing. He was the uncle Nick had mentioned, and the superintendent of the Hopedale division of the Newfoundland Police Department. His wife, Alice, was one of the many O'Connor ladies to come into *Snippy Gals*.

"I know. Really I do, but Kurt, she's everything to me. You know that." Anyone who knew her father knew he thought the world started and ended with his wife. The love they had for each other was timeless.

"I've got most of my men out there," Kurt said.

"Dad," Edward interrupted.

Her father and Kurt turned. Their expression said everything, but when her father's eyes filled with tears, Emily's stomach lurched.

"Nick told us there was a development and you wanted to see us," Edward's voice shook just a little.

Emily grabbed her brother's hand to keep her own from trembling. To her surprise, his hand shook as much as hers.

"What is it, daddy?" Elaine clutched Emily's other hand and squeezed it so hard she was sure her fingers were going to break.

"They found your mother's car in Gander." Her dad blurted out and took a deep breath. "Her phone and purse were still in the car."

"What does that mean? Did someone take her? Did she run off? What?" Elaine almost knocked her father off his feet when she ran into his arms.

"Forensics are checking the car now," Kurt said. "Right now we're just waiting. If there's anything there, they'll find it."

The huge lump in her throat made it impossible for her to speak. It was a known fact, the longer someone was missing, the less likely they'd be found alive. She wouldn't let her thoughts go there, but it was hard.

Emily turned towards the patio doors and focused on the rose bush growing in the middle of the garden. She'd planted it with her mother for the youngest of the Bradshaw children. The one that never got to see her sixth birthday.

It nearly killed her father when sweet Ella passed away. If anything happened to her mother, Emily was sure it would probably kill her dad. He wouldn't be able to function without her. She'd always prayed to find love like her parents, but it didn't seem to be in the cards for her. Right now all she wanted was her mother home safe and sound.

Mom, where are you?

Chapter 2

Keith O'Connor rolled his eyes as he propped himself up against the bar. They were at a wedding, and Aaron was acting as if he was at a dance club. The youngest of the O'Connor Brothers was rubbing himself against a poor young woman. Granted, she was his date, but their parents and grandmother could see him grinding the poor girl. Even though the girl didn't seem to mind.

"Does he ever think with the head on his shoulders?" Ian chuckled as he loosened his tie.

"A.J. only has that brain hanging between his legs." John laughed. Nobody ever called his youngest brother Aaron, it had always been A.J. since the day he came home from the hospital.

"You're just jealous big brother because you got that ball and chain hanging off your leg." Nick pushed his way between John and Keith to grab one of the dozens of shots lined up on the bar.

John being jealous was probably the funniest thing Nick could say. His older brother was married to the love of his life, and Keith had no doubt there wasn't any other woman in the hall, or on the earth for that matter who could ever turn John's head.

"I'll let Stephanie know what you called her." James raised an eyebrow at Nick.

"I'll tell Marina you let Colin have chocolate yesterday." Nick grinned. The narrowing of James' eyes told Keith, John's twin would be in trouble with his wife if that little secret got out.

Keith shook his head. It was the same thing everytime he and his brothers got together. Constant teasing, insults, and threats but even with all that, the seven brothers were thick as thieves.

It had been hard for everyone over the last few months. Especially, Ian's new wife, Sandy. Not only did she find one of her dearest friends, Ruby, had betrayed her, but she found out that same friend was also her half-sister. Then to top that off, Sandy learned the child she thought she'd lost all those years ago hadn't died.

It was difficult for Keith too. Ruby had killed his wife. Tessa was also Ruby's half-sister. It was difficult to get his head around that, and it tore at his heart. Of course, he couldn't let anyone around him know this. Since almost nobody in his family knew he'd been married. His family wouldn't understand why he married Tessa. Probably because they were big on only marrying for love.

Keith did love Tessa, but not the way a man should love his wife. Certainly not the way his brothers loved their wives. He'd married her because she was alone and pregnant. The day he'd asked her, it had just come out. Her brother worked for Keith, and she'd come to see him. Lane was out on a job, so Keith felt obligated to help. When she burst into tears in his office, he told her he'd marry her. He didn't know why, but he followed through.

Keith was raised to keep promises, and mostly he did. Although, he'd pledged to keep Tessa safe, and that was the one he couldn't keep. She'd been murdered, and he didn't know if he could ever forgive himself for letting it happen.

The people that did know about his life in Yellowknife, like his employees, Sandy, and Ian, didn't even know how he felt about it. Keith kept his emotions inside most of the time. It was a character flaw.

Keith had been that way his whole life. He was the peacekeeper in the family and played referee between the brothers when they butted heads. He'd learned to keep his own emotions under control and be the mediator. His father called it middle child syndrome.

There was always bantering between the three oldest brothers, and the three youngest because of the way Mike, Nick, and Aaron liked to play the field. Keith was really not that different. If his siblings knew what Keith did when he wasn't with his family, they'd never let him live it down. The only differences were, he avoided St. John's and he didn't broadcast it.

When Keith got that itch, he'd jump in his jeep and head far enough away so there wouldn't be any chance of running into his younger brothers or cousins. It wasn't that he felt ashamed, but it was something he wanted to keep to himself.

The only person that knew was his best friend and partner Dean Nash, otherwise known as Bull. There were times they would take a weekend and go 'fishing,' as they called it. Although, over the last couple of years, Bull seemed to have stopped 'fishing.' So mostly Keith would go on his own.

"You seem to be a million miles away." Keith felt a familiar hand rest on his shoulder. He turned to a set of eyes similar to his own. His father gave him that look of concern Keith knew so well.

Dr. Sean O'Connor was in his late fifties, but he could still turn the ladies heads. Keith heard someone once describe his father as a combination between Mark Harmon and Liam Neeson, but his father only had eyes for one woman. Kathleen O'Connor was the love of his dad's life, and it could be embarrassing the way they acted sometimes.

"Just a little tired." Keith raised two fingers to the bartender.

The sweet looking girl seemed a little nervous with all the O'Connor boys and their friends hovering around the bar. It didn't help that Nick was hitting on the woman. She placed two bottles of beer in front of Keith, and he winked as he tossed a twenty on the bar.

"Look at that, he does know how to flirt." Mike chuckled.

"Of course he does, look who his father is." His mom sidled up to his father's side, and he wrapped his arm around her.

"Yep, you boys could learn a thing or two from the master," his father dipped his wife and gave her a kiss that had Nick and Mike making gagging noises. Keith just shook his head

"Oh stop it you two. I think it's so romantic how your parents act." Marina smiled as she linked her arm into James'. "I hope we act just like that by the time we're their age."

"Sweetheart, I'm pretty sure we'll be like that by the time we're Nan's age." James wrapped his arms around her and whispered something into her ear that had her gasping.

What seemed like hours later, Keith stood at the corner of the bar staring into his glass of whiskey. He'd had his fill of dancing, drinking and watching all the couples wrapped around each other.

"Another one bites the dust." Aaron plopped down on the stool next to Keith.

"Feeling a little jealous, little brother?" Keith teased, but he knew Aaron was nowhere near ready to follow in the footsteps of the latest O'Connor brother.

"Not in the fucking least." He laughed. "You better watch out, though. The way things are going, you could be next."

13

"I don't see that happening anytime soon." Keith rolled his eyes not because he never thought about getting married again. It was definitely possible, and that was evident when he glanced around the room at John and Stephanie, James and Marina, and Ian and Sandy. Even his parents looked at each other with nothing but pure love.

"Doncha worry Keithy, she's out there. Closer than you think." This was all he needed. Dear Aunt Cora and her freaky cupid power.

"Seeing the future now are you, Aunt Cora?" Keith chuckled.

"I've seen her, Keithy." With that statement, she walked away.

He gaped after her until he heard the familiar snicker of Aaron next to him.

"Don't laugh, A.J. She's working on all of us." Keith chuckled when Aaron nearly choked on the beer he was drinking. Of course, his statement was probably not far from the truth.

Once Ian and Sandy were gone, Keith could finally head home. It wouldn't have looked really great for the best man to leave before the bride and groom. He was ready for a glass of wine and some soft mellow music. Nobody would ever believe by the gruff persona he portrayed that he ended his night like that. Especially, when he pulled out his Harley in the Spring. Pair that with his leather jacket and biker boots and most people expected beer and heavy metal to be his entertainment.

Keith was glad Ian and Sandy decided to get married at the Hopedale country club. He could have a few drinks and walk home. It was a beautiful night, considering it was mid-April. A little brisk, but nice for a walk. He loved Hopedale, and living in the small town he grew up in gave him peace. Even with all the shit that had gone down over the last few years with his brother's wives, there was nowhere else he'd rather be.

He marched up to the security gate of his property or as his brothers called it, *the compound.* Keith bought the property when he was still living in Yellowknife. When he returned home, he had his construction company build his house. He'd also put up bunk houses for his employees to stay when they were in Newfoundland. Although, most of them seemed to be relocating to the quaint town.

He unlocked the gate and was headed inside when his phone buzzed. He pulled it out of his jacket and saw a number he didn't recognize. It was after midnight which meant it was probably a job, and an urgent one. As much as he would've liked to send the call to voicemail, he couldn't neglect someone that probably needed help.

"Keith O'Connor." He closed the gate.

"Keith, I need your help. Someone is threatening my family. I need you to protect my daughter."

Keith froze on the front step of his house. The man sounded completely panicked.

"Give me a minute to get into my house, and you can explain more to me. Can I get your name?" Keith pushed in the code to open his door and quickly ducked inside. After shutting off the alarm, he hurried to his office and dropped into his chair.

"Nelson Bradshaw. Your Aunt Cora told me to call you. You see, my wife's been missing for the last two weeks. I went to school with Kurt as well, and Cora was a classmate of my wife." Nelson rambled, and Keith shook his head as he tried to retain all the information he'd just received in less than a minute.

"I'm very sorry about your wife, Mr. Bradshaw. My company has been lending out resources to the Hopedale P.D. in the investigation." His business had worked with the police for a few years and helped in a lot of investigations. Kurt didn't hesitate to ask for help when Mrs. Bradshaw went missing.

Newfoundland Security Services had two of the best computer analysts in the province. Probably in the country. His new sister-in-law was probably the best one he had hired, but Gage Hodder, otherwise known as Smash, was a very close second.

Like almost all of the employees at N.S.S, everyone was referred to by their nicknames. He didn't like his own but didn't make a big deal about it. After all, he did have red hair, so Rusty worked.

"Thank you for that, but right now I'm scared for my children. Well, more for my oldest daughter. She refuses to stay here at the house where we have security, and she's living over her salon by herself. You may know her." Nelson said.

"I don't think so." Keith tried to remember being introduced to any of the Bradshaws. They lived in SummerBrook, and it was one of the places he didn't go 'fishing' since it was too close to Hopedale and he knew that his cousins had friends there.

"She owns the salon there in Hopedale." Nelson sighed.

"I knew Kim had a partner, but I've never met her. Kim is my sister-in-law's sister."

"Yes, Kim Newman," Nelson said Kim's name with what seemed like destain.

"Mr. Bradshaw it's late right now, but I can set up a time to meet with you and your daughter on Monday." Keith pulled up his schedule on the laptop.

"No!" Nelson shouted. "I'm sorry, I didn't mean to yell. I need you on this immediately."

17

Keith began to get a little annoyed. The Bradshaws were one of the wealthiest families in SummerBrook, but he didn't care how much money the man had. Keith was tired, and a little drunk. Trying to work out the details after having such a long day wasn't going to work for him.

"Mr. Bradshaw, I understand you're worried, but I really can't do anything about it at this moment. My brother got married tonight, and I'm just getting home from that. Also, most of my employees are on other jobs or off. I'm sure...."

"I don't want anyone but you, Keith. Cora said you were the best and I want the best." Nelson was starting to get on his last nerve. Keith had enough on his plate with the security company and his construction company. Not to mention he'd promised to help with Ian and Sandy's daughters while the couple was on their honeymoon.

"My guys are the best, I assure you." Keith clenched his teeth when Nelson refused again.

Keith knew what the girls from SummerBrook were like. He'd gone to school with some of them. Most were snobby bitches who thought their own shit didn't stink. The last thing he wanted was to be dealing with some spoiled rich girl who was slumming it by opening her own salon. Although, Kim had never had a bad word to say about her business partner.

"I'll pay double your fee, but only if you're the one that does this." Nelson blurted out, and it only pissed Keith off more.

He wasn't going to be bought, and he didn't care how much the man was willing to pay. Nothing was worth the hassle of working with people like Nelson Bradshaw.

"Mr. Bradshaw, the money isn't the issue. As I told you, I'm not prepared to set this up at the moment, but if we can set up a meeting for Monday, we can discuss the terms." Hopefully, the man would fuck off, and Keith could relax.

"I apologize for being an ass, but I received a letter today…." Nelson's voice was just above a whisper.

"A letter about what?" That got Keith's attention.

"It said Emily was next." Nelson's voice cracked. "I think it's the same person that took my wife."

"Mr. Bradshaw you need to let my uncle know this." Kurt would be pissed if Keith overstepped.

"I just got off the phone with him. He told me to call you right away." Nelson said.

Keith clenched his jaw. Kurt and Cora really needed to give him a heads up about things. Particularly as he was about ready to tell the man to fly to fuck.

"I'll meet with you in the morning, but I do suggest you speak to your daughter about this as well."

"I've told her, but you've got to understand. Emily's very stubborn and independent. She doesn't like being told what to do, or that she can't take care of herself." Nelson sighed.

"I've dealt with people like that in the past. I'm sure I can handle her." Keith chuckled.

"I hope so, but you'd probably be the first." Nelson sounded a little more relaxed.

"Text me your address, and I'll be there by seven in the morning," Keith said. "And Mr. Nelson, for your piece of mind I'll send someone to watch your daughter's salon as soon as I hang up from you." Keith was beginning to feel like a jerk for thinking the worst of the man on the phone. Nelson just wanted to make sure his daughter was safe, and from what Keith could tell she wasn't going to make it easy.

Just fucking great.

Chapter 3

The man had to be out of his freaking mind. There was no way she was going to have someone following her around twenty-four hours a day. Emily rolled her eyes when her father practically begged her to be civil to the security guy he was sending to her salon, and of course, this would be the week that Kim had taken time off to babysit her sister's daughter and step-daughters so Sandy could go on a honeymoon.

So now she would be stuck dealing with the two hair stylists and receptionist. It also meant that she had to cut down on her appointments so she could deal with the business part of the salon. Emily didn't really mind the paperwork, but she would rather be out in the salon with the clients.

"Dad, my salon is practically across the street from the police station. I'll be okay. I don't need security." Emily tried once more to convince her father to call off the guard dog.

"Emily, please don't fight me on this anymore. You refuse to come here so I can make sure you're safe. I wouldn't be able to handle anything happening to you." Great, now he was pulling at her heartstrings. Her mother's disappearance was slowly aging her dad. He'd turned all his responsibilities in his company over to two of the vice-presidents and made finding her mom his life.

"Fine, Dad, but this guy better be able to be inconspicuous. The last thing I need is my clients feeling like they're in danger." Emily unlocked the door to her salon and turned off the alarm.

"Keith has been doing this a long time, and he knows how to blend in. Trust me and please do everything he tells you. For once in your life listen to what you're being told." She could hear the warning in his voice. She also knew he was clenching his fists because he was aware that Emily didn't like being ordered around.

"Yes, Dad. I'll listen. Don't worry, and please get some rest. Elaine said you've been up all hours of the night." Her sister called several times to say she was worried about his health.

"I'll try. I love you. If you need anything, please call, and be good." There was that warning again.

"I love you, too, Dad. I'll talk to you soon, and I'll try to come to see you over the weekend." Emily dropped her phone on her desk as she flopped down in the chair.

She was no sooner sat in the chair when she heard the chime of the front door opening. Usually, she'd be there by herself for the first hour.

"Great, must be the watchdog." She muttered as she made her way to the front of the salon.

Before stepping out into the front, she took a deep breath. She could be civil to this man. After all, it wasn't his fault her father was pushing this on her. She walked through the curtain and looked around. The place was empty. Goosebumps popped up on her arms, and a chill ran up her spine as she scanned the length of the room.

She slowly walked towards the front door hoping that the wind possibly pulled the door open. It sometimes happened during the winter. Emily stepped in front of the reception desk to get a better look at the front door. As she crept slowly towards the door, a pink head popped up from behind the reception desk.

"Jesus, Aurora." Emily slapped her hand against her chest as if it would slow her now pounding heart.

"Sorry, Em. I was turning on my computer." It was hard to be mad at the young girl. She was so full of energy and always had a bright smile.

Aurora Hanlon was the daughter of one of the stylists that worked for Emily and Kim. Ada was in her mid-forties and a single mother, so when her only daughter needed a job, she asked Emily and Kim about hiring a receptionist.

"It's okay, but for heaven's sake call out to let me know you're here." Emily chuckled.

"I thought that's what that annoying chime was for." Aurora placed her elbows on the desk and rested her chin on her fists.

"Smart ass." Emily gave her a little push.

"I do actually have a smart ass. At least that's what the guy at the club said last night." Aurora wiggled her eyebrows sending Emily into a fit of laughter.

"Should I tell your mother about this guy?" Emily teased.

"Have I told you I've started taking Karate lessons with Jess O'Connor?" Aurora raised a perfectly arched eyebrow.

"Duly noted." Emily headed towards her office to get some accounts entered before her first appointment. "By the way, there's supposed to be a guy coming here sometime this morning. Nothing to worry about, but my dad wants me to have some security for a few days."

"Woohoo, is it one of those hot guys from Jess's cousin's company?"

"Behave yourself. I have no idea. I just know someone will be by today." She didn't really care at this point. The whole thing was going to make it hard to get her mind off of her mother.

Emily was doing her best to be strong for everyone. Her father was ready to fall apart, her brother was doing his best to keep himself from going over the edge, and Elaine spent most of her time in her room crying. Every day it got harder to believe her mother would be found, and if she was, it probably wasn't going to be alive.

The thought of never seeing her mom again caused a huge lump to form in her throat, and her vision blurred. She lowered herself into the desk chair and covered her face with her hands. The tears were hard to contain, but like every day for the last two weeks, Emily swallowed the lump and took several deep breaths.

A few minutes after she'd managed to make herself presentable, she heard the voice of Penny Alyward. Emily loved the woman because she was like the comic relief in an otherwise dark drama. Penny was one of those people that always had a funny story or joke. She was loud but sweet.

"I swear to Jesus it's enough to freeze the balls off a brass monkey out there today. Isn't it supposed to be spring?" Penny walked into the back and shook off her bright orange coat. That was another thing about Penny. She had a fashion that was one of a kind.

"It's supposed to warm up tomorrow." Emily sat back in the chair and glanced at Penny.

"So this is how it is? You with that face and we're gonna chat about the weather." Penny rested her fists on her slim hips and met Emily's gaze.

25

"What else is there to talk about?" Emily turned towards the computer as if she was about to check something, but the truth was she was just avoiding any conversation about her mother.

"Oh, let me see, the fact I got a call from your father at five this morning, and might I say he did hear a few words that I'm sure he didn't think were lady like. I mean who calls someone at that hour? Anyway, he told me what's going on, and I told him not to worry because nobody's gonna get near my girl." Penny continued as she sat in the chair across from the desk. "So, between me and the security, you'll be safer than the Prime Minister."

Emily couldn't help the fit of laughter. Penny was probably no more than one hundred pounds. Being that the woman was five feet seven inches, she was what her mother called the Olive Oil type. Although, she had a massive chest, and Emily wondered how the woman didn't topple over sometimes.

"Don't laugh, Em. Ask my ex how dangerous I can be." Penny stood up and sauntered out of the room leaving Emily shaking her head.

Her phone rang as she was heading out to the front of the salon for her first client. She glanced at the screen and smiled.

"God, I can't even get rid of you when you take a week off." Emily laughed.

"Have you been told to fuck off today?" Kim said.

"Nope but I'm sure you'll love to be the first." Emily chuckled.

26

"Consider yourself told twice." Kim laughed. "Listen, I got one of Ian's brothers dropping by to grab my case. Me and the three girls are having a beauty weekend, and of course, the two older ones want their gorgeous curls straightened."

"Those little girls are lucky to have such a great aunt," Emily said.

"I know. Anyway, he should be dropping by sometime today." Kim said.

"Okay, you have fun," Emily said.

"You know this is great birth control. Looking after the two older girls is easy, but the little one makes me want to pull out my hair. She's not even two yet, and she got a major attitude." Kim sighed.

"And your sister is having another one any day. Good luck to her." Emily laughed. "I still don't know why they went away for a honeymoon when she is ready to pop any day."

"I think she's hoping the honeymoon helps pop it faster." Kim giggled.

"Way too much information. I've got a client coming any minute. I'll call you later to see how you're doing." Emily glanced at her watch.

"Talk to you later," the last thing Emily heard was Kim telling Grace not to touch the garbage.

Emily entered the store front and froze. At the counter stood a man lazily leaning on the reception desk. He was what Penny would call, sweet meat. At that moment he seemed to be blatantly flirting with Aurora, but Emily was shocked to see the young girl didn't seem the least bit charmed.

"Mr. O'Connor could you please get a freaking life." Aurora rolled her eyes and laughed.

Holy shit this was the security guy her father was telling her about. How the hell was he going to fade into the background when he looked like a movie star and seemed to be a huge flirt.

"I've got a life, beautiful. You say yes to a date, and I'll show you." He leaned in over the counter and Emily didn't miss Penny checking out his ass.

"I know what your dates consist of, buddy and I'm not gonna be another notch on your belt. Besides you're too old." Aurora laughed.

"What's eight years?" He smiled, and Emily had to admit the guy was good, but there was no way she could have someone like this in her salon flirting with everyone.

"Oh, Em. Thank God. This ass is looking for you." Aurora pointed her thumb to the guy.

"There must be something in the water in this salon. Lots of hot women around." He winked at Emily, and she raised her eyebrow.

28

"For the love of God, A.J, do you ever stop." That voice was Ada.

"Not when I see a beautiful woman." He wrapped his arm around Ada's shoulder. "Of course age doesn't matter to me."

"You're so gross." Aurora gagged.

"A.J, honey. You'd never be able to keep up with a woman like me, and as for my daughter, I suggest you look elsewhere if you don't want to end up castrated at your age." Ada glared, but Emily could see the faint grin.

"You ladies are a rough crowd. Besides I'm here to see Ms. Bradshaw and…." Emily held up her hand to stop him before someone did hurt him.

"Look, I know my dad thinks I need the security, but you aren't exactly going to blend into the background. I'll call my dad and find alternate arrangements." Emily said.

"What are you talking about?" He looked confused, but when he glanced out through the front window, it was if something clicked. "I'm afraid I'm not the O'Connor you've been expecting. That would be my older brother, and I'm pretty sure it will be even harder for him to blend in." A.J. and Aurora laughed. "I'm here to pick up something for Kim."

Before Emily had a chance to ask what they were laughing at, the chime on the door rang, and in sauntered a walking wall of muscle dressed in black from head to toe. The only other color was the ginger color of his hair, but there was no doubting the family resemblance between A.J. and the large man.

"What are you doing here?" His deep voice echoed through the salon and Emily was sure she felt it right to the tips of her toes.

"Nice to see you too, dick." A.J. snorted.

"That didn't answer my question." The looks were the only thing similar about the two men. This guy was stone-faced and way too dangerous looking.

"Had to pick up something for Kim if you must know." A.J. turned away from his brother and back to Aurora. "Last chance, honey."

"Out, A.J." the huge mountain grumbled.

"Okay, Mr. Happy." He left, but not before he winked at Emily.

"Aurora, nice to see you. I'm here to see Ms. Bradshaw." He stood next to the reception desk, and it barely came to his hips. The man had to be well over six feet tall.

"Nice to see you too, Keith, and you know you could really smile a little more. Might get rid of the frown lines you have." Aurora held up her finger and pointed towards Emily.

"She would be Ms. Bradshaw, but if you don't want to be bitch slapped I'd start calling her Emily." Aurora turned away from him to answer the ringing phone.

Up to that point, Emily hadn't really got a full view of his face, and when he turned towards her, she couldn't breathe. He had the most piercing blue eyes she'd ever seen, and it was as if he was looking right into her soul. For a moment she thought she saw his expression falter, but he cleared his throat and stalked towards her.

Sweet Jesus, he's beautiful. And Huge.

Chapter 4

Keith moved towards the Auburn haired beauty staring at him with wide eyes. It seemed as if Ms. Bradshaw was about to turn tail and run, but as Keith got closer, she straightened her shoulders and raised her eyes to meet his. That was when his heart started to thud. Blue gray eyes stared defiantly into his.

"Ms. Bradshaw, I'm Keith O'Connor from Newfoundland Security Services. Your father hired me as security for you." Keith held out his hand, but she glanced at it and then back up to his face.

"I'm well aware of why my father hired you, Mr. O'Connor but I don't think this is going to work out." She retorted.

"Call me Keith, and I'm sorry, but your father hired me." Fury was building in her eyes.

"I'm sure he'll pay you for your time today, Mr. O'Connor. Have a nice day." She turned around with her head held up and hurried through a curtain in the back of the salon.

Oh no, you don't, princess.

Keith started to follow her, but a woman with wild black hair and way too much cleavage stepped in front of him.

"Honey, I'd suggest you enter at your own risk. She's pissed that her dad has someone here and even a beefcake like you wouldn't make this any easier for her." The woman said

Keith glanced down at the tag on her shirt and saw the name, Penny. Before he got a chance to speak, she put her finger under his chin.

"Eyes are up here, big boy." She raised an eyebrow.

"I was looking at your name tag, Penny. Thanks for the advice but I'm sure I can handle this." Keith stepped around Penny and continued to the back of the salon.

"Don't say you weren't warned," Penny called after him. Ada and Aurora were laughing as he walked through the curtain.

"Dad, the only place where this guy could blend in, is at the World Wrestling Federation or a biker bar. He's going to scare off my clients or have them tripping over themselves flirting with him." Keith stood just outside the door of the office and continued to listen to the one-sided conversation.

"Yes, I realize you want me to be safe, but this is my business, dad. If my clients don't feel safe here, I'll lose them. You know the women from SummerBrook are not the most pleasant people to deal with." For a few minutes, all Keith heard was tapping and a huge groan.

"I know you think this place is beneath me, dad, but it's my baby, and you will never understand what it means to me. So call off the guard dog, or I'll have him removed from my shop." Keith couldn't help the grin forming as he heard her voice rise again.

"I will not be coming to stay in SummerBrook or at Mr. O'Connor's place either, dad. Are you out of your freaking mind?" Keith peeked into the office. She was staring out the small window with her back to him.

"Dad, I'm not dealing with this right now. You call him and get him the hell out of here. I mean it." She tapped the screen and tossed the phone onto her desk while she muttered something under her breath.

"He's just looking out for your safety." Keith should have known that was the wrong thing to say. She turned slowly and glared at him.

"If I were you, I would be checking my phone for a text from my father instead of eavesdropping." She pulled her long hair into a ponytail and then did some twisted thing with it. It always amused him the way women would grow their hair and then put it up.

Keith pulled out his phone as it buzzed. He was really expecting it to be Nelson telling him to forget about everything. He opened the message and chuckled as he read it.

She's going to fight this but please just be patient. She's feisty like her mother, and she has a mouth on her. I'm sure it won't offend you when she starts to curse like a sailor.

"You have a great day, Mr. O'Connor." She grinned when Keith looked up from his phone.

"It's Keith, and I'm sure I will have a beautiful day. I just need you to show me where I can settle in and not be in your way. I also need you to let me know if you're going to be staying at your father's, or at my compound so I can have everything in place before the end of the day." It took everything he had not to burst into laughter at the way her mouth dropped open, and her eyes went completely full.

"My father didn't text you?" She stammered.

"He did, and it was good to know that you curse like a sailor when you're mad." Keith grinned as he shoved his phone back into his pocket.

"I will fu…., I'm going to kill him." She growled.

"I wouldn't say that with me around. I do have four brothers, an uncle and new sister-in-law that are police officers, and I would feel obligated to tell them about a threat of murder." Keith leaned against the door jamb and crossed his arms over his chest.

"You're going to be a pain in the ass, aren't you?" Emily sighed.

"Not as long as you let me keep you safe." Keith watched as she gripped onto the edge of the desk.

"Do you have to be out front?" She didn't look up at him.

"Yes." Keith had already done an outside sweep of the building and knew there was no other entrance except the small window in her office that was not big enough for a person to crawl through. So there was no reason for him to be in the back of the salon and he could do this job by himself.

"You don't have to stand by the door, or anything do you?" She looked up at him under her eyelashes.

"No, I can probably sit behind the reception desk," He wanted to laugh at her expression, but he sensed that would only piss her off.

"I'm sure Aurora will love that." She stood up and pulled down her shirt over her full hips. The woman had curves that would make any man fall at her feet.

"I've known Aurora and Ada for a long time. I'm sure she won't mind me." Keith didn't move out of the doorway as she walked towards it.

"I'll agree to let you be here, but there is no way in hell I'm going to SummerBrook or where ever you live." She tried to push past him, but he put his arm across the door to stop her.

"I live here in Hopedale, and it's probably the safest place you could stay. It's not negotiable. Your dad's place or mine. You've got until lunch to make your choice." With that, he dropped his arm and moved out of her way.

Keith waited for her to argue but she didn't. The way she almost bowled him over when she pushed past him was enough to let him know Emily would be a handful, but he was pretty sure she was going to be fun. Maybe the first job he'd enjoyed in a long time.

Chapter 5

Emily finished her last client and headed back to her desk. Ada had dropped her lunch there when she returned from Jack's Place. It was a small pub just around the corner from the salon and had the best turkey sandwiches Emily ever tasted.

She'd tried to forget about the man behind the reception desk with Aurora. It also pissed her off that he wasn't as big a distraction to the clients as she was expecting. In fact, most of the people knew him.

She shouldn't have been surprised since the O'Connor family were all over Hopedale. You couldn't go anywhere without running into one of them, or at least that was what she was told. Emily didn't spend a lot of time exploring the small town. Not because she didn't like it, but she'd only been living in the apartment above the salon for a couple of months, and then her mother vanished.

"Aunt Alice makes a great sandwich, doesn't she?" Emily snapped her gaze up to the doorway which was filled with the beautiful man she'd been doing her best to ignore all morning.

"I should've known she was related." Emily tried to sound annoyed, but her voice came out all breathy.

"Yep, if you meet an O'Connor in Hopedale, they're related to me." He plopped in the chair across from her desk and proceeded to open a massive sandwich. He popped one of his fries into his mouth and then looked up.

"Is there a reason you're in my office?" Emily didn't feel comfortable being in such close quarters with him. The scent of his cologne was driving her nuts. Not because it was a bad smell but because it was incredible. If she wasn't mistaken, it smelled like, Straight to Heaven by Kilian. It was a combination of spicy and woodsy with a hint of musk. It was also extremely expensive. She didn't know many men that wore it.

"I'm eating lunch and waiting for your decision." He took a bite of his sandwich although she didn't know how he got his mouth around the bloody thing. That was another thing that was too distracting. His mouth. Full lips that could only be described as lickable, suckable, and biteable.

"My decision?" She had completely forgotten what the question was. It was hard to since her thoughts were engulfed in wondering if his lips were as soft as they looked.

"Your father's place or the compound." He locked his gaze on her, and Emily trembled. "I need to know so I can make the necessary arrangements."

"I'm pretty sure I told you that I'm not going to either," She wasn't changing her mind.

"How many bedrooms do you have?" He balled up the empty sandwich wrapper and tossed it into the garbage bucket across the room. Of course, he didn't miss.

"Not that it's any of your business, but there's one bedroom." Emily rolled her eyes.

"I guess I'll have to get a camp cot brought over." He pulled his phone out of his jacket and before she realized what he said, he'd made arrangements with someone to bring a camp cot to her salon.

"Wait one damn minute. You're not staying in my apartment. There's no way in hell." Emily stood up, pressed her fists against the top of the desk and leaned over it.

"Hold on a second, Smash." Keith pulled the phone away from his ear and stood up. She had to lift her head to look up at him. "I'm going to tell you this once more, and it'll be the last. When we know you're not in any danger and only then, will you be rid of me. Until then we'll be joined at the hip. It's pointless for you to cop an attitude with me because, Princess, nobody on this earth has an attitude that can match the females in my family. I'm immune to the pissy moods and complaining. Do you understand me? So if you don't want me staying in your apartment, make a choice." She didn't miss the clenching of his jaw.

"I'm no Princess, and you're an asshole." Emily stomped out of the office into the private bathroom off her office. She slammed the door and pressed her forehead against it.

"Okay, so I'm assuming I'll need the cot." She heard him shout. Emily wanted to march out of the bathroom and punch him straight in the gut, but from what she could see she'd probably break her hand.

Emily paced the tiny bathroom grumbling to herself. Keith was too huge a presence for her dinky apartment. She'd have to hide in her bedroom to avoid being around him, and she wasn't one that liked to hide, but he gave the impression of being a bad boy. The very type of guy she avoided.

It was unusual that she was so attracted to him, especially since she'd just met him. Her whole body reacted to him. Between the pounding of her heart, the palm sweating, and just his near presence, she was ready to go out of her mind. The thoughts of doing a lot of really naughty things to him, and with him were not helping either.

"Get a fucking grip, Emily." She leaned on the small counter and stared at her flushed face. He was driving her blood pressure through the roof, and the big jerk didn't even know. She splashed some cold water on her face and covered it with the small towel that was hung on the hook.

41

"Maybe you're ovulating or something." She whispered as she peered at herself in the mirror again. "And it has been a long while since…." A hard knock stopped her chat with herself and made her almost fall back over the toilet.

"Your next client is here, Em." It was Ada.

"Thanks, can you tell her I'll be right out," Emily called through the closed door.

"Will do." She heard the clicking of Ada's block heels slowly fade away.

Emily took a couple of deep breaths and opened the door. She fully expected to see Keith still sat in her office. She didn't know if she was relieved or disappointed to see the chair was empty. She tugged down on her shirt and headed to the front, and there he was sitting behind the reception desk like he'd been all morning.

"I love that new receptionist." Her client giggled as she motioned to Keith. No surprise that Ginger Dwyer would notice him. The bitch would probably text all her snobby friends in SummerBrook when she left to talk about him.

The only reason she even continued to have clients like Ginger was because they paid top price for anything they had done. Sometimes Emily thought they just came to her place to look down on her.

"Aurora has been here for a while." Emily pretended she didn't know Ginger was talking about Keith.

"I wasn't talking about the girl. I was talking about the bulging wall of muscle in black. He looks like one of those men you'd like to have just once." Ginger whispered.

"I don't think that would work with him. I'm pretty sure he's gay." Emily spoke a little louder than she probably should have, but she wanted Keith to hear her, and from the way, his gaze slowly met hers she was sure he did.

"Wow! Really? What a waste." Ginger sighed as she turned to glance at Keith. Emily tugged on her hair. Hard. "Ouch." Ginger whined.

"Sorry, the brush got tangled." Emily lied.

She felt dead on her feet, and except for Aurora, everyone had left for the day. Emily walked around to check all the stations to ensure everything was turned off. It was weird being there without Kim hovering around. Her business partner had some kind of OCD when it came to checking all the stations.

"I'm gone, Em," Aurora wiggled her fingers as she headed out of the door.

"I'll see you in the Mondy, sweetie." Emily waved as she made her way to the reception desk to grab the cash drawer. She was just going to take it to her apartment and do up the tally. As she picked up the drawer, a deep voice startled her.

"I've secured the windows," Keith sauntered out of the back. Emily dropped the cash drawer sending coins rolling across the floor.

The debit slips and receipts flew into the air, and she almost tripped over it when it hit the floor.

"Shit, shit, shit," Emily grumbled.

"I'm sorry. I didn't mean to startle you." Keith crouched and began to grab the coins that had rolled near him.

"I forgot you were here." Emily lied as she knelt on the floor and began to scoop up the mess. She couldn't forget he was there even if she tried. His scent filled the place, or at least that's what it seemed.

"You forgot, or you were hoping I left." He grinned as he knelt in front of her and tossed the coins he retrieved, into the drawer.

"Hope springs eternal." She couldn't help but smile at him as he continued to help.

"I'm starting to get the feeling you don't like me, princess," Keith chuckled.

Emily shook her head as she picked up the drawer and began to stand. When she looked up, he had his hand held out. At first, she was just going to ignore it but the way her legs felt she was sure she wouldn't be able to get up on her own.

I'm so out of shape.

She accepted his hand, and he pulled her to her feet as if she was a child. When he took the drawer from her hand, she glanced up at him.

44

"Where do you want this? I'm afraid you'll drop it again." He winked.

Emily rolled her eyes, and he smiled. It changed the whole appearance of his face. Softened it somehow. Not that he wasn't gorgeous either way, but that smile could melt a woman's heart.

"My security is also a comedian. I dropped it because of you, jerk." Emily took the drawer back and headed to the door of her apartment in the back of the salon. "I'm taking it upstairs."

As she walked towards the door, she stopped so quickly he slammed into her back. How could she have forgotten he was going to be staying in her apartment?

"What's wrong?" He placed his hand on her shoulder. The slight touch sent a wave of need through her entire body.

"Umm…. Don't you have to go get your things?" She closed her eyes and prayed he'd say yes.

"I thought we'd established I'm your shadow until all this is over. Smash dropped off the things I need, and Ada let me in your apartment to set it up." Emily turned around so fast she hit him with the corner of the cash drawer.

"She did what?" Emily's voice squeaked when he grabbed the drawer before it hit the floor.

"I didn't want to disturb you with your flirty client. You know the one you told I was gay." Keith smirked. She so wanted to slap it off his face.

"You were right earlier. I don't like you very much." Emily yanked the drawer away from him and stomped up the stairs.

When she pushed the door open, there was a large green army cot off to the side of her living room and a duffle bag next to the door.

"That's okay." He plopped down on her sofa, but she ignored him and went to her room to tally up the sales. He could entertain himself.

Emily turned onto her back for the third time. She never had trouble falling asleep after a busy day, but it was after midnight, and she was still wide awake. The only thing going to help was a cup of Camomile tea. She tossed the blankets off and pulled on her fluffy purple robe.

She opened her bedroom door slowly and peeped through the crack. The only light was the one over her stove, and everything was completely quiet. Emily tiptoed towards the kitchen but stopped when she saw him.

He lay on the camp cot still in his clothes. He didn't even have a pillow. With one hand resting on his abdomen and the other behind his head, he looked comfortable enough. His breathing was deep and slow making it obvious he was sleeping. She had to stop staring at him before he woke up and thought she was some weirdo.

She sat down next to the small table and wrapped her hands around the warm mug. Shutting off her mind seemed to be impossible, so she pulled her phone out. The picture on her screen made her smile. It was her mother and sister at the Sweet Heart Ball the previous year. As usual, her mom was the most beautiful woman at the event. Emily was well aware that her sister resembled their mom and looking at the picture it was evident. Emily had some likeness, but Elaine could pass for her mother's twin.

The Sweet Heart Ball was an annual event her mother started after Emily's youngest sister passed away from a heart condition. It was to raise money for the children's hospital that had taken such good care of Ella up until her death.

Ella had a form of heart disease called cardiomyopathy. Her heart wasn't pumping enough blood to her body, and she required a heart transplant. Unfortunately, Ella didn't get a heart and passed away a week before her sixth birthday.

After that, her mother made it her mission to raise money for the children's hospital. She volunteered at least twice a week and made sure if any child was in the hospital for their birthday they had a special celebration.

Her mother had been deep into the preparations for the fundraiser when she vanished. She'd heard her father say he'd move heaven and earth to make sure it still went ahead because it's what she would want. It was not even two months away, and Emily wasn't confident he was going to be able to do it.

Emily wiped the tears that ran down her cheeks. The only time she let her emotions out was when she was alone in her apartment, but she wasn't exactly alone at the moment. Only a few feet away on the other side of the wall was a man that made her pulse quicken and her body ache. It was something she'd never experienced before. She'd never felt the animalistic need to have someone. Not until him.

Emily remembered her mother telling her when she met the right man she'd feel it from the top of her head to the tips of her toes, and he wouldn't even have to touch her. There was no way Keith O'Connor was the one for her, but she did feel it all over.

With a shake of her head, she emptied her cup and placed it in the sink. Quietly she tiptoed towards her bedroom, but as if she had no control, she turned to take another glimpse of him. The light from the moon glowed through the window allowing her to see his form still motionless on the cot.

She spotted the tartan throw on the back of the couch out of the corner of her eye. There was a chill in the room, and it would be rude to let him be cold. It probably would have been more polite to have offered him a blanket and pillow before she stomped off into her room.

Emily grabbed the throw and moved slowly towards Keith. For a moment she stood over him and studied his face. He had a day's growth of beard forming, and it was a little redder than his hair, but it

48

only enhanced his handsome face. His lashes were long and thick but light in color. Across the bridge of his nose, there was a small scar, and she wanted to trace it with her finger, but she wouldn't dare. Her gaze moved to his slightly parted lips, and it appeared as if he was grinning slightly.

"Was there something you needed, princess?" His voice was just above a whisper, but it startled her making her jump back from the cot.

"Yes, … I mean no…. It's cold and…." She stammered over her words.

Keith opened his eyes, and the way they traveled down her body and up again made her shiver.

"I brought you a blanket." Emily tossed it over him, but it slid to the floor. She was thoroughly embarrassed to be caught sizing him up. She crouched to pick it up, but he grabbed her wrist and tugged her towards him.

"I'm not the least bit cold. As a matter of fact, I find it hot." His eyes sparkled, and the heat of his hand around her wrist was unnerving. "But I suggest you go back to bed." His gaze locked with hers and for a moment she thought about throwing caution to the wind.

"Emily, go back to bed." His teeth clenched, and she lowered her eyes but not before she got a quick glance at the large bulge in the front of his jeans.

Holy mother of Jesus.

"I'm sorry I woke you." Emily yanked her wrist from his grasp and practically ran to her room. She ducked inside, closed the door and pressed her back against it.

What the fuck is wrong with you?

It wasn't like she was a virgin. In fact, she was far from it, but the man looked about ready to bust the zipper in his jeans and part of her wanted to see that. Who the hell was she fooling? All of her would have loved to see it.

"It's not like you haven't seen one before." What was she, sixteen? He was just another man that woke up with an erection, and that was it. He probably had his way with some hot blonde in his dream or maybe two. Either way, it had nothing to do with her, and she needed to get some rest. Maybe her brain would return after a good night's sleep because it was evident it had taken a vacation since Keith O'Connor had appeared in her life. There was only one person to blame for the whole thing.

Thanks a lot, Dad.

Chapter 6

Keith gripped the side of the cot and his teeth smashed together as Emily quickly disappeared into her room. She'd obviously seen his aroused condition, and he was pissed she did. Especially since she was the reason for it. Well, that wasn't really true, it was his overactive libido and the fact that he hadn't been 'fishing' in a while. It had nothing to do with how Emily's curvy body sent his brain into full sex mode.

He felt like a teenager around her, or at least his dick did, and that didn't sit well with him. His company was hired to keep her safe. Keith was pretty sure that didn't include stripping her naked and burying himself deep inside her.

"Jesus H Christ," Keith grumbled.

He pulled his hands down over his face and blew out a breath. This was not going to work for him. He needed to talk to Nelson about having one of his guys take over. Giving another reason, besides wanting to bed Emily, shouldn't be too hard to come up with.

The blanket Emily dropped was still pooled on the floor next to the cot, and Keith picked it up. After tossing it on top of his bed, he headed to the kitchen to get something to drink. Hopefully, she wouldn't get bent out of shape if he grabbed a bottle of water.

Her kitchen was tiny, and being in it made him feel slightly claustrophobic. He opened the fridge and sighed when the only thing he saw was cans of soda, and he didn't do carbonated drinks. Not only were they full of sugar but they tasted horrible.

The third cupboard he opened contained a total of three glasses and two cups. He pulled down a glass and turned on the tap. It was a good thing that it was safe to drink water from the tap. It was one of the perks of living in Hopedale. The water was clean.

While he sipped the water, he braced his hip against the counter and scanned the room. Emily didn't have a lot of things around. It wasn't what he would expect from someone who'd come from such a materialistic world. He'd worked for enough wealthy families, and it wasn't uncommon to see a lot of expensive clutter. Even in her small living room the only thing that he would consider unnecessary would be a glass cabinet in the corner that was filled with what looked like glass ornaments.

Emily was such a contradiction to what he expected from a person from SummerBrook. She almost seemed embarrassed about her family's wealth. As if she was trying to separate herself from it. When he'd suggested that she go stay with her father for her safety, he couldn't help but notice the look in her eyes. Fear? Hatred? He wasn't sure what it was, but it told him that wasn't an option for her.

Keith shook his head. The woman's mother was missing. It was possible she couldn't face staying in the house because it had too many memories, or was there another reason?

From the information he'd gotten from the Bradshaw family, they were close. Keith had never had any dealings with them before this, he knew both Emily's parents were old classmates of Kurt and Cora. As far as he knew his father knew them as well. Since many of the surrounding areas all attended the same high school, it wasn't uncommon to have classmates from communities as far as Renews.

Keith didn't know any of the family because he'd gone to a different high school. When it was discovered that he had an eidetic memory, he went to a school that had special classes for advanced students. It had been expensive for his parents, but they didn't want him to lose interest in school.

Keith glanced out of the small kitchen window. He could see the docks that surrounded Hopedale Harbour. He didn't get to see this part of Hopedale very often where his house was located. It was beautiful the way the lights reflected off the water. He could even see the man staring up at the building.

"What the fuck?" Keith glanced at his watch as he hurried out of the kitchen and grabbed his Glock hidden under the cot. He dashed down the stairs and out through the salon. When he unlocked the door and pushed it open an ear deafening siren blared, but he didn't have time to worry about it as he darted to the corner of the shop.

He pointed his weapon in the direction where he'd seen the figure standing. Nobody was there. He scanned both streets but didn't see a soul. He pulled his phone out of his pocket and tapped the last number he dialed. It rang several times before he heard a very grumpy voice.

"What the fuck, Rusty?" Smash grumbled. "It's three in the fucking morning."

"Do you fucking think I'd be calling you at this hour if it wasn't important?" Keith hurried back into the salon and looked around for an alarm panel.

"What the fuck is the racket?" Smash sounded a little more alert.

"Just get your ass down here. I got to figure out how to turn this off." Keith ended the call and shoved the phone back into his pocket.

"I didn't even see her set the fucking thing." Keith wandered around the shop looking for the panel.

"What happened? Did someone break in?" Keith spun around at the sound of her voice.

54

"Can you turn that fucking thing off? Now." Keith held his hands over his ears.

Emily scampered behind the reception desk and reached up to a picture on the wall. She pulled it out and behind it was the panel. Keith wanted to kick himself in the ass because he didn't pay attention to where it was. He didn't even ask if she had an alarm. He really had to get his brain back to his head and out of his dick.

"Why did it go off?" Emily didn't turn around as she punched in the code. Suddenly silence. At least until her cell phone rang. "That's probably the alarm company." She answered the phone and assured them everything was fine. When she ended the call, she turned.

"Well?" She held up her hand motioning for him to explain.

"I saw someone outside looking up here." The color drained from her face, and he wanted to kick himself in the ass. "He was gone when I got outside."

Emily slowly sank into the chair behind the desk. She stared down at her hands. Keith didn't even know when he started to move towards her, but there he was kneeling in front of her holding her hands in his.

"You're safe, Em. I'm not going to let anything happen to you." Keith squeezed her hands gently, and she lifted her face.

Beautiful.

"Are you sure it just wasn't someone out for a walk?" Her eyes pleaded with him to say yes, but he couldn't lie.

"It's possible, but at three in the morning? In Hopedale? I don't think so." Keith wiped a tear from her cheek.

"So this is real. My dad isn't overreacting." Emily sighed.

"I don't think so, Princess." Keith cupped her cheek. What was he doing? "This is why I believe we need to renegotiate where you stay for a bit."

Before she could speak the door opened, and Keith jumped up with his weapon pointed at the door. Smash held up his hands, and Keith lowered his gun.

"What the hell happened?" Smash walked further into the salon.

While Keith explained the events, he heard Emily giggle behind him. Keith turned. She pointed at Smash. When he glanced down, it was evident what had amused Emily. Smash was wearing a pair of pajama pants covered in Sponge Bob cartoons. That didn't surprise Keith because he'd seen Smash's collection of cartoon clothing. It was what he had on his feet that made Keith shake his head. On one foot he had a running shoe but the other one he was still wearing a Sponge Bob slipper.

"Did you drive here?" Keith asked.

"Yeah, Why?" Smash still didn't know what Emily was giggling at, and Keith was doing his best not to laugh himself.

"I bet you have another pair of shoes home just like that don't you?" Emily pointed down.

"What do you expect when someone wakes you out of a dead sleep at three in the morning?" Smash groaned.

"I'm sorry." Emily's smile disappeared, and Keith wanted to throat punch Smash.

"Don't worry about it. I'm used to it." Smash smiled. "I'm Gage Hodder by the way, but you can call me Smash." He introduced himself and held out his hand.

"Why Smash?" Emily asked the question that everyone asked when his guys were introduced with their nicknames.

"Because of the way I smash the computer keys." He grinned.

"That's what he likes to tell everyone anyway." Keith rolled his eyes.

"It's the only answer that matters." Smash laughed and then his smile faded. "Seriously, how do you want to handle this?"

"Emily, you can go back to bed. We've got everything under control." Keith didn't want to scare her. If she was going to be insistent on staying in her apartment, then security was going to have to change.

"Sure, I'll go back to bed and let you men discuss my safety. I mean I really don't need to have a say in this." Keith didn't miss her sarcasm.

"Emily,...." Keith began, but she held up her hand.

"Don't Emily me, Mr. O'Connor. I'm not going to let this person have me hide under my bed." She crossed her arms over her chest and raised her head defiantly. "And you're not going to tell me what to do."

This was exactly what he was afraid of. Emily wasn't going to make things easy in any way, and it seemed she was going to call him Mr. O'Connor when she was being stubborn. He glanced at Smash. He'd suddenly become really interested in a poster of a model showing off her new haircut.

"Please don't be difficult, Emily," Keith said.

"How is me wanting to be involved in my own safety being difficult, Mr. O'Connor?" He was sure her glare could probably cut him in two.

"If you're so interested in your own safety, Ms. Bradshaw, then you'd have agreed to stay with your father or at the N.S.S. compound." Keith didn't miss the roll of her eyes or the way her body stiffened when he called her by her last name.

"Do you have all your clients stay at your compound? I'm guessing, no." She snapped.

58

"If I feel it's the safest option, yes they do." Keith stepped closer to her, but she didn't back down.

"Not sure I remember any staying…." Smash began to say,

"Shut up, Smash," Keith growled.

"Don't tell him to shut up." Emily stepped closer to Keith.

"Look, I'm going to take a look around the outside while you two figure this out. I'm assuming if she's staying here you're going to want some surveillance outside." Smash didn't wait for an answer as he left them alone.

Keith was no more than an arm's length away from her. She glared up at him like a spoiled brat who was trying to get her way, and it pissed him off that it was as arousing as hell.

"Do you always try to bully people into doing things?" Emily said.

"I didn't bully anyone." It took everything he had not to pull her against him and kiss the hell out of her.

"You told poor Smash to shut up. Was that you being nice?" Emily raised her eyebrow. She was baiting him and damn it only made him want her more.

What the hell is wrong with you?

"Just go back to bed, Emily and let me do my job." Keith was about to step back from her but then she moved one step closer.

"Don't tell me what to do, Mr. O'Connor. You work for me, remember." Emily narrowed her eyes and tapped her finger against his chest.

Keith grabbed her shoulders and backed her against the wall. The move had her eyes go wide, and her mouth dropped open. Keith pressed his body against hers and bent over just enough so that his eyes were level with hers.

"Just so we get this straight, Ms. Bradshaw. I don't work for anyone but myself. Your father is a client, not you, and until he says different, I'll do what it takes to keep you safe, but don't pull that princess shit with me." For a moment he kept her pinned and her warm breath fanned his cheek like a gentle caress.

When her tongue flicked out to moisten her full pink lips he stepped back so fast, Emily almost fell. "Now, would you please go back to bed and get some rest." He turned and stomped out of the salon without looking back to see if she was going to do what he asked.

Outside the cold, crisp air took his breath away. He took a couple of deep inhales and let them out slowly. This woman was going to be the death of him, and he hadn't been with her for more than a day.

There was something about Emily Bradshaw that had his brain turning to jelly. She was sexy, smart and defiant as hell, but she had a vulnerability that he could see no matter how she tried to hide it. She was scared, and he wanted to be the one to take that fear away.

I'll protect you with my life, Princess.

Chapter 7

Emily lay on her bed listening for Keith to come back into her apartment. She really should apologize for being such a bitch, she never treated anyone like that. Too many times in her life she'd seen people from SummerBrook treat individuals with the same disrespect, and it made her sick.

She really didn't know where that attitude had come from, but being pinned against the wall by him was the hottest thing to happen in a long time. It should be against the law for a man to be so damn sexy.

"Damn it, Emily. What's wrong with you?" She whispered to herself.

She turned onto her side and glanced out through her bedroom window. It was at that moment the realization of someone possibly watching her place had her shivering. If Keith hadn't been there, maybe whoever it was would have tried to get inside. A chill ran through her entire body. When she heard a knock on her bedroom door, she bolted upright in the bed.

"Em?" It was Keith, and she relaxed.

"Yeah?" She couldn't hide the tremor in her voice.

"May I come in?"

"Yes." Emily pulled her comforter around her and crossed her legs.

The bedroom door opened and he stepped inside. At first, he just stood inside the door and glanced around the room. Emily stared, waiting for him to say or do something.

"Smash is going to set up cameras on the outside of the building. He'll have access to them and will record all the footage." Keith didn't look at her as he stepped closer to the bed.

"Okay," Emily pulled the blanket tighter around herself.

"I'm going to have the lock changed on the doors as well." He took another step towards the bed as he glanced out the window.

"Why?" She studied his profile while he continued to avoid looking at her.

"Your locks suck." He scanned her room again.

"Gee, thanks." Emily leaned back against her headboard.

"You're welcome." He'd apparently missed her sarcasm. "Well, goodnight." He turned and headed out of the room.

"Keith?" Emily sat up straight. She didn't want him to leave her room. At least not until she said she was sorry.

"Hmm…" He didn't turn.

"For the love of God, can you look at me for a minute?" Emily sighed. He dropped his head, and he took a deep breath before he turned and lifted his gaze to her.

"What is it, Emily?"

"I just wanted to say I'm sorry for what I said down in the salon. I was a bitch, and you didn't deserve to be treated like that."

"It's fine. You're not the first princess I've dealt with." He started to turn.

"I'm not a freaking princess, and will you stop calling me that." Emily jumped off her bed and tossed the blanket on the bed.

"I call it as I see it." He chuckled.

"You're an ass," Emily shoved past him and stomped into her bathroom.

"Tell me something I don't know," He called out. "By the way, the stomping of those cute feet actually proves how princess like you are."

Emily clenched her teeth and growled when she heard her bedroom door close. She'd never wanted to punch someone in her life, but right at that moment, she'd be more than happy to curl up her fist and hit Keith Ass O'Connor right in his nose.

Sunday mornings were usually her favorite day of the week. The shop was closed, but she had a few clients that couldn't make it during weekdays, and she'd accommodate them by making their appointments on that day. Usually, it was only one or two, so she'd still have most of the day to herself.

This Sunday was different. Not only was she dead tired but she had to deal with Keith the whole day. He was going to have an issue with her doing her usual Sunday routine. She was in no mood to deal with his bossy ass either.

Emily was showered and dressed when a sweet aroma of cinnamon surrounded her. She pulled her hair up into a messy ponytail and headed out of her room. As soon as she entered the kitchen her mouth watered. Not because of the enormous pastries on her counter. It was because of the incredibly beautiful man leaning next to it holding a cup, and stuffing his mouth with the last bite of one of the buns.

"Morning. I had my cousin drop off some of her cinnamon rolls." Keith nodded towards the counter. "I didn't know if you liked coffee, so I had her bring coffee and tea."

"I like tea. Thanks." Emily picked up the cup with the large T written on the cover. When she turned back, he held out a plate with one of the warm buns sitting on it.

"It's a peace offering." He smiled, and she inwardly sighed.

"Let's just forget last night. I think we're both just tired and if I'm being honest, I was worried." Emily sat at the table, and Keith followed suit, but not before grabbing another bun.

"I'm sure you were, but I don't want you to worry about your safety. That's why I'm here, and I know you want to stay here, but I'd feel better if you'd at least consider staying at the compound." His blue gaze met hers.

"You know when you say compound, I think stone walls with bars and barbed wire." Emily tore off a piece of the bun and popped it in her mouth. The sweet taste melted on her tongue and she moaned. "That's so good."

"Yeah, Isabelle's a genius." Keith smiled. "As for the compound, it's not what you think. Yes, it's highly secure, but there's no bars or barbed wire." He chuckled.

"That's good to know." Emily finished off her delicious bun and drained her cup. "But we'll have to finish this discussion later. I have a client in thirty minutes."

"Wait? What? It's Sunday! Aren't you closed today?" Keith jumped up from the chair.

"Yes it's Sunday, and the salon is closed, but I do have clients that can't make it during the week, so I have them come in on Sundays. It's not like I'm a mile away from the place." Emily rolled her eyes as she tossed her cup in the garbage.

"Emily, you've got to let me know these things." Keith sighed and plopped back down on the chair.

"Okay, Keith, I've got a client coming today." She smiled and sauntered out of the kitchen.

"You're not funny, Princess." She heard him shout as she headed back into her bedroom to grab her phone.

"Wasn't trying to be." Emily sing songed from her room as she fixed her makeup.

"I want your weekly schedule," Keith said from the doorway of her bedroom.

"Well, I want to be three inches taller and twenty pounds lighter, but we can't all get what we want." Emily finished applying her lipstick and turned around. He'd stepped into the room and was standing mere inches from her.

"You don't need to lose weight, and there is nothing wrong with your height. You don't need to change anything, and I don't want to hear you say anything like that again." His voice was huskier than usual.

She held her breath as his hand hovered next to her cheek, but he didn't touch her. When he dropped his hand back to his side, he stepped back.

"Just don't say things like that." Then he left the room.

When she walked out of her bedroom, he was gone. It was doubtful that he'd left since he was dedicated to protecting her. Even in the short time she'd known him, that was the one thing she was positive of.

In the salon she found him sipping coffee and staring out through the door. For a moment, she watched him. His shoulders seemed tense, and it was the first time she'd noticed the tattoo peeking out from the sleeve of his T-shirt. It was hard to make out what it was, but the colors were incredible.

"Who's the client?" He asked as she set up her station.

"Lizzy Bordon." She said sarcastically. Really did he think if someone was out to hurt her that they would make an appointment to get their hair done.

"Emily, I swear you've got to be the most infuriating woman I've ever met." He turned around, and she felt a pang of guilt.

"It's your aunt," Emily sighed.

"I do have more than one of those." Now he was being sarcastic.

"Cora is coming to get her hair colored." She told him, and as if by magic Cora Nightengale appeared in the doorway.

"Emily Bradshaw, are you giving away my secrets. I want my family to believe that I haven't started to go gray." Cora chuckled. "Well, my handsome nephew finally came here to see his future."

That was Cora. She always said the strangest things to Emily, and when asked what it meant, she'd become cryptic. The woman was quirky that was for sure.

Emily's father had known Cora for a long time, but Emily had only met her over the last couple of years. It was all thanks to her mother's charity work. Cora had started to help Emily's mother about two years earlier.

"Hi, Aunt Cora. I promise your secret is safe with me." Emily's heart fluttered when Keith bent down to kiss his aunt on the cheek. It was sweet and made the man even more appealing. If that was even possible.

"Keithy, I know it is. I'm so glad to see you here with Emily." The woman looked giddy with happiness, and Emily had no idea why.

"Aunt Cora, I'm working for her father. He's worried about her safety." Keith groaned.

"I know. Who do you think suggested you?" Cora patted his cheek and walked to Emily's station.

Emily couldn't help but laugh when Keith slapped his hand against his forehead and rolled his eyes.

"It's good to hear you laugh, Emily." Cora took her hand. "Kurt says there's still no news on your mom." The statement made Emily's smile fade.

People who didn't know her probably thought Emily was heartless. Working every day when her mother was missing. The truth was it was the only way she could keep from falling apart. Whenever she thought about her mother, and where she could be, it made her chest hurt so much it was hard to breathe.

"Have you been talking to Pam lately, Aunt Cora?" Keith winked at Emily. It was as if he knew the subject of her mother was too painful to talk about.

"She calls me a couple of times a week. The conversation usually ends with me asking her when she's coming home." Emily didn't know much about Cora's daughter except she'd been living away for a long time.

"I'm guessing that usually ends the conversation pretty quickly." Keith chuckled.

"Yes, but I don't mean to upset her. I just miss having her in Hopedale." Emily's heart went out to Cora.

"I'm sure she'll come home soon," Keith said.

Cora didn't say anything else about her daughter after that, and for the rest of her appointment, she chatted about the rest of her family. Although, over the last couple of months Cora seemed to focus in on Keith and how Emily really needed to meet him. It was evident Cora was trying to set her up with her nephew.

If she'd met Keith under different circumstances, there'd be a little flirting on her part. Who was she kidding? She wasn't the flirty type. One of her ex-boyfriends once told her she didn't know how to flirt, and that when she tried, she looked foolish. He was a huge ass sometimes, but she still tolerated him since his parents were friends with hers, or at least that's the way it appeared.

The Palmers were the big wigs in her father's circle, but Emily, like her siblings, avoided them whenever they could. At least as they got older. During school, it was hard to avoid them. It was how she got involved with Mitchell in the first place. At first, he'd seemed sweet and completely different from his uptight sister.

She'd been friends with him right up until she'd made the decision not to go to Dalhousie. It was when Mitchell's family started to become nasty. Well, not nasty, things they would say were always put off as jokes, but they did sting.

It was also the reason that Mitchell's sister had told her she should dump the ass, or at least that was what the snooty Ms. Tiffany Palmer told her. Emily did find out the truth a few weeks later. Tiffany wanted to set her brother up with one of her friends because they ran in the same circles.

It didn't matter one way or the other to Emily. She knew in her heart that she and Mitchell weren't meant to be. Especially, since he'd once told her, he thought he might be gay. She still wished she could be there when he finally told his family. That would be the icing on the cake.

Now, she only saw him a couple of times a year, and from what she could find out, his family was still in the dark. The only thing that bothered her when she was around him was the touchy, feely way Mitchell acted. Emily figured it was his way of making sure his secret stayed that way.

"Emily, you always do such an incredible job on my hair." Cora studied herself in the mirror after Emily removed the cape.

"It's easy when you work with great hair. I'm assuming it's a family trait." Emily said.

"It is. I'm sure you've seen my niece's beautiful hair, and just look at the lovely curls Keithy has." Cora motioned to her nephew as he entered the salon.

Emily didn't miss his eye roll or the way his jaw clenched, but she wasn't sure if it was because of the compliment or the name Cora used. It was evident that something bothered him.

"Aunt Cora, Uncle Brian is outside." Keith held up her coat. There was no doubt he'd been taught to be a gentleman.

"Here's your coat, what's your hurry, huh, Keithy?" Cora adjusted her scarf around her neck.

"Not at all." Keith smiled, and Emily's stomach fluttered. He wasn't even smiling at her, and it made her swoon. She grabbed the broom and quickly busied herself sweeping up the hair.

"We need to chat, Princess." Emily almost tripped over her feet when she felt his warm breath blow across her neck.

"Stop. Calling. Me. That." Emily turned and poked Keith in the chest for every word.

"Ms. Bradshaw, we need to chat." The quirk of his lips made her want to punch him.

"Chat away." Emily crossed her arms over her chest, but she didn't miss his glance down to her cleavage. When his eyes came back up, she raised an eyebrow. He didn't seem the least bit embarrassed about being caught. With a smirk, he motioned to the row of chairs lined against the large bay window at the front of the shop.

Emily plopped down in the chair, and Keith sat on the table in front of her. The first thought she had was how the table was going to hold up the weight of the giant man in front of her. He rested his elbows on his knees and stared at her.

"You said there was only one entrance to this building." Keith began, and Emily nodded.

"Smash and Crash were doing a check around the building…" Keith stopped when Emily let out a huge laugh.

"Crash? You know the names of these guys are not making me feel very safe." She chuckled.

"Crash is a nickname. His real name is Brent Adams." Keith shook his head.

"What's your nickname? Sourpuss?" Emily giggled.

"It's Rusty for obvious reasons, but only the guys call me that. Nobody else." He raised an eyebrow, and something told her that she probably shouldn't try to use it.

"Continue." Emily motioned her hand in a circle.

"There's another entrance at the back of the building," Keith said.

"It was, but it's sealed," Emily said. "I was told I couldn't close it off entirely because of fire regulations."

"It was sealed." Keith put the emphasis on the 'was' and it was as if someone poured a glass of ice water down her back.

"Wh…what do you mean?" Emily wrapped her arms around herself.

"Someone opened it." He reached out and placed a comforting hand on her knee. The heat from it radiated up her leg to warm her entire body. Calming her. "Em, it was opened from the outside. I've called Uncle Kurt, and he's sending someone over to check for prints, and Smash is going to reinforce the door. This is why we need to chat." Keith met her gaze, and she knew what he was going to say.

"I can't stay here at night." Emily sighed.

"No." He said.

"I'm not going to SummerBrook." Not only would the drive back and forth every day be a pain in the ass but being in her family home would be too difficult with her mother missing. It was heartbreaking to see what it had done to her siblings and her father. He'd aged in the last few weeks, and although she hadn't seen him in a few days, her sister was keeping her updated.

"There's only one other choice," Keith said.

Emily wasn't sure how comfortable she was going to be staying in a place with a bunch of men. Not that she worried about them doing anything, but she really didn't know any of them. Keith's new sister-in-law, Sandy O'Connor, worked for Newfoundland Security Services, but she was on her honeymoon and then she was going on maternity leave.

"Will I have my own room?" Now she really did sound like a princess.

"What do you think we all live in a one room barracks?" Keith chuckled. "Emily, there are eight cottages on my property. Each one has two bedrooms with their own bathrooms, as well as full kitchens, and living rooms. They all have cable and wifi as well. My house has four bedrooms with their own bathrooms and a huge kitchen. There's also a fully functional gym on the property."

"Are you telling me I need to work out?" Emily narrowed her eyes, but of course, she was joking. He'd made it clear earlier that he didn't think she was overweight.

"Don't put words in my mouth, Princess." He warned.

"I guess I really don't have much choice." Emily sighed. She didn't even care that he called her princess.

"I'll call your dad and let him know." Keith stood up and pulled out his phone.

"Dad knows about all this?" Emily groaned

"One of his stipulations was to keep him in the loop." If she didn't know better, she'd think Keith was almost sorry about giving her father any information. Maybe he was, but she knew her dad and when he wanted information he had his way of getting it.

"Great! That's just the melted butter on the hot homemade bread." Emily slouched down in the chair and rested her head on the back of the chair.

"Well, that's one I've never heard before." Keith chuckled. Emily lifted her head so she could glare at him, but the way he was gazing down at her made her body tense.

"He's worried, Em. Don't give him such a hard time." Keith's voice sounded deeper than usual, and it was odd to hear him call her Em. He'd used the name a couple of times, but the only ones that called her the short version of her name were close friends, and she'd only known the man for less than two days. So why did she feel like she'd known him her whole life?

"Where exactly will I be staying?" Emily didn't have time to think about how connected she felt to a complete stranger. She needed to know where she was going to be hanging her hat for the next little while.

"My house." He said as he disappeared outside.

Chapter 8

Keith was at his wit's end. Nelson rambled on about Emily being stubborn and how he wasn't happy about her refusal to go to SummerBrook. Not that he could blame the woman because it seemed Nelson didn't like the way Emily was running her life.

"I understand, Mr. Bradshaw, but you've got to trust me. She'll be safe at my compound." Keith said for the third time.

"She's just so hard headed, and I know why she doesn't want to come home. She doesn't want to hear the truth." Nelson said. "She's got to stop this little hobby of hers."

"I don't think your daughter considers her business a hobby, but that's something you'll have to discuss with her. I'm going to get her moved and settled." Keith was ending the call before he really told the man what he thought. "I'll keep you posted, Mr. Bradshaw."

Keith found her in her room on her bed with her phone to her ear. When she turned to look at him, he didn't have to ask who she was on the phone with. When she flopped back on her bed and slapped her hand against her face, it was all Keith could do to keep from roaring with laughter.

"Yes, Dad. I know you think I'm not taking this seriously, but for the record, I consider my life possibly being in danger very serious." Emily sighed as she listened for another few seconds. "Dad, I'm not going to live in a bubble. We aren't even one hundred percent sure that I'm in any danger and…" It seemed her father had cut that statement off, and Keith coughed to cover his laugh when she shook the phone above her.

"Dad, I think from now on, we need to agree to disagree. You think my business is beneath me, and I think hanging around with snobs is beneath me. Now, I have to go, but I love you." She tapped the screen of her phone and groaned.

Keith studied her as she lay on her bed with her eyes closed. Her lips were moving as if she was silently praying, but with the tension written on her face, she was probably trying to calm herself.

"Is it wrong to want to shake the crap out of your father?" She turned to face him.

"Probably, but I'm sure every child has felt that way at some point," Keith said. "Are you finished here for the day?"

"If it were up to my father I'd be finished here forever." Her growing resentment was evident in her voice as she stood up and shoved her phone into her back pocket.

"If you just want to grab a couple of things for tonight, then tomorrow you can get enough to do you for a few days." Keith had to switch gears because everything in his body wanted to wrap her up in his arms, and he had no idea why. She'd probably kick him in the balls if he even tried.

"About that, I think I'm just going to stay here." Her voice was almost a whisper. She proceeded to smooth her hands over her bed as if she was straightening out wrinkles.

"Emily," There was no way in hell she was staying in her apartment because he'd have to stay with her, and the damn place was entirely too small. It was dangerous to be in such close quarters with a woman who was setting his body on fire, and she had done nothing but glare at him.

"Keith," She mocked him.

"This is what's going to happen. You're going to pack a bag and get whatever girl stuff you need. Then we're going to lock up your shop and get you settled in a room at my house." Keith clenched his fists at his sides.

"I don't see that happening." Emily stood up and crossed her arms over her chest. The motion not only gave her a defiant stance but it pushed her ample breasts up to swell over the top of her T-shirt. His cock twitched, and so did that nerve over his eye that felt like it was ready to pop.

"Either you pack a bag, or I do it for you. You really don't want me going through your panty drawer, do you?" He wouldn't mind because he'd like to see what she was hiding under the curve fitting clothes she wore.

Emily narrowed her eyes, and she bit her lip as if she was trying to keep from saying something sarcastic. With a huff, she pulled her phone from her pocket and proceeded to tap the screen. She put the phone up to her ear.

"Who are you calling, Princess?" Those blue-grey eyes of hers sparkled with defiance.

"Are you writing a book?" She snapped.

"Maybe I am." Keith chuckled.

"Well, skip the chapter on you finding out who I'm calling." She stomped towards him and pushed past him. "And stop calling me princess." She turned in the doorway of her room to glare at him again.

"I call it as I see it, and right now it fits you like a glove." Keith crossed his arms across his chest. He was quickly losing his patience.

"Have you been told today?" She shot at him.

"As a matter of fact, I tell myself every morning."

"Fuck off." She growled

"And now you've told me." Keith stalked towards her and held his hand out for the phone.

"Dream on, Rusty." She grinned at him. It seemed she thought using his nickname was going to annoy him.

Before she had a chance to move, he had her back pinned against him and the phone in his hand. He glanced at the screen. She'd been calling Kim.

"Let go of me you big ass." She squirmed in his grasp rubbing her soft round ass against his growing erection.

"It's okay, Kim. Emily will call you when she gets settled in the compound." Keith said when Kim finally answered.

"Ooookkkkaaayyy?" Kim said drawing out the word.

Keith ended the call and shoved the phone in his coat pocket. She'd kicked him twice in the shin in the few minutes he'd held onto her.

"Will you calm the fuck down?" Keith grumbled when her heel made contact with his leg a third time.

He wrapped his other arm around her waist and tossed her on the bed. She landed with a grunt and scrambled to get over onto her back. Probably so she could say something rude or shoot daggers from her eyes. When she rolled over her eyes went straight to the growing bulge in his jeans. *Fuck.*

"Get a bag ready now, Emily. I'll be back in ten minutes, and if you don't have one packed, I'll pack it." He stomped out of the room and slammed her bedroom door behind him. He leaned against it and took several deep breaths. How is it with all the women he'd been with none of them had him ready to explode with just a look?

He had to get his fucking shit together. The last time he let his emotions get involved in someone, it ended with her getting killed. In his head, he knew Tessa's death wasn't his fault, but in his heart, he always felt like he let her down.

The bedroom door swung open, and he was barely able to catch himself before he fell into the room. Emily was pissed but held a black bag in her hand.

"Why were you blocking my door? Did you think I was going to make a run for it?" She snapped.

"Do you have everything?" He ignored her snarky questions.

"I've got what I need." She stomped by him and snatched her bag back when he tried to take it for her.

"Just because you carry your own bag doesn't mean you're not a princess." Keith teased.

"Remember what I told you earlier?" She didn't turn around but kept walking towards the exit from her apartment.

"Yes." Keith watched the sway of her hips.

"Consider yourself told again." She headed down the stairs to her salon with him behind her shaking his head. This woman was going to be the death of him.

Emily never spoke to him the entire way to his compound. Not that it was far but ten minutes in his jeep with her seething in the passenger seat was slightly uncomfortable. Not to mention the sweet flowery scent coming from her was making him uncomfortable for a whole other reason.

Smash and Crash were still at her salon securing the building, so he didn't even have them to get his mind off the sexy princess next to him. Keith wasn't taking any chances with her safety which is why they were doing it. There was no way she was going to stay away from the place, and with her possibly in danger, it was safer for the other women working there to have updated security.

Keith pulled up to the front gate and punched in the code to open it. The clang of the metal echoed, and the two iron gates slowly opened. He drove through and waited until both gates closed before proceeding to his house.

Keith loved his property and had tried hard to make sure he left as much of the natural surroundings as possible. It's why he didn't pave his driveway and kept as many of the huge pine trees as he could.

As he drove by the building that housed the gym and offices, he eyed a couple of the guys running on the track circling the two structures.

"That's the offices and the gym." Keith pointed to the area. Emily nodded but still didn't speak.

He pulled into his garage after punching in a code on the remote. Once he was inside, he hopped out and circled around the vehicle to open Emily's door. She sat rigid in the seat as she turned slowly to glare at him.

"If you want to sleep in the jeep that's up to you. It's secure, but it can get a little chilly. It's not real comfortable to sleep in either. At least not like the room I've got ready for you. Would you believe it has a bed?" There was no way she was going to miss out on making a snide comment. He'd figured that out about her.

"You're an ass." She hissed as she jumped down from her seat and stomped around him.

"You're not the first to tell me that, and I'm sure you won't be the last." Keith closed the door once she yanked her bag from the floor of the jeep.

He stepped up to the door leading into his kitchen from the garage and punched in the code. It made a small beep, and the door clicked. He pushed it open and motioned for her to go ahead of him.

"What is this place, Fort Knox?" She walked into the kitchen, but he didn't miss the small gasp that escaped her when she entered the kitchen.

"Not what you expected, Princess?" Keith leaned down and spoke close to her ear. She squeaked and moved to the side.

"Well, no… I mean… this is…" She sighed and turned to face him. "Stop calling me princess."

"I'll see what I can do about that. So you approve of the kitchen?" Keith shuffled through the mail that was sitting on his counter. His cousin Jess always picked it up for him and would drop it off when she'd come for her workout.

"It's impressive." She finally moved further into the room.

"Thanks. I like to have a lot of room to move around when I cook." He didn't look up from the letter he'd opened to gage her reaction.

"Hmmm…. Huge property, big jeep, big house, and big kitchen. Seems like you might be overcompensating for something." Emily deadpanned.

Keith slowly lifted his head, and his gaze met hers. She'd propped herself against the counter and had the sexiest grin on her face.

"Oh Princess, I don't need to overcompensate for anything, but you're more than welcome to investigate if you'd like." Keith turned to face her. He was walking a thin line with her, and it was dangerous, but the panicked look on her face was worth it.

"No thanks." She grumbled and quickly turned to adjust the bag on her shoulder. "I'd like to go to my room."

Once he'd showed her to the room where she'd be staying, Emily thanked him and slammed the door leaving him in the hallway wanting to kick his own ass.

He was a masochist. That was the only conclusion. Every time she insulted or attempted to do so, it made him want her more. The sexual attraction to her was unsettling because he'd never felt it so strong before. It terrified him.

Keith sat on the front deck of his house in the oversized captain's chair. It once belonged to his grandfather, and when Jack O'Connor passed away, his grandmother made sure each of them got something that was personal to his grandfather.

It was coming on suppertime, and he was waiting for his cousin Isabelle to drop by with something from her restaurant. He didn't know what Emily liked to eat, but figured he couldn't go wrong with his cousin. Kim had told Keith that Emily frequently ordered from Isabelle's place.

A sound drew his attention to the tree line on the north side of the house. It was where the thickest part of the trees was around his property. He slowly rose to his feet and moved silently towards the side of the deck. As he scanned the trees, he kept listening for the noise. It had been so faint he was beginning to think he imagined it. With his hand pressed against his weapon in his shoulder holster, he leaned around the corner to look. Nothing.

As he turned to make his way back to his chair, he heard it again. He rested his hands on the rail and leaned over to check the side of his deck. Something small and orange was pressed against the lattice. Keith hurried off the deck and moved to the side.

Keith crouched to see a very tiny kitten tangled in the burlap that surrounded the hedge. It looked up at him with frightened eyes and started to hiss as it squirmed to free itself. All it did was tangle itself more.

"Hey, little one. Calm down and let me get you out of that." Keith cooed hoping it would help the kitten calm. It didn't.

"I'm trying to help you here." Keith sighed as the kitten batted at him a third time. "Can you trust me?" The kitten stopped for a moment and then mewled a couple of times. When he reached for it again, the furball crouched down as if it was ready to attack.

"How the fuck did you get so tangled?" Keith held the body of the kitten in one hand and carefully unhooked it's nails from the burlap. It squeaked as Keith finally freed it. He turned it over to see if he was dealing with a male or a female.

"Figures you'd be a female. You're not the first one to hiss at me today." The kitten fit in his hand, and not that he knew much about it, but it didn't seem like it would be old enough to be separated from its mother. It was shivering and wet.

"Don't think you're staying here, but I can't leave you out here to freeze to death." Keith brought the kitten into the garage and grabbed an empty storage container. "This will be your house until I can figure out what to do with you."

He liked animals but considering he was hardly ever home, it would be cruel to have a pet. As he struggled to open the door into his house, the kitten seemed to want to make sure it wasn't going to fall and dug its sharp nails into his chest.

"Ouch, Fuck." Keith flinched.

He dropped the container to the floor and struggled to remove the kitten's needle-like claws from the front of his shirt. He also didn't want the claws to make their way into his skin and draw blood. Although, the thing seemed to be set on doing just that.

He cupped one hand under its bottom and held it up to get a good look. It seemed terrified, and it was shivering badly. The only thing he could think to do was wrap it in a towel until he could get it dry. As he entered his bathroom, he saw the hair dryer. He sat the kitten on the counter as he turned on the loud dryer. The kitten didn't like it and dug its nails deep into his arm.

"You're a little savage," Keith growled as he dropped the dryer and yanked the towel off the shelf. "Fine, I'll wrap you up in the towel."

He headed back to the kitchen with a couple of other towels to put in the bottom of the container. He remembered something about having a hot water bottle for baby animals on a television show he had watched. He didn't have one, but his heating pad should do the same job.

"I hope you're happy. I don't do this for just anyone." Keith crouched on the floor and did his best to make a comfortable, warm place for his guest.

The storage container was big enough that he could put in a couple of small bowls. He didn't really care about the cat doing it's business because it wasn't staying that long.

With the kitten settled in the box, and his sexy guest upstairs hiding in her room, he poured himself a cup of coffee. He was about to put it up to his lips when he heard the scuffle of his cousin coming through the door.

"No, really, I don't need any help." Isabelle dropped the box filled with steaming bags on the counter. He chuckled at her sarcasm because chances were if he'd offered to help she'd have shooed him away.

"That's why I didn't help." Keith winked at her, and she rolled her eyes.

It didn't take more than thirty seconds before Isabelle noticed the out of place storage container in the middle of the kitchen.

"When did you get a cat?" She reached into the box and picked up the kitten.

"I didn't. I found it snagged in the burlap on the side of the house. Be careful that thing's a savage." Keith eyed the kitten as it began to purr at Isabelle.

"Yeah, it's a killer." She chuckled.

"Don't say I didn't warn you. The fucking thing left holes in my arm." Keith started to rummage through the bags.

"Poor Keith." Isabelle teased. "Why bring her in the house then?" She put the cat back in the box.

"It's supposed to get cold tonight, and I'm not a complete ass," Keith said.

"That's a matter of opinion." Keith's jaw clenched when he heard her voice. "Hi, Isabelle."

"Hey, Emily. From that statement, I'm assuming Keith's being his usual charming self." His cousin made herself comfortable as she hopped up on one of the counter stools.

Emily walked around Isabelle and glanced down into the box. It didn't take long for her to coo over the furball, as she and Isabelle talked about changing the style of his cousin's hair. He grabbed three plates from the cupboard and filled them with food.

"What's her name?" Emily asked as she sat next to his cousin.

"Isabelle." Keith chuckled and quickly ducked as Isabelle tossed a bread roll at him.

"I meant the cat, dumbass." Emily shook her head.

"I'm not naming that thing. I'm gonna put a message on social media to see if anyone lost it." Keith shoved another forkful of potatoes into his mouth.

"That could take a while. What are you going to call the little thing until then? Cat?" Isabelle laughed.

"I don't remember asking you to stay for supper." Keith glared at her.

"They say at your age the first thing to go is the mind." Isabelle grinned, and Keith didn't miss the giggle from Emily either.

"One of my customers is a vet. I can give her a call and see if she can drop by. She's not far from here." Isabelle offered.

"A vet that does house calls. No, that won't cost an arm and a leg." Keith said sarcastically as he refilled his plate.

"She owes me a favor. Seriously, that kitten looks really young." Keith stared at his cousin. She was right, and he wouldn't want anything to happen to the tiny thing. He wasn't heartless.

"Fine, but you'll have to meet her at the gate." Keith glanced down into the box. At least the thing was drinking the water.

"She still needs a name." Emily picked up the kitten and cuddled it into her chest, and the first thought that came to his mind was *lucky little bastard*.

"Cat sounds good to me." Keith cleaned his plate and placed it in the dishwasher.

"You're hopeless," Isabelle sighed as she finished her phone call. "You could call her Ginger since her fur is almost the same color as your hair."

"I think next time I order food it'll be from somewhere besides your place." Keith narrowed his eyes and glared at her. Isabelle elegantly lifted her hand as her middle finger slowly raised.

"Did I hear you say you found her tangled in the burlap outside?" Emily asked.

"Yeah, she had her claws hooked in there pretty good." Keith noticed that Emily hadn't touched the food in front of her.

"Call her Burlap." Emily smiled and her nose wrinkled as if waiting for someone to laugh. Her gaze moved back and forth between him and Isabelle.

"That is so cute." Isabelle cooed.

"It doesn't matter I'm not keeping it, but if it makes you feel better, call the thing what you want." Keith rested his elbows on the counter and tapped the edge of her plate.

"So it's settled. Burlap's your name." Emily held the kitten up to her lips and kissed the top of its head. He never thought he'd ever want to be a cat, but it didn't seem all that bad with the attention Emily was giving the fucking thing.

"So now that's settled. I believe you need to eat." Keith tapped the plate again, and she rolled her eyes as she gently put the kitten on the floor.

"Bea should be here in about five minutes. I'm going to meet her at the gate." Isabelle glanced at her phone.

Keith kept his gaze on Emily as she picked at the food. She had to be hungry because she hadn't eaten anything since breakfast and she didn't eat much then.

"If you don't eat you're going to get sick." He never thought he'd utter the line his mother used when they were kids.

"I think I can afford to miss a few meals." Emily picked up a piece of chicken and popped it into her mouth.

"Don't say things like that." Keith leaned closer to her. "There's nothing wrong with how you look."

Her eyes lifted to meet his, and he was sure she could hear the thudding of his heart because it was pounding in his ears. When she met his eyes, it was as if she could see right into the depths of his soul, and that probably wasn't a good thing. Her lips curled up into a sweet smile and then into a soft giggle, but it wasn't until he felt the tiny needles in his thigh that he realized what was happening.

"She thinks you're a tree." Emily covered her mouth with her hand.

"You're really pushing it, cat," Keith grumbled while he tried to unhook the kitten's claws from his jeans. It wasn't going well.

"Her name is Burlap. Let me help." Emily crouched and proceeded to detach the cat from his leg carefully.

Having Emily touch his thigh and kneeling in front of him was putting all kinds of wrong thoughts in his head. He gripped onto the edge of the counter and clamped his teeth together, but he couldn't stop watching how gently she removed Burlap. What was worse, she stayed on her knees on the floor to calm the kitten. How she didn't see the outline of his cock was a miracle because all she had to do was lift her head. He quickly moved behind the island.

"Fuck." He hissed between his teeth as he braced his fists against the counter.

"Oh don't be such a baby. I'm sure the needles they used for those tattoos hurt more than Burlap's claws." Emily teased when she got back to her feet, and he thanked God she was finally off of her knees.

"Just put that thing in the box. I'm not being its pin cushion again."

Before Emily had a chance to put Burlap down, Isabelle and the vet walked into the kitchen. Isabelle introduced Beatrice as Dr. Warren. Apparently, she didn't seem to mind what they called her. The vet proceeded to examine the kitten, and Burlap didn't seem too happy about the whole situation. She mewled the whole time and even managed to let out a little hiss or two.

Emily and Isabelle continued to talk to the cat as if it were a child while the vet finished her examination. Keith couldn't believe that there was so much fuss over a kitten, but before he knew it, he was trying to calm the thing as well.

"From what I can see, she's small, but I'd say about eight weeks maybe seven. Other than her size she's healthy. I've brought some food we use for underweight kittens and deworming medication. Chances are it wasn't done, and I can feel a few small ones in her belly." Beatrice explained as she worked to keep Burlap from jumping off the counter.

"So she's okay?" Emily seemed to be itching to take the kitten into her arms again.

"Yes, and I can see she doesn't have a litter box. I have a disposable one in my car that will do until you can get a permanent one."

Burlap had calmed some since Beatrice had let her wander around the counter. The stupid cat bounded towards him and pressed its head against the hand he had rested on the marble. He knew what was going to happen but damn if he didn't want to admit it.

"Looks like you have a healthy kitten, Keith." Isabelle smiled.

"So I hear." Keith stared down at the copper-colored furball and knew at that moment, Burlap was home.

"You're keeping her?" Emily sounded both hopeful and surprised.

"Unless someone gets back to me on social media, I might as well." Nothing could prepare him for what happened next. Emily ran around the counter and wrapped her arms around his waist. He stiffened as she hugged him tightly.

"I knew you had a heart in there somewhere." She squeezed once more before she let go. It was as if she'd taken all the heat from his body when she stepped away. This wasn't good. Not good at all.

Fuck!

A week later Keith stood in his kitchen listening to Emily argue with her father. Nelson had come to see her, but it wasn't turning out to be a civil visit. Probably because five minutes after he arrived he growled about her working on a Sunday. Emily had turned down his invitation to spend the evening with him in SummerBrook, which had provoked his visit.

"Dad, I don't have time to fight about this. I've got to get to the salon." Emily took a deep breath when Nelson slapped his hand down on the counter.

"Emily, when are you going to at least acknowledge that this isn't the life for you."

Emily opened her mouth and then snapped it shut again. She walked around her father, and before Keith knew what had happened, she was gone.

"Emily, come back here," Nelson yelled after her.

"I'm sorry Mr. Bradshaw, but I need to go after her." Keith ran out through the garage in time to see her pull out in his jeep.

"How the fuck…" Keith didn't even see her grab the keys and he'd made the mistake of letting her know all the codes.

"You're losing your touch, Rusty." Keith turned. Rex had his back braced against the garage door. He was a guy Keith hired from the Atlanta, Georgia. His name is Caden Dixon, and he was former military. Keith didn't know where the nickname came from, but that's what everyone called him.

"I'm losing it all right." Keith grabbed the keys for the car in the garage that he hardly used. "Tell Bradshaw I'll call him later and take him home."

He drove to the salon, sure there was probably steam coming from his ears. Not only did Emily take off with no security, but she took his jeep. He never let anyone drive his baby.

"Grandda, give me the patience to deal with this because I'm pretty sure I've met a younger version of Nan." Keith always found himself talking to his grandfather when he was overly stressed. Probably because before Jack O'Connor passed away, he was always the one Keith would talk to about his problems. The man gave great advice.

By the time Keith pulled up in front of the salon, Emily was already inside with her client. *Kristy*. His cousin waved at him as he walked into the building.

"Hey, How's it goin?" Kristy smiled, but Keith didn't feel very cordial at the moment.

"It was goin great until someone stole my jeep." Keith glanced at Emily. She didn't seem to be the least bit worried.

"How the hell did someone get into your compound to steal your jeep?" Kristy didn't realize he was talking about Emily.

"I took it to get here." Emily groaned. "I borrowed it. I didn't steal it. Don't be so dramatic, Keith."

"Oh, oh, pot meet kettle." Keith threw his hands up in the air. "You took off because you didn't want to deal with your father. Not to mention that you took off without taking your safety into consideration."

"I had an appointment as you can see," Emily shouted.

"I'm sure Kristy would have been fine with you being late." Keith raised his voice.

"Jesus, you two sound like a married couple." Kristy laughed but stopped when both Emily and he glared at her.

Keith was about to speak, but Emily ended the conversation by holding her hand up. He didn't want to fight with her, so he stepped outside the salon and let the smell of the ocean help calm him.

Exactly forty-three minutes later Kristy was gone, and Emily had disappeared into her office. If she thought their conversation was over, she was sadly mistaken.

"Emily, you've got to come back to the compound." Keith blocked the exit of her office. He'd calmed himself and figured he was better able to handle her mood.

"Look, Mr. O'Connor.." Emily snapped

"Keith."

"Mr. O'Connor," Emily glared at him. "I've got a business to run, and I need to be here." She picked up some papers on her desk and glanced through them. He knew it was the same ones she had put in the basket to file the day before.

"Your father…." Keith began but Emily's eyes snapped up, and they were beautifully dark with anger.

"I really don't give a flying fig what my father says." She plopped down in the chair behind her desk. "He thinks my business is beneath me. I should be striving to be something important." She mocked as she turned on her computer. "So standing here telling me what my father thinks, is not helping your case any."

"Your father loves you, and he's hurting." Keith tried to play on her sympathies. Although, hell if her attitude did not make him want to clap his hands. Emily didn't bow down to what was expected. It was good to know that not all the women from SummerBrook were spoiled brats.

"I know he misses mom. We all do, and I know he loves me. Really. I love him too, but you don't know what it's like to love something so much and to constantly be told it's not a good enough career for a fucking Bradshaw. Like we're above the typical blue collar jobs. It's been worse since mom vanished. I love my business and what I do. There's nothing more fulfilling than when a client thanks you because they feel beautiful after a haircut or having their makeup done." Emily sat back in the chair and blew out a breath. Damn, she was so passionate and beautiful. Especially when she was pissed.

"Mom understood how I felt about this place, but I can't get dad to understand, and when he does this, I just walk away before I say something I'll regret."

"I see your point." Keith leaned against the wall and crossed his arms over his chest.

"Well, hall-a-fucking-luia. Someone outside of my employees and clients sees my point. I'm so fucking overjoyed." Keith tried very hard not to laugh. The girl had a mouth on her.

"I'm glad you're overjoyed, but we still have a problem." Keith raised an eyebrow when she slammed her hands down on her desk.

"We don't have any problems. I'm perfectly happy. You may have a problem, but you know what? I don't give two fucks about your problems, Mr. O'Connor." Emily stood up and narrowed her eyes. She was baiting him. She only called him Mr. O'Connor when she was pissed.

"You know I could easily take you over my shoulder, carry you out to the jeep and bring you back to the compound." Keith almost lost it when her face turned purple with fury.

"You put one of your big meat hooks on me, and I'll kick your balls so hard, your father will feel it," Emily growled through gritted teeth.

"That sounds really painful, and I don't think Dad would appreciate it either. Plus, I said I could. I never said I would. Besides, if I was going to throw you over my shoulder, it sure as hell would be for something a hell of a lot more fun." For the first time since he met her, she was dumbstruck. "Wondering what would be more fun, Ms. Bradshaw?" He smirked.

"Fuck off." Was all she could say.

"Great come back, Emily." Keith chuckled.

"You know, I've done more cursing since I met you than I have my entire life." She flopped back in her chair.

"I'm glad I'm helping increase your vocabulary," Keith said.

When she stood up, again he fully expected her to continue their banter, but she walked around him and flicked off the lights in the office.

"I'm done if you're ready," Emily called from the front of the salon. "I can drive back."

"Let's get something straight," Keith informed her once they were outside. "That was the first and only time you drive that."

"What is it with men and their trucks?" She rolled her eyes and tossed the keys at him.

"It's not a truck. It's a 1974, FJ40 Land Cruiser. It's in mint condition because nobody drives it but me." He probably sounded like a complete idiot, but the jeep was one of his most prized possessions.

"Wow. I'm so impressed." Emily faked a yawn as she shuffled to the jeep. He was convinced she was swaying her hips more just to get to him as she walked away. It was working because his cock was twitching and his balls ached.

"God, help me," Keith whispered as he walked behind her.

Chapter 9

Ten days Emily had been at Keith's house, and it wasn't terrible. They had that little spat, but that was mostly because of her father. Well, that and the fact she'd stolen his jeep.

Keith brought her to work every day and managed to stay out of her way. Most of the time he'd sit behind the reception desk and even helped with the clean up at the end of the day.

Even the girls had gotten used to him being underfoot. Most of the time he was teased by Aurora about his big feet in her way, or Penny making sure she reminded him to keep his eyes off her chest. Of course most of the time Penny was just doing it to embarrass him. Emily was sure the woman enjoyed showing off her assets.

"I don't know how you get any work done with that beautiful specimen around." Her customer motioned towards where Keith had just disappeared into the back of the salon. Cinnamon Dwyer was not her favorite client, and Emily dreaded the days when she'd have an appointment, but like her sister Ginger, she paid well.

"It's a struggle." Emily smiled as she put the finishing touches on the woman's hair.

"I've heard stories about those O'Connor boys," Cinnamon whispered.

"Well, you know what they say? Believe half of what you see and none of what you hear." Emily pulled the cape off a little rougher than she should. It didn't stop the bitch from continuing her gossip.

"Oh, I found out from a reliable source. This person spent a weekend with one of them and said he made her scream more times than her husband ever did." Cinnamon cupped her hand around her mouth as if she was telling a secret only to Emily, but from Ada's tutting, Emily was pretty sure everyone in the salon heard it.

"Young lady, I've known those boys since they were kids and I assure you if a married woman told you she was with one of them, she's lying, because no matter what, they would never do anything to jeopardize someone's marriage." Ada chastized Cinnamon, and Emily wanted to cheer her on but kept quiet.

"She was separated from her husband if you must know, but you probably shouldn't be eavesdropping on private conversations." Cinnamon stood up and lifted her nose at Ada.

"Honey, if that was supposed to be private then you should probably check the volume on that whiney voice of yours." Penny sashayed by with an armful of towels.

"Emily, if this is how you allow your employees to treat clients, I think you need to have a chat with them." Cinnamon pulled on her coat and huffed to the reception counter.

"I'm not sure they're the ones that need to be spoken to." Emily spun when she heard the gruff voice behind her. Keith had apparently not missed the conversation either. He placed his large hand on Emily's shoulder and leaned towards Cinnamon.

"What's that supposed to mean?" Emily almost laughed when Cinnamon pressed her hand against her cheek and fluttered her eyes at Keith.

"You see, a true lady doesn't spread gossip or tell people about other people's conquests, real or imagined. As for your friend, I can't say if she's truthful or not, but if she is, I'm sure my brother did make her scream. We know how to please a lady, but they have to actually be a lady." Keith gave Emily's shoulder a little squeeze. "It's why the ladies in this salon don't gossip. They are true ladies." Then he was gone, and Emily immediately missed his touch.

"Emily, I'm just letting you know I will not be coming back here again, and I'm going to make sure everyone knows how poorly I was treated." Cinnamon grabbed her card from Aurora's hand and stomped out through the door. As soon as it closed everyone, including the clients waiting in the lounge burst into laughter.

"Thank the Lord for small favors," Penny yelled over the laughter.

Even though Emily was laughing with them, fear filled her stomach. The Dwyer family knew a lot of people and could probably ruin Emily's reputation. She was sure it wouldn't kill her business, but she had a lot of clients from SummerBrook that would listen to Cinnamon and never come back. The worst would be all this getting back to her father and giving him another reason to rant about how she was ruining her life.

Emily made her way to her office for a little peace and quiet. She'd give it about two hours before she'd receive a call from her dad. Even with her mother still missing, and him out of his mind with worry, he never missed the chance to put down her choice of careers.

Sitting in her chair, she rested her elbows on her desk and covered her face with her hands. *Breathe in, breathe out, breathe in, breathe out.* Her mother's advice never failed. Whenever Emily would be at her breaking point, her mom would tell her to sit quietly and think of nothing but breathing. It worked most of the time, but something else eased her frayed nerves this time.

"I'm sorry, Princess." His voice startled her, but she'd been aware of his presence before she even realized it. His scent was the something else that calmed her.

"Can you stop calling me princess?" She didn't move. "I'm not a princess, and I've never been one."

"Em, I'm not using that as an insult." He'd come closer, and his woodsy scent played havoc with her senses.

"It feels like one." She turned her head. He was crouched next to her with his arm rested on her desk.

"It's not, and I'm sorry about overstepping with that …. Woman." He seemed to be struggling with calling Cinnamon anything but what she was.

"Don't worry about it. She's a bitch, and everyone knows it. The only one of the spice family that's down to earth is Basil." Emily smiled.

"Did you say the spice family?" Keith raised an eyebrow. "Penny said that woman's last name was Dwyer."

"It is, but all the kids are named after some sort of spice or herb." Emily giggled at his reaction. "There's Ginger, Clove, Basil and Cinnamon."

"Who the fuck does that shit? What are the parent's names, Salt, and Pepper?" Keith laughed and then stopped to look at her. "That's not their names is it?"

Emily burst into a fit of laughter because at that moment, between his question, and the look of horror on his face, it was the funniest thing she'd ever seen. Every time she'd calm a little, she'd glance at him and fall into another fit of laughter.

"Hey, want to fill me in on the joke." Emily glanced towards the office door. Kim stood there with her hands on her hips. "We can hear you out front."

"Keith,…" Emily burst into laughter again.

"Yeah, he's kinda funny looking." Kim moved into the office and flopped down in the chair next to the desk.

"Bite me, Kim." Keith stood up and walked towards her.

"Sorry, you might like it too much." Kim grinned. "So come on, what's the joke?"

"He asked if Cinnamon's parent's names were salt and pepper," Emily managed to get out between giggles.

"Are they?" Kim said seriously, and that sent Emily into another fit of laughter.

"I'm thinking probably not, she's been laughing about it since I asked." Keith chuckled.

An hour later Emily's stomach hurt from laughing so hard, but the stress of waiting for her dad's call had started to build again. Kim and Penny told her to go home and get some rest. Not that she considered Keith's place home, but since he wouldn't let her stay in her apartment, it was home for now.

Emily had to admit Keith made her feel at home. He gave her full access to the house and kept his distance. They did eat together every evening, and he'd entertain her with stories of his nieces and nephews. The sad thing was the more time she spent with him, the more she liked him.

Then there was her night time tossing and turning. Nightmares of her mother and what could have happened to her. Then there were the dreams of Keith and her doing things that had her waking up sweating and aroused.

They'd just finished supper, and she helped Keith tidy up the kitchen. Almost simultaneously the doorbell rang, and Keith's cell phone chimed.

"Can you get that?" Keith asked as he put the phone to his ear.

Emily hurried to the door but had to jump back when it flew open, and a very pregnant Sandy stomped through inside. She stopped on the front porch and pressed her hands against her lower back. Emily stepped around her and closed the door so the kitten wouldn't escape. Burlap had a tendency to appear out of nowhere and run into rooms Keith tried to keep her out of.

"Hi, Sandy. How was the honeymoon? Kim said you came back early." Emily motioned for Sandy to go ahead of her into the kitchen.

"It was either we came back early, or I was going to go to jail for murdering my husband," Sandy grumbled as she eased her large body into one of the kitchen chairs.

"Can I get you something?" Emily glanced at Keith's amused expression.

"You know what I'd like? A hot cup of black coffee, but nooo, I'm not allowed to have coffee because Dr. Asshole says caffeine is not healthy for the baby, but do you know what's not healthy for the baby? Having his mother thrown in jail for killing his father because if Ian doesn't back off, I'm going to snap, and that wouldn't be good because I own guns." Sandy snarled when Keith laughed.

"Ummm…. I don't know what to say to that, but what about some tea?" Emily stammered.

"Yes, thanks, Emily. I'm sorry I'm just irritated and uncomfortable and horny," Sandy sighed.

Emily stared at Sandy for a moment. There was no way the woman said she was horny. In her condition, there was no possible way the woman wanted to have sex.

"That's way too much information, kiddo." Keith chuckled as he filled the kettle.

"Fuck off, Keith. Ian is a freaking doctor, and he knows it's fine to have sex while you're pregnant. I need this baby out, and they say sex works." Sandy glared at Keith, and Emily could now see what the words 'if looks could kill' meant.

111

"Three or four times a day, kiddo. Ian says he can't keep up with you lately." Keith leaned his hip against the counter.

"Keith, I swear I can make it a double murder. Just keep it up." Sandy grumbled.

"Oh, calm down," Keith moved over behind Sandy and rubbed her shoulders. Emily's stomach clenched. How could she be jealous of Keith touching another woman? Especially one that was married to his brother.

"I just want him out." Sandy sounded as if she was going to burst into tears.

"I'm sure you do, kiddo. It won't be long now." Sandy stood up, and Keith hugged her. Again that sick feeling of jealousy hit the pit of Emily's gut.

"Oh. Shit." Sandy gasped, and her gaze slowly moved to the ground. On the floor where Keith and Sandy stood was a pool of water.

"Is that what I think it is?" Emily quickly moved next to Sandy as Keith stepped back and pulled out his phone.

"I'm calling Ian," Keith shouted.

"Why are you yelling?" Emily asked as she held Sandy's hand.

"I don't know." Again he yelled.

"Just get me to the car." Sandy rolled her eyes.

"Ian, Sandy's water just broke." Keith was still shouting, and Emily giggled when Sandy swirled her finger next to her temple, indicating she thought Keith was crazy.

"Are you in any pain?" Emily wrapped her arm around Sandy as she guided her out of the kitchen.

"No, not yet," Sandy said.

"Ian said he's leaving the gym and should be here in a minute," Keith's voice boomed behind Emily.

"For the love of God, Keith, stop yelling." Emily groaned as she grabbed her purse.

"Sorry," He lowered his voice and gave her that heart melting smile. "I don't like not knowing what to do."

"So yelling helps that?" Emily laughed.

"You better get something to put on your seat," Sandy motioned down to her wet pants.

Once Keith had placed a garbage bag and a couple of towels on the back seat, he helped Sandy into the back of his jeep. He yanked open the passenger door and motioned Emily to get in.

"I can stay here." She didn't feel comfortable interfering in a family affair.

"Emily, no arguments. I'm going with my brother and Sandy, and you aren't staying here alone." Keith pointed to the front seat.

113

She was about to argue, but a deep groan from the back seat of the vehicle had her jumping in and turning to make sure Sandy was okay. Before Keith made his way around to the other side, the back door opened and Ian jumped in beside his wife. He lifted Sandy's hand up to his lips and kissed it tenderly. Emily was astounded at how quickly Sandy's face relaxed.

"I'm sorry about being a bitch today." Sandy sighed.

"Churchie, you weren't a bitch. I love you. You ready to meet our little slugger?" Ian wrapped his arm around Sandy and pressed his hand against her swollen belly.

"I'm sure I told you I was ready to meet him a week ago." Sandy giggled and then gasped. "Ouch."

By the time they got to the hospital, Sandy was saying a lot more than *ouch*. She'd also made a few comments on how Ian was never getting sex again. Emily didn't miss Keith's chuckle, and since only minutes before Sandy had been complaining about not getting enough.

Emily shouldn't have been surprised when within an hour the waiting room was filled with most of the O'Connor clan. She felt completely out of place. It didn't help that Cora made comments about how she was part of the family. Keith's body tensed next to her when his aunt hugged Emily and said it wouldn't take long.

"Well look here. Young Emily come ta join us." It was Keith's grandmother. Emily knew her well since she came to the salon every couple of weeks to have her hair done. She was Kim's client but when Nanny Betty walked in everyone knew it. The woman was a whirlwind. Emily knew she was in her late seventies, but she didn't look it and certainly didn't act it.

"Hello, Mrs. O'Connor," Emily smiled as the tiny woman sat next to her.

"Oh lass, Mrs. O'Connor was me mother-in-law, and she was a witch. All me girls call me Nan. I'm sure I told ya dat before." Nanny Betty patted Emily's hand.

"Uh oh, you're one of Nan's girls." Jess chuckled.

Jess was Keith's cousin. Emily knew all of the women from the family because they came to the salon. She'd met a few of Keith's brothers but only in passing when they'd come pick someone up.

Emily had gone out to a few parties with Kim, and the O'Connor girls had joined them most of the time. They were such a friendly bunch and were nothing like the girls in SummerBrook. They accepted everyone no matter who they were or where they were from.

"Yes she is, and Keithy will take good care of her." Nanny Betty said.

Keith looked as uncomfortable as Emily felt. It seemed his grandmother thought there was more going on between her grandson and Emily than there actually was. Someone had to set the poor woman straight.

"He's keeping me safe." Emily smiled.

"A course he is. Dat's what a man does fer his girl." With that comment, Nanny Betty jumped up and made her way to the older man who'd walked in. Emily was pretty sure the man's name was Tom, and he was dating Nanny Betty.

"I'm sorry about that." Emily jumped at the sound of his voice. For someone so large he moved like a shadow. "That's Aunt Cora's fault for putting things in Nan's head."

"She's never wrong." Kristy teased as she walked by.

"Shut up, Brat," Keith growled through clenched teeth.

"What's the big deal with Cora?" Emily spoke quietly to make sure nobody else could hear besides Keith.

"It's nothing really. She has this weird reputation and because she's been right a few times everyone believes she has some sort of superpower." Keith rolled his eyes. "The family calls her Cora the cupid."

"Seriously?" Emily laughed.

"Yes, and don't dare joke about it with Nan." Keith chuckled as he leaned back in the chair and glanced around the room.

No matter how many times she studied his features, she was in awe of how perfect his face was. Strong jaw covered with a beard a little redder than his thick hair, and his nose the perfect size for his face. Then there were those blue eyes. Emily knew if she let herself look into them she'd be lost.

"Something wrong?" Keith grinned, showing perfect white teeth.

"I was just wondering if you had a nose job." Emily lied, because what was she supposed to say? *I was just admiring how absolutely gorgeous you are.*

His laugh boomed in the room, and everyone turned. Suddenly Emily felt exposed with all eyes on them. It was as if she was back in high school and standing in front of the whole school to do her speech on World War Two. Her stomach tightened, and she clasped her hands together.

"I've never had a nose job." Keith leaned close to her ear. "Do you think I need one?"

Emily turned. A small gasp escaped when she realized how close his face was. The blue in his eyes was the color of a summer sky, and his scent filled her senses. Her gaze dropped to his full lips.

"Don't do that, Em," Keith growled.

"Do what?" She managed to whisper as her eyes moved back up to his.

"Stare at me with those big beautiful eyes," Keith whispered.

"She's eight centimeters dilated." The boom of Ian's voice broke the spell, and Emily jumped to her feet.

"It won't be long now." Keith's mother cooed. "I'm going to facetime the girls and let them know they'll have a baby brother soon."

Ian and Sandy already had three daughters between the two of them. Emily didn't know the whole story, but it seemed they were a blended family and were now adding a little boy to the mix. They had what Emily had always wanted. A beautiful family and they were deeply in love.

"Who wants to bet Sandy punches Ian?" Emily glanced across the room at the man she'd mistaken for her security that first day. She now knew his name was Aaron, but everyone called him A.J. He was the youngest of the O'Connor brothers and from what she'd seen a huge flirt.

"Not a fair bet. She already did that in the jeep." Keith laughed.

Just before they'd gotten to the front of the hospital, Sandy had curled up her fist and swung it at her husband. For some reason, him telling her she was doing a great job pissed her off. Apparently, she thought he was being sarcastic.

"And you didn't record it." The man standing next to A.J. laughed. Emily heard someone call him Nick when he arrived. He was obviously another of the O'Connor brothers because he looked so much like Aaron they could be twins.

"Did anyone call Kurt and Alice?" Sean asked.

"Alice is on her way, but Kurt had something urgent he had to attend to at the station," Cora informed everyone.

"Dat man works too hard." Nanny Betty complained. "It's time fer him ta retire."

"I don't see that happening anytime soon, Nan," James said. "He's not gonna retire until they make him." A round of nods and agreeing went around the waiting room.

Emily sat back on the seat she'd jumped up from. Keith hadn't moved, and his amazing fragrance engulfed her. It still made no sense how his spicy scent made her relax and tense at the same time.

To distract herself, Emily pulled her phone from her purse. Maybe playing a game of cookie crush would help, but when she opened the screen, there were several missed calls from her sister and brother. It wasn't unusual for them to call but not so many times without at least leaving a message or text

Keith's phone chirped as she was about to tap her sister's number. He turned it so she could see her father's number and held up his finger as he touched the screen.

"Hello," Keith answered in a quiet voice. He listened for a moment, but Emily didn't see any change in his expression. He could be so stone-faced.

Her phone buzzed in her hand, and her sisters face appeared on the screen. When she held it up for Keith, he shook his head. Why wouldn't she answer her sister's call? Being her usual defiant self, she answered.

"Hello," Emily pulled the phone from her ear when Elaine's voice screeched into her ear.

"Emily, where the hell have you been?" It was so unlike her sister to sound so panicked.

"Keith's sister-in-law went into labor, and we brought her to the hospital," Emily explained.

"Em, which hospital?" Elaine asked.

"The Health Science Center." Keith was still talking on the phone, but his gaze hadn't moved from her.

"Em, they found her." Every bit of air whooshed out of her, and it took a moment before she could remember how to breathe again.

"They… found her…. Mom?" Emily's voice cracked.

A million questions ran through her head, but she was terrified to ask them. The first. Was her mother alive?

"She's alive," Elaine answered the unspoken question.

"She is?" Huge tears overflowed and streamed down her cheeks.

"Yes, we're in the Emergency Department," Elaine told her. Without another word, Emily grabbed her purse and ran out of the waiting room. Before she made it through the door, a hand wrapped around her arm and yanked her to a stop.

"Where are you going?" Keith backed her up until she was against the wall.

"My mother's down in the emergency department." The tears wouldn't stop, but she didn't care. "She's alive."

"I know, but you can't go running off without me." Keith held her shoulders in his strong hands and heat radiated through her body.

"Keith, I'll be fine. You need to stay with your family." Emily tried to shrug off his grasp, but his hands slowly slid down her arms and took her hands.

"Princess, almost all my family's in that room. I'm not letting you out of my sight. Just let me tell them what's going on, and we can go." He didn't release her hand until she nodded, and even after he disappeared into the waiting room, she could still feel the warmth of his touch.

Emily realized she hadn't hung up her phone, but when she looked at the screen, the call had ended. She texted her sister and told her she was on the way. While she listened to the low rumble of Keith's voice explaining things to his family, she rested her head against the wall and stared up at the ceiling.

A cold chill ran down her spine, making the hair on the back of her neck stand up. She stood up straight and looked around. Out of the corner of her eye, a dark figure disappeared around the corner. She started to head in the direction, but a hand caught hers.

"Are you ever going to listen to me?" Keith shook his head and squeezed her hand gently.

"I thought I saw someone staring at me." Emily motioned towards the elevator and then shook her head. "I'm just being paranoid."

"Stay here." Keith never gave her a chance to answer as he dropped her hand and jogged down to the elevators. He scanned both ways and then turned around. When he shrugged his shoulders, Emily wanted to crawl under a chair and disappear. She'd never been the type to overreact.

Great! I'm going crazy.

Chapter 10

The Emergency room was overcrowded as usual, and Emily frantically searched for her family. Keith kept her hand in his because it seemed to be the only thing to keep her from falling apart, or at least it was the reason he told himself. Her mother had been missing for almost three weeks, and Keith was sure the things going through Emily's head were horrific.

"Could you tell me where the family of Lynn Ann Bradshaw is waiting?" Keith asked a stern looking nurse.

"Who are you?" Nurse crappy attitude asked as she looked him up and down.

"This is her daughter, Emily and I'm her…." Keith glanced at Emily. For some reason, he was at a loss as what to call himself.

"This is my good friend," Emily interjected.

"I'm sorry, I can only let family inside." The woman snapped at Emily. Keith had to press his lips together to keep himself from giving the nurse a piece of his mind. For someone that was supposed to make people feel better, the nurse was not the best example of a health care professional.

"I'm in no mood for this," Emily muttered and stepped in front of Keith. "I don't know who stuck a stick up your ass, but I need you to bring me to my family. Keith will be coming in with me because he's here to support me. If you can't do that, then get me someone who can."

Keith cringed. To hear Emily sound so rude didn't sit well with him. It was obvious she was scared but acting like a spoiled brat wasn't going to work with nurse cranky ass.

"There are regulations, Ms. Bradshaw and rules state only the family are permitted." It seemed the woman wasn't intimidated easily.

Emily pulled out her phone and Keith saw her tap her father's number. From the way her face fell, her call didn't go through. She tried tapping her brother and sister's number, but Keith could see she wasn't getting anywhere.

Keith dug his phone out of his pocket and scrolled down to the number he knew would get results. It only rang once, then he heard the southern twang of Rex.

"Hey, Rex. Could you come out to the emergency department and show us where Emily's family are located. We aren't getting any luck from nurse Cratchet out here." Keith kept his voice quiet.

"Gray hair and pointy nose?" Rex asked.

"Yeah."

"Yep, she's a ray of sunshine that one." Rex chuckled. "I'll be there in ten seconds.

Keith turned to speak to Emily, and he swore he could see smoke coming out of her ears.

"Could you at least go get one of my family and tell them I'm here," Emily growled.

"I can't leave the triage." The nurse snapped.

"You know, you're a ...." Keith tapped Emily on the shoulder to stop her before she got herself kicked out of the hospital.

"It's okay." Keith motioned to Rex holding open the security door.

Before Keith could stop her, Emily turned back to the nurse who was glaring at them. Emily lifted her hand and raised her middle finger, but Keith stepped in front of her and guided her through the door.

"She can have you removed from the hospital," Keith whispered next to her ear as the door closed behind them. He didn't miss her sudden intake of breath or the shiver. "Stop acting like a spoiled little rich girl. I know that's not you, Princess."

The statement probably stung, but he'd learned Emily was not that type of person. He was learning pretty quickly she didn't like the snobby way the women from her town acted.

Emily sighed several times as she tried to walk by Rex, but his guy went by the book, and since he was one of the security for the family he stayed in front. It was obviously pissing Emily off. Rex was former American military, and there was no doubting it with the way he held himself.

Emily stopped at the door of the waiting room. Her father sat with his hands clasped in front of his face, elbows rested on his knees and his eyes closed. Edward sat in a similar position, but his eyes were focused on the small window in the room. Elaine was curled up on a couple of the chairs with her eyes closed. From the smooth rhythm of her breathing, she was asleep.

Nelson told him that they'd tried to get in touch with Emily for hours. They'd been at the hospital for a while, and they were all exhausted.

Keith scanned the room out of habit. There were other people in the room which wasn't surprising. He'd met the two men who's heads snapped up from their phones when Emily walked in. The Becker brothers Ken and Elliot worked for Nelson. When Keith had first met them, they looked at him as if he was no better than a piece of dirt on their shoes. He didn't like them and figured out pretty quickly they probably had their noses so far up Nelson's ass they'd have to come out for air. It did make him really uncomfortable the way they were ogling Emily.

The couple was new to him, but from the glare the woman gave him, she didn't seem to like the look of Keith. The man glanced up from his phone when they walked in but didn't appear to think their entry was as important as what was on his phone. The woman whispered to the man and then stood up.

Here we go.

"Dad," Emily moved towards her father as the woman walked towards him. Keith did his best to ignore what he knew was coming and focus his attention on Emily and the leering asshole.

"Emily, thank God you finally got here." Her father stood up and seemed to wince when he got to his feet.

"Dad, are you okay?"

"I'm fine. Just tired and fed up. They're not telling us anything." He wrapped his arms around her, and she clung to him.

"Let me see what I can find out," Emily kissed his cheek.

It was the last thing he'd heard before his attention was drawn to the woman who'd put herself in his line of vision.

"I'm Judy Palmer, and I'm a dear friend of the family. I don't think you should be in here with us. Who exactly are you?" She said with a hint of detest.

"I'm Ms. Bradshaw's personal security, Mrs. Palmer." Keith didn't show any emotion as he met the woman's glare.

"We're keeping this room strictly for the family, so we'd appreciate all employees of the Bradshaw's to wait outside the room." Keith didn't want to cause a scene so when the woman motioned to the door, Keith went with it, but not before he turned to see what could only be described as an enraged Emily.

Emily stomped over with her hands fisted at her sides, and her face was so red that Keith was waiting for it to explode.

"Excuse me, Judy," Emily's voice was surprisingly calmer than she appeared.

"Emily, I was just showing your security detail where he can wait with the other one." Judy touched Emily's shoulder softly.

"Thank you, Judy, but with all due respect, it's neither your duty or business as to who can stay in the room with my family. First of all, there are already several people here who are not family. Keith may be my security detail, as you put it, but he's also my friend, and he'll be waiting inside the room with me." Keith was doing his best not to laugh, but damn if the woman didn't make him want to give her a round of applause, or maybe a kiss.

"Emily, I didn't realize you were seeing anyone." Judy's gaze traveled up and down Keith as if he were nothing but a piece of garbage. Which was what the bitch probably thought.

"First of all, Judy, I said friend, and secondly, I wasn't aware you were supposed to be informed about my dating life." Emily put Mrs. Palmer in her place.

"There isn't a need for being so rude, Emily. Your mother would be very upset with how you've treated her friend."

"Judy, the only reason you even acknowledge my mom is because she's the chair of the Sweet Heart Ball, and you're only here to find out if that position will need to be filled." Emily stood in front of him putting herself between Keith and Judy. "Just so you know. If anything happened to mom, Elaine takes over for her. If you still want to stay, I suggest you go back and sit with your husband and mind your own business."

Without waiting for a response, Emily turned and linked her fingers into Keith's large hand. He wrapped his fingers around hers, and it felt so damn good.

"Dad, I'm going to find the doctor," Emily called as she tugged Keith's hand. He almost laughed at the curious glances from everyone in the room, but what surprised him was Nelson's smile.

"Not that I mind you telling that lady off, but can you please fill me in on what just happened," Keith whispered as he walked next to her.

"I hate fake people and ones that don't know how to keep their noses out of other people's business." Emily looked into the small room across from the waiting area. Nurses and doctors scurried around and didn't seem even to notice them standing there.

"You were a little harsh with her." Keith squeezed her hand gently.

129

"You don't know what it's like to deal with those type of people all your life. Just because I didn't want to cow down to being an uptight snob, they all treated me like I was lower than low, and when you're dating any of their sons, well, they do everything to end that."

"You dated her son?" Keith couldn't see Emily dating some uptight asshole.

"I don't want to talk about this right now." Emily didn't seem comfortable talking about her ex, but the thought of her with anyone made that green eyed monster crawl to the surface. "Excuse me could you tell me what doctor is caring for my mother? Her name is Lynn Ann Bradshaw."

Thank God it wasn't the bitchy nurse from the reception area of the hospital. Emily probably would have punched her.

"It's Dr. Adam Cramer. He's in with her now. I'll let him know that your family is anxious for news." The young nurse's gaze moved to Keith, and he smiled at her. The sweet thing blushed.

"Thank you, we appreciate it," Keith guided Emily away from the doorway.

"You enjoy doing that, don't you?" Emily leaned against the wall outside the waiting room.

"Doing what?" She still hadn't let go of his hand, and he didn't care. It felt good. Too good.

"Come on, you give a little smile and girls give you that 'I'm available' look." Emily batted her eyes at him.

"I've got no idea what you're talking about, but I like the way you flutter your eyes." Keith grinned.

"Nice distraction technique there." Emily rolled her eyes. He wasn't naïve. He could tell Emily was attracted to him. Not that he was arrogant.

"Just so you know. I know Dr. Cramer. He's a good doctor." He glanced down into her beautiful blue-grey eyes. "He saved my brother John's life."

"John almost died?"

"He hit a moose on the Southern Shore highway a few years back. Dr. Cramer saved him." It was the same day that they'd buried James' first wife and the family was so terrified. Keith couldn't remember being so scared in his life.

"Stephanie's husband? Right?" Emily asked.

"Yes. She was actually his physical therapist. They fell in love, and the rest is history." Keith shrugged and leaned against the wall next to her. He glanced over at Rex, who raised his eyebrow and gave him a smirk. That was going to happen a lot if he continued to let himself get close to Emily, like this. He didn't care.

Emily was getting impatient waiting for Adam, but when she started to fidget, he'd say something to make her smile or give her hand a gentle squeeze. He wasn't sure how he was doing it, but she would seem to calm a little everytime.

"There's the doctor," Keith saw Adam coming through the door.

"How are ya, Keith?" Adam shook his hand.

"Hangin' in there, Adam." Keith released Emily's hand and felt the loss immediately. "This is Mrs. Bradshaw's daughter, Emily."

Adam glanced down at her and nodded his head.

"Ms. Bradshaw, It's nice to meet you. I understand the rest of your family is inside the waiting room." He motioned towards the door.

"Yes, but there's others in there as well. Do you think we can find a room to talk to the family in private, Adam." Keith asked.

"Of course, there's a room just up here. Meet me there." Adam nodded and headed down the hall.

Keith entered the room and told her father the doctor wanted the family to meet him in the room down the corridor. Judy and the Becker brothers stood up to follow.

"I'm sorry but family only," Keith said with great satisfaction.

The Becker brothers sat right back down and shrugged. It didn't seem to bother them that they were being kept out, but Judy was a whole different story. Her eyes narrowed as she glared at him and Keith really expected her to cause a fuss. That was until her husband sat back down and clasped his hand around her arm. Judy didn't say a word. She eased back down in the seat and rested her hands in her lap

Keith stepped back so Nelson, Edward, and Elaine could exit the room. Nelson stopped just outside the room and turned towards him.

"Thanks, for that Keith." He slapped Keith on the shoulder. "They all showed up just before you and Emily, and I honestly don't know why they're here."

"You're welcome, Mr. Bradshaw." Keith nodded.

"From what I just saw, I think you can start calling me Nelson." He turned before Keith could respond and headed towards the room where Emily stood with the door held open.

"What's going on there, Rusty?" Rex whispered.

"Not really sure," It was the only response he could come up with because he really didn't know.

The only thing he was sure of was, he had an overpowering urge to protect Emily, not because he was hired to do it. He'd heard his brothers and father talk about how they felt the first time they met the women they loved. Was this what it felt like? Then there was Cora and her little comments that first day. Was Emily the one?

Chapter 11

"Keith, can you and Rex come in here as well?" Emily needed Keith close to her. She was terrified to hear what the doctor was about to say, but if she asked just for Keith, it would look a little odd.

Emily managed to arrange herself so that she was sat next to Keith. She was also trying to control the urge to take his hand again. What the hell was wrong with her? He wasn't her boyfriend, but he was the one keeping her calm the entire day.

"First of all, Mrs. Bradshaw is going to be fine." The doctor must have sensed everyone was expecting the worst. With his words, he eased all the tension in the room. Well, maybe not all of it.

"I know that's your first concern. However, she's going to have a bit of a recovery time. She's severely dehydrated, and apparently hasn't been fed very much while she was in captivity." He continued. Emily bit her tongue to keep from firing a million questions at him.

"Dr.Cramer, I hate to ask, but I need to know. Was.... She.... I mean.... was she assaulted... Sexually, I mean." Her father stammered over his words. Emily wanted to know too, but then again, she didn't.

"Mrs. Bradshaw assured me that she wasn't, and we did examine her to verify that as well."

"Thank God." Elaine sobbed.

"The bad news is she was treated very poorly, and although the physical injuries will heal, she will probably need help with the psychological ones." The doctor explained.

"Can we see her?" Her father asked, and it broke her heart that he now had tears in his eyes.

"We did give her a sedative, and are putting fluids into her, so she is resting and will probably be sleeping most of the night. I know you're all anxious to see her so you may go in two at a time for a few minutes." Dr. Cramer nodded to her father. "She did ask for you several times, Mr. Bradshaw. She said she would like to talk to you privately, but I doubt she will be alert enough to talk tonight." Her father jumped to his feet.

"I have to see her. Please." She'd never seen her dad so unhinged in her life. "I'm not going home."

"She's in a private room, as you requested, so we'll make arrangements for you." He turned to her and her siblings. "Before any of you go in you need to know that she's lost weight, and she has several bruises on her body, but she'll be okay. If there's anything, you want to know just ask." He nodded towards her father and they left the room.

"I think maybe we should just let dad be alone with her tonight." Edward stood up and shoved his hands into his front pockets.

"I just need to see her." Elaine was still sobbing.

"We can all go in and see her, but just to see for ourselves, she's really okay." Emily wrapped her arms around Elaine.

"Let's give dad a few minutes alone with her first." Emily felt her brother's strong arms wrap around her and Elaine. She glanced towards the door. Keith had his shoulder propped against the wall, and he was staring down at his phone. She stepped back from her siblings and went to him.

"Is something wrong?" Emily asked when she saw the look on his face. He held up his phone. The screen showed the sweetest baby she'd ever seen. He had a head full of dark hair and was snuggle against the chest of a very teary eyed Sandy.

"Oh, my goodness." Emily pulled the phone from Keith's hand without even asking. "He's so cute."

"Meet Alexander Ian O'Connor," Keith was obviously a very proud uncle.

"Sandy looks so exhausted, but happy." A pang of jealousy hit her. At the rate she was going, she would never be a mother.

"You'll be happy to know that Ian's still alive as well." Keith chuckled when she handed him back his phone. Sandy had threatened Ian's life a number of times in the jeep when he'd tried to get Sandy to control her breathing.

"Your father wants all of you to come see your mom. The doctor said it's okay as long as you only stay a few minutes." The nurse she'd spoken to earlier peeped into the room.

Emily glanced at Keith, and he nodded. She wanted him to hold her hand when she entered her mother's room, but that would be pushing it. The doctor was probably bending all kinds of rules to allow all of them in to see her mother at the same time.

She entered the room linked into one of her brother's arms, and Elaine was clinging to his other hand. The nurse tried to prepare them for what they were about to see, but it didn't work.

Her mother was asleep, and wires and tubes were running everywhere around the bed. The nurse told them it was to keep an eye on her vital signs. Emily assumed the bags of what looked like water was to make sure her mother got all the fluids she needed. It was a little hard to see her mom like that.

"She's sleeping." Her father whispered from next to the bed. He was holding his wife's hand as if she would disappear.

Emily swallowed the lump in her throat and blinked her eyes to keep tears from spilling out. She had to be strong for her father.

"She looks so skinny." Elaine slowly moved to the side of the bed.

"She's still the most beautiful woman in the world." Her dad gently touched her mom's cheek.

"We'll get her a big cheeseburger when we get her home." Edward tugged Emily towards the foot of the bed.

"She loves dad's homemade burgers." Emily forced a smile.

"I'll make her a burger every day if she wants." Emily had never seen her dad so shaken. He'd always been a strong and overbearing man, not that Emily doubted his love, but when it came to his wife, he was a pushover.

"Dad, are you sure you'll be comfortable staying here tonight?" Emily asked.

"Yes, I'll be fine. They're bringing in a recliner for me to sleep in, but I doubt I'll move from here." He glanced up at her and smiled. "Emily, go home with Keith. Get some rest. Rex will take Elaine and Edward home."

"Dad, you need Rex here," Edward said.

"I've messaged Keith. He's got another guy on the way here." His gaze moved back to her mother.

Emily walked around the bed and wrapped her arms around her dad. When she kissed his cheek, she felt the dampness of the tears he'd been trying to hide.

"I'll be here tomorrow first thing. I'll get Kim to take my clients." Emily whispered. "I hope to see you awake tomorrow, mom."

Emily leaned over the bed and kissed her mother's cheek. It was so hard to keep the tears from falling especially with her sister sobbing, but it was what she did.

The drive home was quiet, and Keith didn't push her to talk. The only time he did, was when he drove through the Tim Horton's drive-thru to ask if she wanted anything. She shook her head and continued to gaze out the window. The sun was going down, and by the time they got back to Keith's house, she knew it would be dark.

As usual, when they walked into the door, Burlap howled and wrapped herself around their legs. She had settled into Keith's house, and although he hadn't said anything, Emily was pretty sure Keith liked the little kitten more than he admitted.

"Okay, you weren't here that long by yourself. Chill out." Keith reached down and picked up Burlap in his huge hand.

Emily watched as he ran his fingers over the kitten's tiny head making Burlap purr and snuggle into Keith's chest. He was such a gentle man.

As if someone had dumped a bucket of cold water over her Emily started to tremble, and she had no idea why. Her heart pounded in her chest, and she felt slightly dizzy. She grabbed onto the counter and took several deep breaths, but she couldn't stop it. Tears started to spill down her cheeks, and thick heavy sobs escaped.

"Shit, Em, what's wrong?" Keith put the cat on the floor and was next to her in seconds. He wrapped his arm around her waist.

"I….I…. d….don't know. I…I…. f….f….feel like I'm falling apart." She stammered.

Keith pulled her against him and wrapped her tightly in his arms. She fisted his shirt and sobbed. Tears she'd been holding in for hours, days and even weeks flowed like a river. She cried with happiness that her mother was home. She sobbed for what her mother had been through, and she trembled because she was wrapped in the arms of the man that she was quickly falling for. The only man that could break her heart.

Chapter 12

The freaking cat was climbing up his leg, and her nails were digging into his thigh painfully, but he couldn't move. Emily was crying in his arms, and he wasn't one hundred percent sure why. It was probably because the entire day had been overwhelming, and although she seemed to be hiding her emotions from everyone, he knew.

"Let it out, Em," Keith whispered. "You've been holding this in for way too long."

Burlap finally gave up and jumped down from his leg. Keith was relieved, but with Emily so close it did things that were so wrong, considering the situation. She wanted comfort, and he had a hard on from having her pressed against him.

Such an asshole.

"This is so ridiculous." Emily hiccupped and sniffed. "Mom's safe."

"Princess, you've been holding in everything for so long. Nobody can keep their emotions in forever. No matter how strong they are." Keith kissed the top of her head without even thinking.

Holding her in his arms felt good. Felt Right. It was as if she'd been made to fit perfectly in his embrace. It was so wrong to think about Emily as more than a client, but he couldn't help it. He was falling for her and damn if he could keep fighting it.

"I'm sorry," Emily pressed her forehead against his chest.

"You've got nothing to be sorry for," Keith whispered.

Emily tipped her head back, and Keith gazed down into her eyes. They glistened with tears, and red circles surrounded them, but she was the most beautiful woman he'd ever seen.

"Keith," Emily whispered and dropped her gaze to his lips.

"Emily," Keith cupped her cheek in his hand. He slowly lowered his head until his lips were a breath away from hers. "Tell me to stop." He said it, but there was no way he wanted her to say it.

"I don't want you to." Emily pressed her lips against his before he could respond. It was like a shock jolted through his body as soon as their lips touched. Her hands were fisted in his shirt, and she was pulling him closer as her mouth opened to his. *Damn*, she tasted like the damn berry candies she'd been eating while they were at the hospital.

Her tongue glided across his lower lip as she tilted her head and slid her hand up his chest. He moved his hand to the back of her head and fisted her hair, and she whimpered, but her tongue delved into his mouth flicking against his.

He turned her, so she was between him and the counter. He ground himself against her. There was no doubt she could feel what she was doing to him. When she pressed her hips forward to meet his, he almost lost it.

Keith didn't know where he got the strength to stop, but he tore his lips away and pressed his forehead against hers.

"Emily, we've got to stop," Keith gasped.

"Why?" She threaded her fingers through his hair and kissed his chest where his shirt was open. "I can feel you want this as much as I do, and I need this."

"Emily, I was hired to keep you safe." Keith moaned when her tongue flicked against his Adam's apple, and she pressed her hips forward again.

"Well, I can't think of a safer place than in your arms," Emily whispered.

"I don't know if my arms are the safest place at the moment." Keith chuckled.

"I want you, Keith." Emily pressed her hands against his cheeks. "I'm not asking for anything beyond tonight, but I want you more than I've ever wanted anyone."

Keith was lost in her eyes. Here she was offering herself to him for one night, and he was actually thinking about saying no. Probably because one night with Emily was never going to be enough for him.

"Do you have any idea what you're saying right now?" Keith tucked a stray piece of hair behind her ear.

"Yes," Emily's hands had moved to the buttons on his shirt, and she'd opened the first two. He wrapped his hands around her waist and lifted her onto the counter.

"I want you too, Princess but it's not ethical for me to sleep with the woman I was hired to protect." Keith groaned when her hands pressed against the bare skin of his chest. He was trying hard to ignore the fact that she now had his shirt completely open and her touch was doing wonderful things to his body.

"You're fired." Emily grinned as her nail flicked over his nipple.

"You didn't hire me." Keith gritted his teeth.

"Are you going to make me beg, Keith?" Emily moved back from him and leaned back on her hands. The position pushed her breasts up, and his gaze dropped to where her nipples were poking through the fabric.

"No, but I don't want you to regret this in the morning. You've had a very emotional day." He couldn't tear his eyes from her breasts.

"I won't." Emily put her finger under his chin and lifted it until he met her eyes. "You'd probably enjoy looking at them more if I was naked." She grinned.

The woman was a vixen, and she tempted him to the point of no return. When she ran her finger down between her tits and looked up at him through her lowered lashes, he was finished. He lifted her off the counter. She squeaked, but it didn't take a second for her to wrap her legs around his waist.

Keith hurried down the hall to his bedroom, and although it was awkward, he managed to open his bedroom door without dropping her. A miracle really, since she'd started to suck on his earlobe and whisper some pretty dirty things in his ear.

He kicked the door closed and eased Emily down on the bed. She stared up at him, and for a moment he thought she'd changed her mind.

"You have the most beautiful blue eyes," Emily whispered.

"Thank you." Keith moved back from her and rested on his elbow.

"I like the five o'clock shadow. It's a little redder than your hair but sexy as hell." Emily rubbed her hand against his cheek.

"Thank you again. You're kind of sexy yourself." Keith ran his finger across the swell of her breast. She gave a little sigh.

"You're the only one of your brothers with red hair," Emily said.

"Ian's is close, but yeah, I'm the only ginger." Keith dipped his finger inside the edge of her bra, and her eyes drifted closed.

"Are you a true red head?" Her eyes slowly opened.

"Are all these questions your way of changing your mind, Emily?" Keith stared into her eyes. "Because if you've changed your mind just say so."

"I haven't changed my mind. I'd just like to know if you're a real ginger. You know, red everywhere." Her hand cupped his groin, and he groaned.

"Guess you'll have to check for yourself." Keith slowly unbuttoned her blouse as she popped the button of his jeans.

Emily slowly lowered the zipper of his jeans as he flicked open the clasp of her bra. The person who invented bras that opened in front was a bloody genius. He pushed the silky material aside and cupped her firm, full breast in one hand. She was so much more than a handful.

"So beautiful," Keith said with reverence as he circled her nipple with his finger.

146

Her hand slipped inside his opened jeans, and her eyes darted up to meet his. It seemed she'd discovered he didn't wear underwear. He always found them too constricting.

"Commando man, huh." She grinned as her hand wrapped around his rock hard erection.

"Fuck, yes." Keith's eyes closed as she gently stroked him. "Emily, that feels so fucking good." Never had a woman's hand felt so good on his cock.

"Can we get rid of the clothes, please?" Emily squeezed him gently. "I really want to see what I'm feeling."

Keith reluctantly rolled away from her and ripped off his shirt. He tossed it in the corner as he kicked off his boots. The whole while his eyes never moved from Emily. She'd removed her blouse, bra, jeans and was kneeling on the bed in a pair of the skimpiest pair of panties he'd ever seen. They were white with see-through lace, and he could see her bare pussy through them.

"Fuck, you're completely bare," Keith growled.

"The perks of owning a beauty salon." She slid her fingers inside the waist of her panties and slowly slid them off.

"That right there is the most beautiful thing I've ever seen," Keith whispered as he crawled onto the bed.

"Oh, no. You still have jeans on." Emily pushed him back. "I told you I wanted to see what I was feeling."

Keith backed up and stood next to the bed. Her gaze traveled down his body to where his cock was now peeking out of his opened jeans. He dropped them to the floor and watched as her eyes widened. It was a reaction he got from most women he slept with.

"I know I had my hand wrapped around it, but wow. You're kind of large." Emily crawled to the edge of the bed, and he held his breath. His cock was now seeping with pre-come, and when she flicked her tongue against the head, he almost fell to his knees.

"Baby, if you keep doing that I won't get a chance to be inside that bare pussy." Keith pushed her back on the bed and grabbed her knees. He pulled her to the edge of the bed and ran his hands up her thighs. "You've got the sexiest legs I've ever seen."

"I've got chubby thighs, but I like the way you touch them." Emily rested on her elbows as he worshiped her legs.

"Your legs, like the rest of you, are beautiful and there is nothing chubby about them," Keith whispered as he slowly alternated his kisses from one leg to the other, going from her knees right up to her wet heat. "Fucking beautiful." Keith rubbed his nose against her wetness. He could smell the scent of her arousal, and he couldn't keep himself from tasting it.

"Keith," Emily gasped with the first flick of his tongue against her clit. The second pass was slow between her folds, and she made the most amazing sound. A cross between a gasp and a moan. It was incredibly hot.

"Emily, you taste so fucking good." Keith used his thumbs to open her so he could sink his tongue inside.

She raised her hips to meet the thrusts of his tongue. She'd lay back on the bed, and her hands were threaded through his hair. He sunk his finger inside her as his tongue worked her hard nub.

"Oh. Fuck. Keith." The loud groan from her sweet mouth made him almost come then and there.

Keith pulled her clit into his mouth and quickly flicked his tongue against it as he pushed a second finger inside her. On the third thrust of his finger and sucking hard on her clit, Emily's hips raised off the bed, her body shuttered, and she clamped around his fingers.

"Yes." She screamed as her body shook. Keith didn't stop until she collapsed on the bed. Her breathing was coming in fast gasps, and he pulled his fingers from inside her.

"Oh dear lord. What the hell did you just do?" Emily gasped.

"Made you come." Keith chuckled as he hovered over her.

"No shit. I've never orgasmed like that. I mean not from just oral." She lifted her head and brushed her lips against his.

"Princess, you were with the wrong men." Keith bent down and placed soft kisses on the top of her breasts. He didn't like the thought of another man having touched Emily like this.

"I guess so." Emily moaned when he pulled her nipple into his mouth.

"Fuck, Em, I need to be inside you." Keith groaned as he ground his cock against her wetness.

"Well, why are you still talking about it?" Emily giggled.

A realization hit Keith, and he cursed himself. He didn't have a condom, and there weren't any in his house because he didn't bring women home. When he'd go on his 'fishing' trips with Bull, he'd usually pick them up just before he needed them.

"Em, I'm a fucking idiot. I don't have a condom." Keith dropped his head into the crook of her neck, but when she started to giggle, he raised his head and stared down at her.

"Do you think men are the only ones that should be carrying condoms?" She pushed him until he lay on his back and hovered over him.

"Well, yeah. I mean no, but…" Emily pressed her lips against his stopping him from putting his foot in his mouth.

"I've got some in my purse." Emily pulled back from his lips and jumped off the bed. A few seconds later she returned with her purse and opened it. "Ta-da," Emily said as she pulled out a small box.

Keith reached for it, but she pulled it away from him.

"Woman, you're killing me." Keith groaned.

"Slow down there big boy." Emily crawled over him and settled herself between his legs. "You got to taste me. Now it's my turn."

150

Before Keith could say a word, Emily wrapped her lips around the head of his erection and circled her tongue slowly.

"Holy fuck." Keith groaned through gritted teeth. As good as her mouth felt on him, he wouldn't last a minute with her sucking him the way she was.

"Mmm." Emily slowly slid her lips over his length, but there was no way she could take the full length of him in her mouth. At least that was what he thought.

When her lips moved back to the top of his cock, he was ready to pull her off and roll on the condom. Then she did it. She took the entire length of his cock into her mouth, and he roared out. When she took him almost entirely out a second time, he shook as he tried to keep back the orgasm that was inevitable if she continued to deep throat him. Before she could do it again, he pulled her up on top of him.

"Sorry, Princess. If you keep that up, I'm finished." Keith rolled her onto her back. "I want to be deep inside you when I come, and I don't mean inside your mouth, but fuck let me tell you, that was fucking incredible." Keith grabbed the box of condoms that had gotten tossed aside and ripped it open.

He pressed his lips against hers as he spread her legs with his knee. He was about to cross a line that he couldn't return from. Hell, he'd pretty much passed it the minute he kissed her, but there was nothing he could do to turn around now. He needed to be inside her.

"Keith, why are you stopping?" Emily cupped his face.

"I'm waiting for you to change your mind," Keith admitted.

"I'm not going to," Emily whispered just before she guided him to her entrance. "I want you."

With that, Keith covered her mouth with his and pushed into her. She sucked his tongue into her mouth the same way her pussy sucked his cock deep inside.

"Fuck, baby. You're so fucking hot." Keith groaned as he pumped into her. He wasn't going to last, but he was taking her with him. He reached between them and pressed his thumb against her clit as he thrust in and out of her.

"Keith, don't stop." Emily grabbed his ass and dug her nails in as he took them both over the edge.

He felt her close around him right before she screamed his name as her hips pushed up off the bed. He was sure she'd broken the skin on his ass as she dug her nails in, but he didn't care as he pumped once more and spilled into her.

"Fuck, Em," Keith yelled as he drove deep inside one last time. His body shuttered with the most intense orgasm he'd ever experienced and for a moment he didn't think it would stop.

"Yes, you did." Emily giggled when Keith rolled off her and flopped onto the bed.

"I did what?" Keith turned his head to look at the beautiful woman laying next to him. She was curled on her side and her arm under her head.

"You said, 'fuck, Em,' and I said, 'yes, you did,'" Emily grinned, and Keith chuckled.

"I need to take care of this," Keith rolled off the bed. "Don't move."

"Jeez, can I breathe." Emily teased.

"As long as you're still in that bed when I get out of the bathroom," Keith winked as he made his way to the ensuite off his room.

He disposed of the condom and grabbed a cloth for Emily. As he passed the vanity, he caught sight of himself in the mirror. The sudden realization of what just happened between them hit him in the gut like a punch.

"You fucking idiot." Keith plowed his hand through his hair and sighed. It was too late to change things now because now that he'd had Emily there was no going back.

It had been less than ten minutes, and he already wanted to be inside her again, but what he wanted wasn't worth a crock of shit. What was important was what Emily wanted. Yes, she did say she wanted him tonight, but did she just need an outlet for all the stress in her life over the last few weeks, or did she feel the same as Keith?

He'd never been one to pull punches, but asking Emily where she saw them going was the scariest thing he would ever do. Keith wasn't sure he wanted to know the answer.

Do you want it to go somewhere?

Chapter 13

Emily stared at the door long after Keith closed it. She didn't move from her position on the bed. Not because he told her to stay there, but because she didn't want to. This was his bed, and his scent was everywhere. Besides, she wasn't sure if her legs would work since he'd just given her the most intense orgasm she'd ever experienced.

The last thing she expected when she left the hospital was to be laying in Keith's bed. Not that she didn't think about it since she met the man, but he was way out of her league. He'd told her she was beautiful and sexy, but she chalked it up to being caught up in the heat of the moment.

Emily rolled onto her stomach and rested her cheek on her folded fingers. Was this just a *wham-bam* thing, or was this the start of something? When Keith wrapped her in his arms after they arrived home, everything she'd been trying hard to keep inside overflowed. Yes, that included the growing feelings for him. It was probably why she'd been so bold in telling him what she wanted.

The click of the door had her heart pounding. She closed her eyes waiting for him to give her the, 'that was awesome now can you leave' speech. It seemed like forever before she felt the bed dip next to her and she felt a damp cloth being pressed into her hand.

"I thought you might want to clean up, but then again maybe you want to go to the bathroom." Keith pushed back a lock of her hair and smiled.

"I would like to visit the bathroom, but you said I wasn't permitted to move off the bed." She forced a grin so he couldn't see the fear.

"So, this is the first time since we met that you're actually going to do what I tell you?" Keith laughed.

"Well, why break a perfect defiance record." Emily hopped off the bed and skipped to the bathroom. She turned and stuck her tongue out as she closed the door.

"Keep that tongue in your mouth, Princess." She heard him shout just before the door closed.

Emily leaned her back against the door and sighed. She was starting to love when he called her princess. Not because she believed she really was one, but because when he said it, she felt like it was with affection.

When she finally got the nerve to come back out of the bathroom, Keith was propped up against the headboard. He had the comforter pulled over his legs, and he was staring off into space. She should probably make it easy on him and say goodnight. She didn't want to go to the other room, but she didn't want things to be awkward either.

Emily started to pick up her clothes, but before she could put them on she felt a strong hand grab her around the waist and toss her on top of the bed.

"What the hell?" Emily grumbled.

"My question exactly. What the hell are you doing, Em?" Keith pulled her shirt from her grasp and tossed it on the floor.

"I was going to make things easy for you, and just go to the other room," Emily admitted as she avoided his eyes.

"Is that what you want?" Emily's gaze snapped up to meet his.

"Is it what you want?" Emily asked.

"I asked first." He grinned.

"A gentleman always lets the lady go first." Emily retorted.

"I'm letting you go first. You can answer the question first." Keith ran his hand across her belly and grasped onto her hip.

"I want you." Emily snaked her arms around his neck and pulled him closer.

"Emily," Keith groaned when she threaded her fingers through his hair. "I need to know if you just want tonight, or do you want more?"

Emily stared at the man hovering over her. She knew the answer to his question, but telling him was going to be the hardest thing she'd ever done. Admitting she wanted more with him left her open to his rejection. That would completely break her since she'd never wanted a man as much as she wanted Keith O'Connor.

"What is it, Princess?" He'd apparently seen her internal struggle, and she closed her eyes.

Just freaking tell him and let the chips fall where they may.

"I don't just want tonight." She blurted out but kept her eyes closed. She really didn't want to see the expression on his face.

"Open your eyes, Emily," Keith said, but she didn't.

"Nope." Emily squeezed them tighter. "Gonna live in my little fantasy world where you don't laugh and tell me I'm crazy."

He chuckled, and she opened one eye to peek at him. It wasn't there. The expression she expected. The one where his face was filled with horror because she wanted more. What she saw had her opening both eyes and staring into his smiling eyes.

"I like your fantasy world," Keith whispered and brushed his lips against hers.

"It is pretty impressive." Emily sighed as he kissed his way down to her chin.

"Just so you know, I want more than tonight." Keith stopped kissing her and pulled his head back. He cupped her cheek and glided his thumb across her lip.

"But," Emily could see there was a 'but' by the way he studied her face.

"What makes you think there's a but?" Keith smiled.

"That little twitch in your jaw when you clench your teeth." Emily ran her finger along his strong jaw line.

"Okay, it's just… I don't want to lose focus on the job. I was hired to keep you safe, and mixing my job with feelings can only lead to something going wrong." Keith looked genuinely torn.

"So, who are you going to put on my protection detail?" Emily assumed he would pursue their relationship and get one of the other guys to be her security.

"I'm it. It's not that I don't trust my team, but I need to be the one to protect you against whatever could be out there to harm you." Keith had started rubbing his hand up and down her arm.

"That's not good." Emily groaned.

"I know, but I'd never forgive myself if I lost my focus and something happened to you." Keith threaded his fingers with hers and squeezed gently.

For a few minutes, Emily stared at where their hands were joined. He'd rolled onto his back and pulled her into his side. It was warm, and she felt at peace. Her head rested on his chest, and she could hear the steady rhythm of his heartbeat.

"Your compound is pretty secure, right?" Emily knew it was because when she'd moved to his house, it was as if she was entering Fort Knox.

"Yes, it is," Keith replied.

"So, how about when we're inside the compound, which by the way is a stupid thing to call your home, we can be together, but when we're outside you're strictly my security?" Emily closed her eyes and waited for his answer.

When he didn't respond after a few minutes, she tilted her head back to look at him. He was staring at the ceiling, and there was that twitch in his jaw.

"What are you doing?" Emily asked.

"Thinking."

"That's dangerous." Emily deadpanned.

Keith rolled her over and pinned her hands above her head. He narrowed his eyes as he stared down at her. When she started to giggle, he smiled. Then his expression turned serious.

"Emily, your suggestion would work, but only if outside the compound, by the way, it's not a stupid name, you do what I tell you to do." Keith looked deep into her eyes, and she could tell he was seeing her doubts and fears.

"I don't really do well with orders." Emily gave him a weak smile.

"I've noticed." Keith chuckled.

"All I can promise is I'll do my best to listen. I know it's for my own safety, even though I don't think I'm in any danger." Emily tried to pull her hands free.

"That's probably as good as I'm going to get from you, isn't it?" Keith held her hands tighter and rolled his large body over hers. "Let's do an experiment." He wiggled his eyebrows.

"Jesus, I don't know if I like the sound of that." Emily groaned.

"I want you to keep your hands above your head while I ravish you." Keith's smile was the sexiest she'd ever seen it.

"And if I move them?" Emily asked.

"Then I know if you can't listen in my bed, you won't outside." He spread her legs with his knee and knelt between them.

"Go for it." Emily gripped the comforter above her head. If keeping her hands off him while he did wicked things to her was the only way to keep him doing those things. She'd hold on for dear life, but when his lips first wrapped around her nipple, Emily cursed. This was going to be the hardest and most amazing thing she ever did in her life.

Emily rolled over on the bed and stretched. Her body was deliciously sore. Keith had made it do things she never thought it could. His stamina and recovery time was something she'd never experienced before. After the third time, she'd fallen asleep with his arms wrapped tightly around her. Since she'd managed, just barely, to keep her hands above her head while he kissed, sucked and touched her, he'd agreed they could try things her way.

Emily realized she was alone in the bed when she rolled over to snuggled into the human heater. She scanned the room and glanced towards the bathroom door. It was open, but she could smell Keith's body wash. He'd apparently showered and left her to sleep. She jumped out of bed and pulled on his T-shirt. Once she had all her discarded clothes in her hands, she headed to the other room to shower and dress. She wanted to get to the hospital as soon as possible.

He was standing at the counter with a cup in one hand, and his other hand tucked down in his jeans pocket. The white T-shirt stretched across his broad chest, and it looked as if the sleeves were going to rip when he lifted the cup to his lips. Those lips. She could still feel them when she closed her eyes.

"Sleepwalking, Princess," Keith chuckled, and she snapped her eyes open.

"No, just making sure I didn't dream last night." She propped her shoulder against the doorjamb.

Keith raised his eyebrow and slowly lowered his cup to the counter. As he stalked towards her, her heart started to race.

"If you think you were dreaming, then I must've done something wrong." He grabbed her hips and pulled her against him.

"Nothing I can think of." Emily rubbed the palm of her hands over his chest, and his pectoral muscles flexed.

"Did you want to eat before we go to the hospital?" Keith kissed her forehead.

"I could eat the leg off the Lamb of God right now." Emily laughed.

"I don't have any lamb of God at the moment, but I do have eggs and ham." Keith brushed his lips across hers.

"Mmmm… That sounds good, but your lips taste better." Emily sighed.

"Too bad we've got to get out of here as soon as you eat." Keith pulled back and pushed her hair from her face. "Just keep that thought in mind for when we get back here."

Emily was putting her plate in the sink when the doorbell chimed. Keith popped up from his chair and sauntered to the entrance. Emily followed him thinking it was probably one of the guys or his family. Her heart sunk when the door opened to a beautiful strawberry blonde who threw herself into Keith's arms. The worst thing was, he seemed happy to see her.

"Superman." The woman screeched.

"Lois Lane." Keith chuckled as he pulled the woman into his arms.

Emily's breakfast suddenly felt like it was going to come up in her throat, and she did her best to keep it down.

"I've missed you so much." The woman cooed, and Emily's body trembled.

"I've missed you too." Keith kissed the woman's cheek, and that was all Emily needed.

"Hey, I'm going to run over to the gym and see if one of the guys can take me to see mom. It'll give you two some time alone. You know, to catch up." Emily grabbed her coat off the hook and pushed by the woman.

"Emily," Keith roared.

"It's fine." Emily didn't turn as she started walking faster. "You two catch up."

Before she got a chance to get to the end of the driveway someone grabbed her arm. Emily turned, but it wasn't Keith that stopped her. It was the woman. Now that Emily looked at her she really wanted to throw up. The woman had a flawless complexion and the most beautiful blue eyes.

"I didn't get a chance to introduce myself." The woman smiled as she glanced back at Keith. "I'm Pam." She held out her hand, and it took Emily everything she had not to slap the woman's hand away.

164

"Nice to meet you, I'm Emily," Emily really wanted to choke on those words.

"I know. My mom told me all about you." Pam smiled. Emily glanced over her shoulder. Keith glared at her with his arms folded over his chest.

"Your mom?" Emily tore her gaze from Keith and back to the woman.

"Yes, Cora's my mom." It took a second for it to register, but when it did Emily wanted the ground to open up and swallow her.

"Cora's your mom, so that makes you Keith's…." Emily groaned and covered her face with her hands.

"Cousin," Pam finished.

Emily looked up at the woman expecting to see her laughing at the way Emily had behaved, but she wasn't.

"I'm sorry for being so rude. It's just…. I thought…." Emily sighed.

"No problem at all. I'd probably have punched me in the nose." Pam chuckled.

"Pam, can I talk to Emily alone for a moment?" Keith's voice was the way she'd heard it the first time she met him.

"Keith, don't go getting bent out of shape." Pam turned towards her cousin and put her fists on her hips. "I'd be pissed too if I thought some woman was coming to the house and jumping in my man's arms."

"Pam, go inside. Make yourself a tea." Keith didn't pay any attention to her as he stalked towards Emily.

"Bossy as ever," Pam grumbled as she turned and gave Emily a sympathetic smile.

The next thing Emily knew, Keith had her face cupped in his hands and was kissing her mouth harder than she'd ever been kissed by anyone. Including him.

"What the hell?" Emily pulled back and pressed her fingers to her lips.

"Just so you know, you're the one and the only woman who has been inside my house or my bed. I haven't been a monk, but I keep my sex life out of Hopedale. At least until you." Keith still had her face between his hands.

"Okay." Emily managed to squeak out.

"I've heard the rumors about my younger brothers, and though most of them are probably true, that's them. Not me. I don't jump from bed to bed or woman to woman. I haven't been in a long term relationship in a while, but when I am, I'm entirely devoted to that woman." Keith brushed his thumb across her lip. "Understand?"

Emily nodded and smiled. She'd never been the jealous type. The fact she felt physically sick from seeing Keith with his arms around another woman concerned her. Even if it was his cousin.

"Now come inside, and we'll have a quick chat with Pam before we head to the hospital. Okay?" Keith searched her eyes, and she smiled.

"Okay, and I'm sorry." Emily rested her hands on his hips. "I'm really not the jealous type."

"It's okay, but you should know, I am." Keith squinted his eyes and then smiled.

"Ugh, great." Emily exaggerated a sigh and rolled her eyes.

Pam was funny and reminded Emily of Keith's other cousin Kristy. Of course, when Emily took a better look at the woman, the family resemblance was there. The blue eyes and dimples seemed to be an O'Connor trademark.

Keith had asked Pam if she was back in Hopedale for good, but his cousin didn't really answer the question. She just said she'd see how it goes. Keith had given her a raised eyebrow, but Pam didn't seem to notice.

An hour later they were pulling into the parking lot of the hospital. Keith cursed everyone who'd ever parked in the lot, especially when a man almost rammed into the side of the jeep. Keith shoved the vehicle into park and was about to jump out, but Emily grabbed his jacket and pointed to an empty spot.

She'd received a text from her sister to let her know that her mother was awake and asking for her. Emily hurried through the hallway to get to the room. She couldn't wait to see her mom actually awake and talking.

Just before she pushed open the door to enter she heard the raised voices of her parents. It sounded as if they were arguing, but it was odd because her father never raised his voice to her mother.

"I said no, Lynn. She doesn't need to know anything about it." Her father snapped.

"Nel, he said he wanted her. He knows the very thing we've kept hidden all this time. Sweetheart, she needs to be told, and we'll deal with the fallout later." Her mother pleaded.

"Lynn, please don't. She'll hate me." Her dad sounded scared. "We've kept it from everyone this long. This ass isn't going to ruin it all with threats."

"What if he gets to her?" her mom's voice was muffled.

"What are you doing?" Keith whispered next to her.

"Shhh," Emily put her finger to her lips and continued to eavesdrop. Something in the pit of her stomach told her, the 'she', they were referring to, was her.

"What if he takes her? Nel, it's time. She needs to be prepared." Emily could hear the crack in her mother's voice.

"He's not going to get anywhere near her. I've taken care of that. That O'Connor boy will keep her safe." They were talking about her.

Emily stepped back and stared at the door as if when it opened her world would be blown to pieces.

"What are they talking about, Em?" Keith must have heard them as well.

"I don't know." Emily barely heard her own voice.

With everything she had, and knowing Keith was there next to her, Emily took a deep breath and pushed open the door. Both her parent's heads snapped towards her.

"Emily," Her mother covered her mouth with her hands and tears poured down her cheeks.

"Mom," Emily couldn't stop the emotions. She ran to her mother and got swallowed up in her mom's embrace. "I've missed you so much."

"Me too, baby." Her mother always referred to Emily and her siblings as babies. It didn't matter how old they got.

"How are you feeling?" Emily pulled back and looked into her mother's face. She was still very pale, and her cheeks were sunk in.

"I'll survive." She smiled weakly.

Her father hadn't said a word. He stared out through the window, and Emily knew it was wrong, but she had to know what the hell they were keeping from her.

"I heard you talking just before I came in the room." Emily blurted out and glanced back at Keith. He was next to the door with his hands shoved into his pocket.

Her father still didn't move, but her mother's eyes widened for a moment. When her mom glanced towards her dad, Emily walked around the bed and obstructed her mother's view.

"Mom, what is it I need to know?" Emily met her mother's eyes.

"It doesn't concern you, Emily." Her father's voice interrupted. "I don't know why you would think we were talking about you."

"Do you have another O'Connor boy looking after someone, Dad. Stop the bullshit." Emily grasped her father's arm and forced him to turn and look at her.

"Watch your mouth young lady." He said sternly, but she could see the tremble in his jaw. "It's nothing you need to concern yourself with."

"Really, Dad. Really? Then tell me why I would hate you if I knew." Emily wanted him to know exactly how much she'd heard.

"Nel, maybe we should…." Her mother obviously wanted her to know, but he cut her off.

"I said, no. I'll take care of it, and Emily doesn't need to be concerned about it. Now, that is the end of this discussion." He turned on his heel and stomped out of the room.

Emily stared at the door for a moment. This had to be bad. Her father had never walked away from a disagreement in his life. Especially, when he thought he was right.

Her gaze moved to Keith. He looked as confused as she felt, but he nodded his head towards her mother. Whatever was going on, her mother had the answers.

"So, who's this handsome young man?" Her mother motioned towards Keith.

"This is Keith O'Connor." Emily didn't really know how to introduce him after what happened between them. "He's …."

"Your husband hired me as security for Emily, but we've become good friends," Keith said.

"O'Connor?" Emily's mom stared at him for a moment. "You're not related to Kurt O'Connor and Cora Nightengale, are you?"

"My uncle and aunt." Keith smiled.

"Then you're one of Sean and Kathleen's boys." Her mother seemed very excited about meeting Keith.

"Yes, mam." Keith nodded.

"Well come over here and let me get a good look at you." Her mother held out her hand towards Keith. He slowly walked to the side of the bed and glanced at Emily.

"There are those eyes. Your whole family has those beautiful blue eyes. You know your aunt is the reason I'm married to Nelson." Her mother took Keith's hand and squeezed it.

"Really?" Keith chuckled.

"I'm sure you know about her little gift."

"Yes, I'm very aware of it." Keith laughed.

"Emily, his aunt can meet a person and tell them who they are meant to be with. She's simply amazing." Her mother didn't take her eyes off Keith.

"I've heard the stories." Emily watched Keith shift from one foot to the other.

"I'm feeling a little tired." Her mother closed her eyes, but Emily didn't miss the tear that ran down her cheek.

"You sleep, mom." Emily leaned over and kissed her mother's cheek. "I'll see you later."

Emily couldn't upset her mother by hounding her about what they were keeping from her. She closed the door quietly so she wouldn't wake her mom and turned to Keith.

"I need to find my father." Emily snapped.

"I don't know if it's a good idea for you to be talking to him in that mood." Keith took her hand, and she pulled it from him.

"We're not in your house." Emily knew that it was kind of bitchy to be taking her frustration out on Keith, but at the moment her father wasn't in view.

"You're father has gone home to change." Keith stepped back and showed her his phone. Of course, he texted Keith.

"Fuck." Emily stamped her foot and realized how it must have looked to anyone nearby.

"Really? That was a very princess move." Keith chuckled but quickly stopped when she narrowed her eyes.

"He's going to talk to me and tell me what the hell is going on." Emily stomped by the large man standing next to the door. It was strange she hadn't seen him when they arrived, but Keith seemed to know him.

"Good luck with that." Emily heard the man say to Keith. She spun around and glared him.

"Thanks, Shadow. Nothing I can't handle." Keith fist bumped the man.

So he thought he could handle her. That pissed her off more than her father running off to avoid telling her the truth.

"We'll go home, and you can get in touch with your dad later." Keith pushed the button on the elevator.

"Oh, he's going to talk to me later even if I've got to tie him down." Emily walked onto the elevator.

Keith didn't say another word. Probably because she was being a complete bitch, but this big secret being revealed by someone who wasn't supposed to know scared her to death. What was so bad that it had her parents fighting, and how did it all involve her? The fluttering in her stomach told her that whatever it was, her world was about to be turned upside down.

Chapter 14

Emily hadn't spoken the whole way home, and Keith hadn't pushed her. He understood why she was so upset. He wondered since his uncle and aunt knew her parents if they had any idea about this big secret, but from what he could get from the whole conversation, nobody knew. That's what worried him.

The rest of the day was relatively quiet, Keith brought Emily to the salon because she wanted to work. He couldn't blame her. He knew from experience that secrets always had a way of coming out, and most of the time it caused more harm than good.

Emily seemed to relax a little more when she walked into her salon, but when Keith saw who was waiting, he suddenly wasn't so relaxed.

"There's me handsome grandson." His grandmother motioned for him to kiss her on the cheek.

"Good to see you, Nan." Keith smiled as she took his hand and stood up.

"Emily, I'm so glad dat yer mudder's back and gonna be alright." Nanny Betty quickly shuffled to Emily and hugged her. "I've been prayin' fer her."

"Thank you, Mrs. O'Connor." Emily didn't seem to mind his grandmother's affection.

"Ya call me Nan. Mrs. O'Connor was me mudder-in-law and let me tell ya she wasn't a very nice woman." Keith shook his head. He'd heard that statement from his grandmother anytime someone called her Mrs. O'Connor. He really didn't know why Nanny Betty disliked her mother in law, and nobody wanted to ask.

"I'd love to call you Nan." Emily smiled as Nanny Betty released her.

"Kim tells me Keithy's been spendin' a lotta time here lately."

Keith glanced at Kim, and she shrugged. There was no way anyone knew what happened between him and Emily, and he'd warned Pam not to say a word.

"Keith's just here as my security until they figure out what happened with mom." Emily's eyes flicked to him and then back to his grandmother.

"I see, but I'm sure dere's more." Nanny Betty patted Emily's cheek. "My Cora's never wrong."

176

Keith heard the honk of a horn and was relieved to see Tom parked outside the salon. He hopped out of the car and walked around.

"Nan, Tom's outside," Keith informed his grandmother before she started to go on about Cora the Cupid.

"He can wait. Emily, my lass, Keithy's a wonderful man, and you'll find dat out next week at Sean's birthday party. We're gonna have baby Alexander's christening dat same day."

Keith pulled out his phone and opened his calendar. *Shit*. How the hell did he completely forget about his father's birthday party? He also didn't realize they'd planned the baby's christening so soon. Sandy wasn't even out of the hospital yet.

"I think that's just for family, Nan." Emily smiled.

"My dear lass, ya are family." She kissed Emily on the cheek. "We'll see ya soon."

With that, the whirlwind that was his grandmother waved and scurried out the door to where Tom was holding open the car door for her.

"Those two are so stinking cute." Penny chuckled.

"Yes, they are." Keith had to agree. It was a little weird in the beginning when Nanny Betty started to see Tom, but he quickly became part of the family.

"You forgot about the party, didn't you?" Ada snickered while she combed out an older woman's hair.

"I hate to admit it but yes." Keith flopped down on one of the chairs.

"Do you have anything for him?" Emily asked.

"Yes, I bought it a while ago online. It's all wrapped in the closet." Keith's eyes locked with hers.

"Then you've got nothing to worry about." Ada laughed.

Keith had lots to worry about. The party was nowhere on the list. His biggest concern was the woman who'd just disappeared into the back of the salon. Emily appeared to be chipper and happy, but Keith didn't miss the tears welling in her eyes.

She shouldn't be on the verge of tears. Her mother was safe and going to make a full recovery, but her parents were hiding something from her and from what Keith could see, it was killing Emily. Mainly since it concerned her.

"Is Emily okay?" Keith smiled at the young girl behind the receptionist desk. He'd known the kid all her life. Then again she wasn't really a kid anymore. Aurora had turned into a sweet young lady with the same sassy attitude that Emily had. No wonder the salon was called *Snippy Gals*.

"She's just overwhelmed right now." Keith headed towards Emily's office. He'd learned it was where she went to get herself together.

"I bet." Aurora smiled.

Keith stepped into the office and glanced around. Emily stood in front of the small window with her arms wrapped around herself. He closed the door to the room and moved behind her. Screw keeping things professional outside his house. He wrapped his arms around her waist and pulled her against his body.

"Isn't this breaking the rules?" Emily teased, but her voice was soft and tense.

"I made the rules so I can bend them when I see you need a hug." Keith kissed the top of her head, and she turned into his chest.

"What are they hiding from me?" Emily hiccuped and sighed.

"I wish I knew, Princess." Keith wrapped her tighter in his arms.

"It can't be so bad that I'd ever hate him. I mean yes my dad pisses me off sometimes. A lot actually but I could never hate him." She sobbed softly.

"We just have to try and make them understand it's best that you know." Keith pressed his lips against her forehead.

"We?" Emily lifted her head away from his chest and gazed into his eyes.

"Sweetheart, I'll do my best to convince your parents to tell you. I don't know if it will make a difference, but I'd do anything to take those tears away." He swiped his thumb against her cheek to wipe away a tear.

"That has to be the sweetest thing anyone has ever said to me." Emily smiled.

"There it is." Keith brushed his lips against hers. "That smile should never leave that beautiful face. Let's get you back to the compound and figure out what our next step is."

"I need to get a couple of things done here before I go. I hate leaving all the paperwork for Kim. She doesn't mind, but I like to do my share." Emily stepped back from his embrace. "It shouldn't take too long, but can we just go back and not think about anything else tonight but me and you?"

"If that's what you want, it's done like dinner." Keith kissed her cheek.

"Dinner would be great as long as you cook." Emily giggled when he pulled her back against him and nuzzled her neck.

"I'll cook dinner as long as you're dessert." He whispered in her ear and then chuckled when she moaned.

"Get out of here, or I'm not getting nothing done." Emily pushed him away.

"Anything I can do to help?" Keith knew what it was like to run a business and how paperwork piled up if a person didn't keep up on it.

"No, I have a system." Emily sat down behind her desk and turned on her laptop.

Keith saluted as he sauntered through the office door and left Emily to her work. It was probably a good time to catch up on his own business. The phone in his pocket had been buzzing with incoming emails for the last twenty minutes or more. He plopped down behind the reception desk and pulled out his iPhone to deal with the emails.

It was so hard to concentrate on his emails while a very heated discussion between Aurora and her mother got louder by the minute. It was hard not to burst into laughter.

"Aurora, if you come home with a tattoo I'll bust your arse," Ada warned while she was pounding her fist on the desk.

"For the love of God, Mom. It's just a little tattoo." Aurora didn't move from where she sat on top of the counter behind the desk.

"You know they hurt like hell?" Ada seemed to think the fear of pain was going to stop her daughter. Keith rolled his lips in to keep from smiling.

"I'm sure it does, but that's not going to change my mind." Aurora folded her arms over her chest.

"You're too young to be defacing your body." Ada slammed her hand on the desk.

"Mom, I'm almost twenty." Aurora sighed.

"Do you hear her?" Ada grumbled.

At first, Keith didn't realize she was talking to him, but she called out, and his head snapped up.

"You're going to get someone who has several tattoos to talk to me about how bad they are?" Aurora scoffed.

"Keith, tell her she's too young." Ada looked about ready to explode.

"Sorry Ada, I was eighteen. It's a right of passage in our family. We all get the family crest." Keith tried not to smile when Ada glared at him.

"But she's a girl." Ada pushed.

"So is Jess, Isabelle, Kristy, Stephanie, Marina, Sandy, and Pam. They all have them." Keith almost lost his composure when Ada tossed her arms up in the air.

"You're no help at all." Ada walked away from the desk and left Aurora giggling.

"That was so awesome," Aurora whispered.

"No, it wasn't. She's your mother, and you shouldn't be talking to her like that. As for the tattoo, she wasn't wrong. They hurt like hell." He was exaggerating about the pain, but he was pretty sure Aurora was only doing it to rebel against her mother.

"I don't mind pain." She jumped down off the counter and stopped. "How painful exactly?"

Gotcha!

"Very." Keith was doing his best to keep his expression serious.

"Fuck off. I'll ask Jess. You're just siding with mom." Aurora kicked the toe of his boot with her shoe.

It still amazed him how this was the same kid that lived down the road from his parents, and they had to search the woods for her when she was five.

"I'm ready to go." Emily's voice brought him out of his head. "Unless you want to try and scare Aurora some more."

"I don't think anything scares that girl." Keith stood up and walked around the desk. "Let's go."

He'd barely said the words when there was a loud explosion, and the large picture window shattered sending glass flying into the salon. Keith wrapped his body around Emily and took her to the ground.

"Stay behind this desk," Keith warned as he crouched on the floor. Emily nodded.

"Is anyone hurt?" Keith shouted so he could be heard over the screams of panic.

He scanned the salon to make sure nobody was injured. Kim was crouched behind her chair. Luckily, she didn't have a client. Penny had been in the back room getting something and came running out. Keith looked towards Ada's area but didn't see her. Her workstation was closest to the window.

An ear-splitting scream had him jumping to his feet and running in the direction. Next, to the waiting chairs, Ada lay on the floor with Aurora kneeling next to her.

"Aurora, get over behind the desk with Emily." Keith cupped the girl's face in his hands forcing her to look away from her mother's bloody body.

"Sh….sh…. she's …d…dead." Aurora sobbed hysterically.

"Aurora, go to Emily. Now." Keith shouted.

"Come over here, honey." Penny's head poked out behind the desk where she hid with Emily.

Once she'd moved away from Ada. Keith pulled out his phone and called 911. Ada wasn't dead because she was still breathing, but the bleeding was bad. He pulled off his leather jacket and tossed it on one of the chairs. He glanced around for something to put on a large wound near her neck. It seemed to be where most of the blood was coming from.

"I need a towel or something." He shouted behind him, and within seconds several were tossed in his direction.

"911 What's your emergency?" The operator answered

"There was just an explosion at Snippy Gals Salon on the corner of Harbour Street and Middle Road in Hopedale." Keith tried to stay calm as he watched the towel he held against Ada's next turn from white to red.

"How many injured?" The operator asked.

"I have a woman with several cuts and the worst is a large one on her neck." Keith continued to explain the best he could. He could hear Aurora sobbing and Emily's voice trying to calm the young girl.

"Is she conscious?" The operator asked.

"No, but she's breathing." Keith took a chance and raised his head so he could take a look out through the broken window. He couldn't see anything from his vantage point that could have caused the explosion.

"We've got help on the way, sir. Can I get your name?" The woman on the phone asked.

"My name is Keith O'Connor. My uncle is Kurt O'Connor. He's the superintendent of the Hopedale division of the NPD." Keith told her. Hoping someone would contact his uncle. "The woman's name is Ada Hanlon."

"Keith, help is on the way."

He could hear the sirens before the woman said the words and he dropped the phone on the floor.

"Hang in there, Ada. Help's coming." Keith whispered.

Aurora was sobbing from behind the desk, and he wished he could check on Emily. He didn't know if she was hurt or in shock. He glanced behind him to see Kim crawling next to him.

"Is she ...." Kim's voice squeaked.

"No, and she's gonna be fine. Kim, I need you to go over behind the desk." The way Kim was staring at Ada he couldn't help but wonder if it brought back memories of when she'd been stabbed.

When Kim didn't answer him, he had to raise his voice to get her attention. Her head snapped up, and he saw her wide eyes fill with tears.

"Kim, go behind the desk with everyone else. I'm not sure what happened, but you'll be safe over there." She didn't move, and he hated to yell at her, but she seemed to be going into shock. "Kim, now."

It worked because Kim jumped up and ran to join the others. Seconds later the loud scream of the fire trucks became deafening as they pulled up in front of the building.

"Keith?" The voice was familiar, and he glanced over his shoulder to see Brad King. Not only was he a firefighter, but he was also Sandy, Kim, and Lane's brother. Keith saw the frantic look on his face as he searched the front of the salon.

"Kim's behind the desk, but I need help here. Ada's hurt bad." Keith shouted over the sirens.

Brad didn't hesitate, he ran back through the now windowless door yelling for medical assistance. Within seconds Keith was pushed aside as paramedics took over Ada's care. Keith managed to grab his phone and jacket and still stay out of the way.

When he turned, he came face to face with his uncle and his brother James. Before they said anything, he saw several firefighters wrapping blankets around the girls and escorting them from the salon. He didn't see Emily.

"What the hell happened here?" James asked.

"I don't know, but where the fuck is Emily?" Keith quickly moved behind the desk. He sighed with relief when he saw her huddled under the desk with a firefighter trying to coax her out.

"Miss, I promise you it's safe." The man spoke softly. "I just want to get you out of here."

"No….no…. I need Keith." When Keith heard her shaky voice, his chest swelled. Not because she was okay, but she wanted only him.

"It's okay, Em. I'm right here." Keith crouched next to the firefighter that he knew as Dustin Fisher. He'd met him at a bar with Brad a few times. "I've got her Fisher."

Fisher handed Keith the blanket and stepped away. Emily looked up and grabbed his hand as if her life depended on it.

"Ada?" Emily whispered as she threw herself into his arms.

"She's alive, they're taking her to the hospital." Keith wrapped the blanket around her shoulders, but she plastered herself against his body and her arms wrapped around him. "It's okay, Princess. I got you."

"Keith?" He looked up at his uncle and shook his head.

"Not now Uncle Kurt." Keith walked Emily out towards the exit. She stopped when she saw the shattered glass of the doors.

"Come on, Em." He managed to get her to move and guided her outside.

He joined the other women huddled next to the ambulance that was now being loaded with Ada. Emily trembled as she clung to him. He wanted to put a severe beating on whoever did this.

"Can I go with my mom?" Aurora asked one of the paramedics.

"You can sit up front. We need room to care for your mom." The woman helped Aurora into the seat of the ambulance.

As the emergency vehicle pulled away and headed towards the highway. He glanced back at the building they'd just exited. Every window in the front of the salon was gone on the first floor. The second-floor windows seemed to be fine. The pharmacy next door hadn't seemed to receive any damage either. Whatever caused the explosion, it wasn't meant to cause significant harm. It was a warning. He just didn't know what the message was, or who sent it.

Chapter 15

Emily couldn't stop shaking as she watched the fire chief walk into her salon. There were police searching outside and placing little yellow signs here and there. She figured they were something to do with important things they were finding. Only because she'd seen that kind of stuff on television.

The only thing keeping her from collapsing at the moment was being wrapped in Keith's arms. She had her head against his chest, and she could hear his heart pounding. Either he was scared or angry.

"Emily," She glanced to her left. Kurt O'Connor placed his hand on her shoulder and squeezed it gently.

"Can I take her to the hospital before we do this, Uncle Kurt?" Keith sounded irritated.

"Yes, I was going to let you know James will take you both," Kurt said.

"What about the girls?" Emily glanced around, but she couldn't see any of them.

"Nick already has them on route to get checked, but for what it's worth they looked unharmed." Kurt bent a little to look into her eyes.

"Except Ada." Tears filled her eyes and started to run down her cheek.

"Ada's going to be fine." Keith kissed her temple. "She's a tough cookie."

Keith sat in the back of his brother's cruiser with Emily tucked into his side. Her trembling wasn't as much, but the front of his shirt was getting wetter by the second.

"I'll get in touch with your family, Emily," James pulled in front of the emergency entrance. "Ian also has a doctor waiting for you. You won't have to wait."

"I'll call my family." Emily sat up straight. What she meant was she was going to call her brother and sister. She was still too angry with her father, and her mother was still recovering.

"It's not a bother, really." James turned in his seat.

"It's fine, bro," Keith answered. "Let her do this."

James nodded and exited the vehicle. Once he'd let her and Keith out of the back, he got back in the car.

"Make sure you call if you need anything, bro," James said just before he drove off. What Emily needed was something to wake her up from this nightmare. Had all this really happened?

It seemed that Dr. Adam Cramer was the doctor that Ian had waiting for her. Keith seemed happy to see him, but Emily didn't even know why she was wasting the man's time. She wasn't hurt. Not like Ada. Poor Aurora had to be scared to death.

"I'm fine, Dr. Cramer." Emily sighed as Adam checked her eyes. "Keith pushed me to the floor and covered me."

"I still need to make sure you're okay." He smiled as he had her follow his finger with her eyes.

This is so stupid.

The only thing she wanted to do was find her friends and make sure they were all okay. They'd all been swept away before she got a chance to speak to any of them, but most important, she had to find out how Ada was.

"From what I can see, you're all right." Adam wrapped his stethoscope around his neck and tilted his head. "I hear your mom's doing very well."

"Yes," Emily answered, and it probably sounded rude.

Before he said another word, there was a knock on the door. Adam opened it, and Emily breathed a sigh of relief when Keith stepped through the door.

"Is everything okay?" Keith glanced back and forth between Adam and Emily.

"She's good. I was just about to come get you." Adam glanced back at Emily. "You should get some rest, though."

Emily stopped the urge to roll her eyes and hopped down off the examining table. Luckily Adam didn't ask her to wear one of those ridiculous hospital gowns.

"Thank you, Dr. Cramer." Emily tried to step through the door, but Keith caught her by the hand.

"Yeah, thanks, Adam. I really appreciate this." Keith said.

"No problem, but it might cost you a beer someday." Adam chuckled as he left the room.

"I need to find out how everyone is." Emily tried to pull her hand from Keith's, but it was futile.

"They're all with Aurora. I'll take you there, but Uncle Kurt does want to ask you some questions. He's going to meet us at my place as soon as you're ready."

Emily didn't know what she could possibly tell Kurt. She didn't know who would do this or why. Something was telling her that this was only the tip of the iceberg.

By the time they tracked down Aurora and the girls, the doctor had just left. Penny told them the artery in Ada's neck had been nicked by the glass, and she'd been rushed into surgery as soon as she arrived at the hospital. The surgeon repaired it, and she had to have a couple of bags of blood, but she was going to make it.

Nobody wanted Aurora to go home alone, which was probably why Keith invited her to come to his house with Emily. Aurora had refused because she wanted to stay with her mother. It took a little persuasion, but later that evening, Penny finally convinced Aurora to stay with her.

They pulled into Keith's driveway, and Emily sighed. She hadn't been there two weeks, but the sight of the house made her feel like she was home. Keith had even managed to get most of her clothes from her apartment. Something in her gut told her she'd never be staying in that apartment again.

"Kurt texted me. He's going to wait until morning. I told him you needed to rest." Keith reached over and placed his large hand over hers.

"Thanks," Emily murmured.

"How about we go inside, and I'll pour you a glass of wine. We can watch a movie or listen to some music, or if you want you can take a hot bath and call it a night." Keith lifted her hand to his lips.

Emily turned her head so she could look at him. He'd been hired to protect her, but he'd become so much more. Spending time with him was getting to be her favorite thing.

"A hot bath sounds good, and so does the wine." She forced a smile.

"Well, that's settled." Keith kissed the palm of her hand.

Emily had two glasses of wine while she was in the bath. Keith brought her one when she first slipped into the water and came back to refill it for her a little while later. Now she was curled up on the couch sipping the third glass. Keith had country music playing softly in the background while he read.

Emily studied him while he sat in his huge arm chair. Burlap curled up on his shoulder, glasses resting on his nose while he read. The man was full of contradictions. He had tattoos, wore a leather jacket and army boots. A person would expect him to listen to heavy metal music, not read books like *Finnigan's Wake*. Which wasn't what he was reading at the moment, but it was one of the hundreds of books he had on the shelves in his living room and bedroom. He looked like someone who would only read magazines with half-naked women on the front. He looked like a biker.

"Do you ride a motorcycle?" The question popped out before she could even stop it.

Keith's gaze slowly met her's and he grinned. That panty-melting smile made her forget her own name most of the time. The one that was making the last twenty-four hours fade into the background.

"Do I look like I should own one?" He pulled his glasses off and folded them.

"Honestly, yes." Emily sipped her wine.

"What makes me look like I would own one?" It pissed her off when he answered questions with questions.

"Tattoos, leather jacket, and I don't know. You just look like a biker." Emily shifted on the couch, and her robe slipped open exposing her leg. Keith's gaze went there immediately.

He placed his book and his glasses on the table next to his armchair. Burlap was carefully removed from his shoulder and put on the arm of the chair. Keith slowly rose to his feet and stalked towards her.

"Not everyone with tattoos and leather jackets is a biker." Keith crouched in front of her and ran his finger from her ankle up her leg until he reached her knee. "Just like not every wealthy person is a snob."

"You have a point." Emily gasped as his large hands covered her bare thighs. There was something about having his hands on her legs that made her so hot.

"To answer your question, I do have a motorcycle." Keith's hand moved under her robe.

"I've never been on one." Emily sighed when he started to massage the tense muscles of her thighs.

"I take mine out after the May twenty-fourth weekend. I can take you for a ride." Keith's hand slid up to her hips as he lowered his knees to the floor and pulled her towards him.

195

"I'd like that." Emily placed her glass on the side table and wrapped her arms around his neck.

Keith slipped his hands from under her robe and grabbed the remote from the coffee table. He pointed it at the stereo. She found it amusing that he used a stereo that was probably twenty years old. As the volume increased, he took her hand and stood up.

"Johnny Reid," Emily grinned because the singer was one of her favorites.

"Dance with me." Keith tugged her to her feet.

"It's appropriate that it's the name of the song too, huh." Emily stepped into his arms.

"Yes, it is." Keith pulled her tightly against him, and she pressed her cheek against his chest.

"You're a mass of contradictions." Emily closed her eyes and swayed with him.

"How's that?"

"You listen to country music, you read the most challenging books, and you let a kitten sleep in your bed, but if someone off the street met you, they'd probably say you liked Metallica, read Playboy and had a Pitbull." Emily listened to the soft beat of his heart.

"I let you sleep in my bed too." Keith chuckled.

"You're so funny." Emily tipped her head back and peered up at the man that had come to mean so much to her.

"I like all sorts of music, Em. Country music is what I grew up listening to. It gives me a sense of calm. I read a lot of books because I can't read the same book twice." Keith brushed a lock of hair behind her ear.

"Because you remember everything." Emily smiled.

"Yeah, and I haven't really let that damn cat sleep on my bed. She kind of snuck in there." Keith cupped her cheek and brushed his lips against hers. "The only one I like sleeping there with me is you."

"Good, cause your bed is really comfy." Emily smiled.

"Moreso since a princess slept in it." Keith pulled her against his chest again. "Are you okay?."

The question made her wince because she'd been trying to put it out of her mind. It also forced her to have to think about the events of the day. Her parents refusing to tell her what the hell was going on and what they were keeping from her and then the explosion. She could still hear the crash of the glass when it shattered. She trembled.

"You're safe, Princess," Keith kissed the top of her head.

"I feel safe in your arms." He made all the bad things fade into the background.

She didn't know how long they stayed swaying to the music there in the middle of his living room, but it was several songs. She was fine until George Canyon came on. The song called *Let It Out* had been one she'd heard before, but never actually listened to the words.

Then as they were swaying to the song, Keith began to sing, and she actually listened to the lyrics. She couldn't keep the tears from falling if she tried.

While he sang to her, Emily let all the emotions of the last couple of days flow down her cheeks and let Keith hold her through it.

"That's it, baby, let it out," Keith whispered as he picked her up in his arms and carried her to his bedroom. Emily trembled as he lay her on the bed and stretched out next to her. He held her tight against his side and softly hummed.

It seemed forever before she finally stopped sobbing and took a deep breath. She wanted desperately to gaze up at the man who'd let her cry more tears over the last two days then she'd cried in the past 10 years, but she was sure her face was a mess.

"You're an incredibly patient man," Emily whispered as she traced the pocket of his jeans with her finger.

"Why would you think that?" He chuckled.

"Let me see, I've been acting like a spoiled brat at one moment and then like an emotional wreck the next." He put his finger under her chin, but she wouldn't lift her head. Instead, she turned her face into his chest. "I can't look at you now. My face is probably all blotchy and red, and my nose is running."

Keith flipped her over onto her back and forced her to look at him. She kept her eyes closed tightly as if that would keep him from seeing the mess she was in.

"Open your eyes, Princess." Keith cupped her cheek, but she shook her head. "I don't know what you were taught, but just because you have your eyes closed doesn't mean I can't see you." Keith chuckled.

"Hey, it works for kids." Emily opened one eye and peeked at him.

"Not this kid." Keith brushed his lips against hers.

"Okay, you can run away now that you've seen me looking like a complete mess." Emily threw her arm over her eyes, but Keith pulled it away.

"Woman, will you open your eyes and look at me." He sighed.

Emily gazed up into his sparkling blue eyes. He was smiling as he pushed her hair behind her ear.

"You're the most beautiful woman I've ever met. Yes, you are frustrating because you're stubborn and independent, but none of that changes how incredibly stunning you are to me. I'm patient with you because I know you're going through a lot, and if you need to cry it all out every night, then I'll hold you while you do. Just do me one huge favor." He brushed his thumb across her lower lip.

"What?"

"Don't ever let me hear you say that you aren't exactly what you are. Beautiful. Stunning. Exquisite." Keith smiled.

"I…" She stopped before she made a complete fool of herself and told him she loved him. He would probably run for the hills, but the way he was looking down at her made her want to test it.

"You what?" He rested his cheek on his fist as he twirled her hair around the finger of his other hand.

Damn.

She couldn't tell him she was falling in love with him. It was way too fast, and her life was in such a limbo it wasn't possible the way she felt was real.

"I'm drained." Emily couldn't meet his eyes. Knowing Keith, he'd know she was not telling him the truth.

Keith didn't say anything, and his silence had her glancing at him to gage his reaction. He had a sweet smile on his full lips, and he seemed to be studying her.

"Why are you staring?" What was going through his beautiful mind?

"Just wondering why you feel the need to hide things from me."

Busted.

"I'm not hiding anything." Emily sighed. "It's just been a very long day."

He stared at her for another few seconds then shook his head.

"I won't push it, but just so you know, you can tell me anything, Emily." With that statement, he jumped up from the bed and reached behind his neck to pull his shirt over his head.

"What are you doing?" Emily was torn between wanting to see his incredible body and being too tired to move, but when his hands moved to the button on his jeans, she started to get a second wind.

"I'm getting ready for bed." He dropped his jeans, and there he stood in all his naked glory.

"I like the way you sleep." Emily kneeled in the middle of the bed and untied her robe.

"I really like the way you think, but you're exhausted and all I'm going to do tonight is hold you in my arms while you sleep." Keith pulled back the comforter and pointed underneath.

"You really are bossy." Emily pulled off the robe and slipped under the covers in just her panties.

"Yes I am, and you're trying to kill me by crawling into bed like that." Keith groaned.

Emily glanced down to see his partly aroused state. She lay on her back, and her eyes slowly moved back up to his eyes.

"Don't look at me like that, Princess," Keith growled as he pulled out a drawer in his dresser. He tossed a T-shirt at her and pulled on a pair of shorts. "You need to sleep, and to make that happen we are going to need a clothes barrier."

"And here I thought you had good control." Emily pulled the shirt on.

"Not when it comes to you." Keith crawled in next to her and pulled her into his side. "Now, sleep, Princess."

Even if she tried to defy him by staying awake, she couldn't. She was exhausted, and being wrapped in Keith's warm embrace was just what she needed to fall into a deep sleep.

Keith slipped out of bed being careful not to wake Emily. She'd slept all night, but had a few times where she was restless. The only thing that calmed her was when he'd pulled her tightly against him.

Keith made his way to the kitchen and poured a cup of coffee. It was a little after five in the morning and Bull walked through the front door. Keith could tell that his friend had something on his mind.

"Coffee?" Keith held up the pot.

"Yeah, and a favor." Bull grabbed a cup from the cupboard.

"Sure, what's up?"

Dean Nash was his best friend and business partner. His nickname Bull, fit him like a glove because of his large size. He was covered in tattoos from the neck down to his waist, but each tattoo had a meaning for him. Keith knew that if Bull was asking for a favor, it was something big.

"I need to go back home." Bull plopped down on one of the stools.

"Something with your family?" Keith knew there was trouble with Bull's family. His parents and older sister were deceased. Bull believed they were all murdered by someone with a grudge against him. It's why he'd placed his sister's daughter in a safe house.

"I'll fill you in when I get back. I feel awful for leaving in the middle of this." Bull folded his hands and pressed them against his lips.

"Go do what you need to and if you need back up just call." Keith bent over and rested his elbows on the counter. "I got your back."

"I know." Bull stared at the wall for a moment. Keith didn't need to ask why he was apprehensive about leaving. Bull had it bad for Kristy but kept her at arm's length until he figured out what was going on with his family.

"Anything else on your mind, bud?"

"Nothing I want to discuss. I just need you to give this to Kristy." Bull handed him an envelope.

"A letter?" Keith raised his eyebrow because Bull wasn't the love letter type.

"It's a congratulations card. She graduates from nursing school next month. I may not be here to give it to her." Bull tossed the card in front of Keith.

"You'll be gone that long?"

"Maybe longer." With that statement, Bull stood up and held out his hand.

"Call if you need anything." Keith shook Bull's hand and watched him as he walked through the door.

"He seemed kind of melancholy." Emily's voice came from behind him.

"He always seems that way." Keith chuckled. "Why are you up so early?"

"It got cold in the bed without you." Emily wrapped her arms around his waist and pressed her head against his back.

"I'm sorry, I've got an internal alarm clock that won't let me sleep past five." He pulled her around so he could wrap his arms around her.

"What time do you think Kurt will be here?" She sighed.

"Probably around eight." Knowing his Uncle, he'd be on this first thing.

For a moment, she didn't move or speak, but there was tension in her body. It was hard to believe that he'd known her less than two weeks, but he could easily gauge when she had something on her mind. Why wouldn't she, considering what she'd been through, it was surprising she wasn't a puddle on the floor.

"Want to tell me what's going through that beautiful brain of yours?" Emily tipped her head back and gazed up at him.

"I was about to ask you the same thing." He wanted so much to take away anything that could harm her.

"I just want to know who hates me so much they'd want to destroy my salon and almost kill poor Ada." Emily's eyes filled with tears.

"We'll find out who's behind this," Keith promised.

"I can't stop thinking that what happened with mom and my salon is connected."

"I think you may be right, Princess." It was too coincidental for both incidents not to be related.

Kurt walked in through the front door of Keith's house along with Aaron. After a couple of minutes of catching up, Kurt turned to Emily. She stiffened, and Keith covered her hand with his. Emily took a deep breath and nodded.

"Emily, before I ask you any questions, I wanted to let you know that Ada is doing fine. I stopped by this morning when I checked on your mom." Kurt said. "Your mom is looking a lot better today as well."

"I'll go see her after I get off…." Emily stopped and her body tensed.

"Don't worry, Emily. It won't take long to get your salon up and running again. As far as I know, the inspectors will be there today to check for structural damage." Keith squeezed her hand.

"I thought that would take weeks to get done." Emily sighed.

"That's the perks of having a friend who owns a construction company. He has inspectors on retainer." Aaron winked.

"Thank you." The way Emily looked at him made him want to puff out his chest.

"Emily, I talked to your parents. They say they don't know anyone who would do this." Kurt said.

"Why would you talk to them?" Emily asked, but Keith knew why. He'd made sure Kurt knew about the conversation Emily had overheard.

"With your mom's return and the explosion happening so close together, I'm pretty sure it wasn't a coincidence."

It seemed that Keith and Emily weren't the only ones to see the connection. Keith was sure that all of it stemmed from whatever her parents were keeping from Emily.

"Kurt, nobody told me. Where was my mother found?"

Keith hadn't asked either, but with everything that had happened, the only thing he had been concerned about was Emily.

"She was left in the parking lot of the hospital in Gander." Kurt began. "A nurse found her when she arrived for her midnight shift. Whoever left her there knew that there wasn't any video surveillance in that part of the parking lot."

"That says the dick is probably from that area," Aaron interjected.

"Your mother said the man that abducted her kept her in a small room. The only thing that was in it was a bed and a bathroom. She said there were no windows and for the last week she was in the room the water and power had been off."

Emily gasped, and Keith's stomach clenched. He couldn't imagine what it was like for Lynn in that situation.

"Are you sure you want to hear this, Emily?" Keith asked.

"Yes." Emily breathed the word more than spoke it.

"Up until the last week, he fed her once a day, but she had access to water. He'd turn off the lights every evening and bring her food into the dark room. He'd pass her a phone with a number already on the screen. All she had to do was tap the call button." Kurt stopped.

"Who did he want her to call?" Emily's voice was just above a whisper, and she was clinging to Keith's hand as if he would disappear.

"He wanted her to call you, and ask you to come get her. When she'd refuse, he'd hurt her." Keith could see it was killing Kurt to tell Emily about her mother's experiences.

"Why didn't she just call?" Emily wasn't crying, but her voice cracked, and her eyes were full of tears.

"He's obsessed with you. According to your mom, he didn't speak, but he would pass her notes. Some of the things he had written tells me the man is probably stalking you." Kurt said.

"But why destroy her salon?" Keith didn't see the reason, but it was hard to understand someone out of their mind.

"I think it was a distraction that didn't work," Kurt explained. "He probably hoped in all the confusion he could get to Emily. I don't know for sure, but right now it's the only thing that seems plausible."

"Which means he's probably really pissed that he missed his chance," Aaron said.

"Emily, you're going to have to be extra careful," Kurt explained.

"Nobody will get near her. I promise you that." Keith's body felt like a spring about to uncoil. There was no way he was letting this crazy bastard near Emily.

Emily had excused herself before Kurt and Aaron left. It was something he'd figured out about Emily. When she was emotional, she wanted to be alone.

"Bro, just so you know. If you need any help with this, I'm here." Aaron said after Kurt left.

"Thanks, A.J," Keith said. "I may just take you up on that. Bull had to go out of town, and it leaves me one man short."

"I'm sure all of us can pitch in." Aaron stepped out on the front porch with Keith behind him.

"I know. I can't let anything happen to her." Keith had the words out of his mouth before he could stop them.

"Mike owes me twenty bucks." Aaron chuckled.

"Huh?" His brothers were always making stupid bets on the weirdest shit.

"I told Mike that there was something between you and Emily. Mike told me I was nuts." Aaron laughed.

"You're a fucking ass, A.J," Keith grumbled.

"Yeah, but a loveable one." Aaron chuckled as he jogged down the front steps.

"Whatever gets you through the day, dick," Keith yelled, and Aaron gave him the finger before he hopped in his car.

He found Emily curled up on his bed with her arms wrapped around a pillow. She'd been crying, that was obvious, but at that moment she was focused on the window. She looked lost, and he had no doubt she was blaming herself for what happened to her mother.

"Why would someone be so obsessed with me they would hurt my mom and my family?" She didn't look at him.

"I don't know why someone would want to hurt good people, Princess." Keith sat next to her and touched her arm.

"I thought you were a genius." Emily sat up and smiled, but he knew it was forced.

"I never said I was." Keith pushed her hair back from her forehead.

She moved closer and rested her head on his shoulder, and he instinctively wrapped his arms around her.

"I need to go see mom and dad. I've got to find out what they're keeping from me."

"I figured you would."

"Can we go now?"

"Whatever you want, Princess." Keith kissed the top of her head and pulled back so he could see her face. "I just don't want you to be disappointed if your father refuses to tell you."

"Oh, he's going to tell me." Emily popped up on her knees. "This is about me not him, and if he knows something, he's going to tell me whether he likes it or not."

"You're a real firecracker, aren't you?" Keith chuckled.

"Hello, red hair!" She held up a piece of her hair. Keith never considered her a ginger like him, but most people would say she was.

"Let's go," Keith stood and held out his hand to her. When she took it, his heart seemed like it flipped in his chest.

At that moment he knew Emily was the one for him. He never thought he could fall in love so fast, even after he'd seen it happen to his brothers. No nutcase was going to hurt her.

I know you're up there Grandda. I really need you to watch over her.

Rhonda Brewer

Chapter 17

The entire drive to the hospital Emily couldn't keep still. There was no doubt her father was going to fight her every step of the way. Her mother always told Emily she got her stubborn streak from her dad. So she knew when she butted heads with him it was like two bulls clashing, but she wasn't backing down. She needed to know what her parents were hiding.

Walking into the hospital, Emily grabbed Keith's hand and clung to it as if it was a lifeline. At this point, she didn't care who saw or what they thought. Keith kept her calm, and she needed his strength.

When she walked into her mother's room, her father wasn't there. Her heart dropped for a second, but it was probably better to start with her mother. Not that her mother was a pushover, but from the conversation Emily had overheard, her mother wanted to tell Emily.

"Emily, I'm so glad to see you." Her mom looked so much better. She was still really skinny, but her color was back. "When Kurt told us what happened I was so worried. How are all your girls? I heard Ada was hurt, but she's going to be okay."

"All the girls are shaken a bit, but they're fine. Ada was injured pretty badly, but she'll be okay." Emily sat on the bed next to her mother and took her hand. "Mom, I know dad didn't want to talk to me about this big secret, but we think it has something to do with what happened to the salon and to you. I need to know."

Her mother opened her mouth and closed it again. She was definitely struggling with whatever this was.

"Mrs. Bradshaw, this could be important, and trust me if it doesn't have a connection we'll make sure it doesn't leave this room." Keith appeared at the other side of the bed, and her mom reached for his hand.

"I don't want to go against Nel's wishes." She sighed.

"Mom, please. This is important." Emily wasn't above begging.

"Emily." Her father's voice boomed from the doorway.

Emily squeezed her mother's hand and stood up. She turned to face her father with all the stubbornness she'd inherited from him.

"This is what you do. You ambush your mother when she's recovering." Her dad closed the door and glared over her head at

Keith. "And you. I hired you to keep my family safe, and what happens? Someone blows up my daughter's salon."

"Mr. Bradshaw…." Keith started, but Emily held up her hand.

"Don't you dare blame Keith for this. He has been keeping me safe." Emily fisted her hands at her sides.

"Watch your tone with me, young lady." Her dad growled.

"Dad you can chastise me later. Right now you need to tell me what you're hiding. There is nothing you can tell me that would ever make me hate you. I'm not backing down on this, Dad." Emily could see her father's face go from angry, to concern and then fear.

It was the fear in his eyes that had her going to him. Whatever her parents were holding in seemed to bring out an emotion in her father that she rarely saw.

"Dad, please." Emily took his hands. "I need to know."

Her dad squeezed her hands, and his gaze moved to her mother. Emily saw the tears in his eyes, and it tugged at her heart, but she couldn't back down.

"Nel, it's time." Her mother's voice came out in a whisper.

"It amazes me how much you look like her." Her father looked down at Emily and smiled.

"Dad, Elaine is more like mom. Stop stalling." Emily sighed.

"Not your mother, sweetheart. You look like her sister." He closed his eyes and dropped his head.

Emily knew her mother had a sister that had died years before in an accident, but her mother never actually talked about it. Emily knew the pain of losing a sibling, so she never asked.

"What does Aunt Nora have to do with this, dad?" He dropped her hands and slowly sat in the chair next to the door. He rested his elbows on his knees and folded his hands in front of him.

Emily glanced at her mom who clung to Keith's hand, and she nodded.

"Dad," Emily whispered as she knelt in front of him.

"I killed her." He choked out.

Did she just hear him correctly? There was no way her father would hurt anyone let alone take a life.

"You killed her?" Emily said the words as if they were another language. "I thought it was a car accident."

"It was." Her mother said.

"Dad, I don't understand." Emily cupped his hands in hers, and he raised his head.

"Start from the beginning, Nel." Her mother encouraged.

Her dad pulled his hands out of Emily's grasp, and he cupped hers in the same way she'd just been holding his.

"You know I've been in love with your mother since I was seventeen years old." He forced a smile and Emily nodded. She'd heard the story of him chasing after her mother until she finally agreed to go out with him.

"She was beautiful, and there was never any other woman for me." He glanced over Emily's shoulder obviously looking at her mother.

"There was never any other man for me, either." Her mother's voice cracked.

"Your Aunt was younger than your mom."

"I know." Emily's heart raced, and at the rate, her father was telling the story they were going to be there forever.

"She had a huge crush on me, and I was flattered, but she knew I loved your mother."

Emily was getting more anxious, but it seemed so hard for him to get this out. She knew her aunt had died when she was just sixteen years old.

"Emily, we've kept this buried for forty years because we didn't want to tarnish Nora's reputation." Emily could see he was trying so hard to keep the tears back.

"Or yours?" Emily cringed at the words, but he'd said she would hate him if she knew.

"Yes." He sighed and sat back in the chair letting her hands drop. Emily still kneeled on the floor in front of him, and she rested her hands on his knees like she did as a little girl when he would read to her and her siblings before bed.

"I'd finally convinced your mother to go to a movie with me just after I turned twenty. Nora was sixteen and was starting to hang around with a crowd of hard cases from school." He sighed.

"I remember mom saying she was wild." Actually, her mother had said Nora was hell on wheels.

"Your mom was really worried about her, and since she knew Nora was crushing on me, she asked me to talk to her."

"You spoke to her?" Emily didn't have to ask because knowing her father he would do anything for her mom.

"I took her out for ice cream one day and asked her about the people she was partying with. She told me she was seeing some guy from town and he drove a motorcycle, and he told her when she turned eighteen he was taking her away." Her father seemed to be finding it easier to talk, so Emily just continued to listen.

"I did the asshole thing and laughed at her. Told her to grow up. She threw her ice cream at me, told me I was going to be sorry I was ever born and ran out of the soda shop." He shook his head.

"I tried to catch her, but by the time I got outside, she was gone. I went straight to your mother's house and told her what happened. I asked your mom not to tell her parents. I wanted to find her. It's something I regret to this day."

"That's when she had the accident?" Emily asked.

"No. I knew where the teenagers went to party, so I went there to find Nora. When I got there, I didn't see her at first, but it didn't take long to find her. She was huddled in the grass with a really rough looking guy and let's just say they weren't even trying to hide what they were doing." He sighed and cursed before he continued.

"She was drunk, and I pulled the guy off her. You know I still don't remember the guy's name. I should have killed him for taking advantage of Nora in her state, but I grabbed her by the arm and dragged her to the car. She was screaming that she would tell her parents I raped her and ruin my relationship with her sister."

"She was drunk, dad." People could be asses when they drank.

"I know, and that's why I didn't pay attention to what she said. I put her in the car and brought her home. Drunk or not she did exactly what she said she would. I was thankful your mom or grandparents didn't believe her."

"They knew a good man when they saw one." Her mother said, and he smiled at her.

"Dad, I still don't know how any of this has to do with me," Emily said.

"Em, let him continue," Keith said. Emily nodded.

"A couple of days after that I got a call from your mom saying that Nora had taken off with the guy she'd been forbidden to see. He'd picked her up on his bike when her parents went out. Your mom tried to stop her, but she punched her and broke her nose." Emily gasped.

"I was so angry. I should've just called your grandparents, but I didn't. I went off like a hot head to find Nora and that ass. I drove around SummerBrook, Hopedale, and some of the other communities. I couldn't find them. Then, I was on the way back home, I saw him turning onto one of the backroads with Nora on the back of his bike. I couldn't help it. I saw red and hit the gas. I caught up with them and kept honking the horn to get them to pull over. He wouldn't, and like I said I wasn't thinking I floored the car and pulled in front of him. He turned to avoid me and lost control of the bike."

Emily glanced back at her mother because she knew where the story was heading. It was the accident that killed Nora and all these years her father blamed himself. She just didn't know why it was this big secret.

" I jammed the car into park, and when I got out of the car, I ran right to him. He was getting up, and I'm ashamed to say I pounded the shit out of him. By the time I got myself under control, he was unconscious. I turned to talk to Nora…." Her father stopped and swallowed several times before he finally continued. "She was under the bike…." He swallowed again. "Her eyes were open and …." He pulled his hands down over his face and took a huge intake of breath. "You don't need to know that part, but she was gone."

None of this was explaining why there was a crazy man obsessed with Emily. It made sense why her father felt guilty but not why it had to be kept from her, or anyone for that matter.

"What happened to the guy?" Keith asked.

"Between Lynn's parents and mine, he was paid off to keep his mouth shut and take responsibility for the accident. I never saw him again, and neither of our parents would tell us who he was." Her father took her hands. "Emily, it's why I butt heads with you so much. I know you were never wild like Nora, but you look so much like her and every time I look at you, it reminds me of what I caused."

"Dad, it wasn't your fault." Emily didn't know when the tears started to run down her cheeks, but she wrapped her arms around her father and hugged him.

"I love you, Emily, and I'm sorry I've given you such a difficult time with your shop." He was squeezing her tightly.

"Mr. Bradshaw, you don't know what happened to the guy?" Keith asked.

"No, my father told me never to mention it again, and Mr. Miller told me to follow his story to the letter. I was to say that I saw the accident and nothing else." Her father kissed the top of her head. "I don't know how Lynn's dad never blamed me."

"He knew it wasn't your fault and I've told you to stop blaming yourself." Her mom's voice was soft and shaky.

The room was quiet for a few minutes except for the quiet sniffing from her mother and the soft sobbing from Emily. She was still clinging to her father because she couldn't believe that he'd been keeping this from everyone for so long. Keith was the first to break the silence, and from the way her father's body tensed, he didn't like what Keith was saying.

"Mr. Bradshaw, I know this has been kept quiet for a long time, but you need to tell Uncle Kurt. This guy could be the one that took your wife." Keith said.

"You think he's trying to get back at dad by hurting mom or me?" Emily turned around to look at Keith.

"You want to know what I think?" Keith asked.

"You think he sees me as Nora." Emily didn't need Keith to say it. She'd seen enough crime shows to know people could snap and see things that weren't there.

"When he told you to call Emily, what did he say?" Keith asked her mother.

"He didn't speak. Just showed me a picture and handed me the phone with Emily's number punched in. The only noise he made was growling when I refused and when he would…." Her mother swallowed. "Hit me."

"You never heard his voice?" Keith asked, and her mother shook her head. "And you didn't see his face or anything that you would recognize?" Her mother shook her head again.

222

"Kurt asked her all these questions." Her father sat on the edge of the bed and rested his hand on her mother's leg.

"Kurt didn't have all the information." Keith raised an eyebrow at her father, and Emily really wanted to punch him.

"Keith, don't start," Emily warned him. She didn't know why he seemed so angry, but she could tell by the way his jaw was clenched.

"I'm sorry Mr. and Mrs. Bradshaw, I know this has been something you've hoped wouldn't have to come out, but when you knew what this guy wanted you should have filled me in. I need all the information to do my job. You need to call Uncle Kurt now and give him this information." Keith turned to glance at Emily. "I'll be just outside the room."

"Keith," Emily called out as the door closed behind him. "What the fuck?" Emily tossed her arms up in the air.

"Watch your mouth, Emily." Her father warned. "I understand why he's upset and he's right."

"Dad, just so you know. I don't hate you, and how you ever thought I would because of this, I'll never know. I do believe you need to call Kurt and also tell Elaine and Edward."

"I know. I do feel lighter just telling you." He stood up and opened his arms.

"I love you both. Now I've got to give Mr. O'Connor a piece of my mind for being an ass." Emily turned to leave the room.

"It's difficult for a man to see the woman he loves could be in danger." Her father said stopping Emily in her tracks.

Emily turned slowly to face her parents. Her father was sat next to her mother again, but he wasn't looking at Emily. His eyes were glued to her mother.

"I don't think that applies to me, Dad," Emily said.

"I believe it applies to you more than you believe, sweetheart." Her father turned to her and smiled.

Emily glanced between her mother and father. They were serious. How could they think Keith was worried because he loved her? Sure, she was falling faster than a wheel rolling downhill, but there was no way Keith felt the same way.

Emily turned without saying a word and opened the door. Keith leaned against the wall with his arms crossed over his chest talking to Rex. His gaze met hers as soon as she left the room.

"You ready to go?" Keith pushed off the wall.

"Yes," Emily replied and without waiting for him started toward the elevator.

By the time she got to the elevator which was about ten steps from her mother's room, Keith grabbed her hand to turn her around.

"I'm sorry." He whispered as they stepped on the elevator.

"You shouldn't have made my dad feel bad. He's been holding this in for almost forty years and now because of it some crazy person kidnapped his wife and hurt her, blew up my salon and for some reason is obsessed with me." Emily closed her eyes and took a deep breath. "Why would someone be obsessed with me?"

Emily's eyes flew open when the elevator jolted to a sudden stop. Keith was just pulling his finger away from the panel and turned to her.

"Are you fucking kidding me? Keith, what are you doing?" Emily shouted.

"Do you want to know how someone could be obsessed with you?" Keith's eyes locked with hers. "Well, Princess, I'm going to tell you. For one, you're beautiful, smart, sexy as fuck and do you know what the best thing is?"

Emily didn't speak.

"Do you?" He apparently wanted an answer.

"What?" She whispered.

"You have no fucking idea just what people see in you. You want to know something else?" He rested his hands on her hips and pulled her towards him.

"What?" She smiled up at him.

"I'm fucking obsessed with you." He brushed his lips against her ear making her shiver. "You've invaded my house, my room, my thoughts, my dreams and I wouldn't want it any other way."

"You're crazy." Emily pressed her forehead against his chest.

"You're not the first one to tell me that, but everything I said was true." He kissed the top of her head.

"Can we start the elevator?" Emily mumbled into his chest.

"Yeah," Keith kissed the top of her head again as he leaned towards the panel. The elevator jolted and started to move.

It's difficult for a man to see the woman he loves could be in danger.

Her father's words echoed in her head. Keith hadn't said he loved her. He was obsessed with her wasn't the same thing, but it did warm her heart.

The warm feelings that she'd gotten from Keith started to fade. With the realization that there was someone out there that hurt her mother to get to Emily was terrifying. Her body suddenly felt icy cold, and as if Keith sensed it, he wrapped his arms around her shoulder and pulled her into his side.

"I got you, Princess. I always got you." Keith whispered as the elevator doors opened.

Yes, you got me. More than you know.

226

Chapter 18

Keith jogged up the steps to his front door and nodded at Crash. He still felt the need to make sure someone was there to watch over Emily even though he was just at the gym on his property. It was probably a little too cautious, but he wasn't letting anything happen to her.

It had been three days since the explosion, and they were still waiting on the results of the investigation. Ada was still in the hospital but doing very well. Emily and Kim had decided to pay everyone's salary until they could reopen, which probably took a lot of stress off the women.

Nelson wanted to wait until Lynn was out of the hospital before he met with Kurt to tell him everything. So it gave him and Emily the last three days to themselves. The only time they left his compound was to visit her mother and Ada. Everyone seemed to know that Emily needed peace, and for the most part left them alone.

The rest of his evening would be a different story. Kurt was dropping by to give them the results of the investigation into the explosion. Emily's mom was out of the hospital, and she and Nelson insisted on coming to Keith's place to talk to Kurt. They felt it was the safest place for Emily.

"I feel I should give you a heads up." Crash stepped in front of him.

"What?" Before Crash could answer his door opened, and the noise of a houseful of people made him want to run the other way.

"Keithy, dere you are." Nanny Betty motioned for him to go inside.

"Good luck," Crash chuckled and tried to step around Keith, but he was brought to a halt by Nanny Betty.

"Ya get in dis house, Brent." Nanny Betty grabbed Crash's arm. "We got enough food fer everyone."

Crash looked almost fearful as he glanced at Keith, but like everyone else, he obeyed the five-foot tall woman.

Keith entered his kitchen and just as he suspected his house had been invaded by all the women in his family. He stood in the doorway and scanned the room for Emily. Not that he would have missed her because he seemed to have some sort of radar for her. His eyes locked onto her on the other side of the kitchen holding his newest nephew.

Emily's face was glowing as she smiled down at the baby. As if she sensed his eyes on her, she looked up to meet his gaze. It was as if all the din of the chatting women disappeared while they stared at each other. That was until he got shoved into the kitchen by one of his asshole brothers.

"You know blocking the door isn't going to keep us out." Mike slapped him on the back as he squeezed into the room.

"Sorry, bro. Nan texts we show up." James walked in followed by John and Nick.

"Who the hell taught her how to text anyway?" Aaron chuckled.

"You know, I love all of you but why exactly did Nan order this family gathering?" Keith caught Ian as he was about to squeeze by him.

"I think you must be the only one who didn't get the text." Ian pulled him aside. "Mom, Dad, and Nan decided that because of the danger Emily could be in, that it wouldn't be a good idea to have the party where it wasn't secure. Nan suggested your place. Well, it wasn't actually a suggestion. Plus, Kurt wanted to talk to you, and from what Marina said, he made the mistake of saying it in front of Nan."

"I checked my phone, but I don't have a message from him or Nan," Keith said.

"As far as I know, it has to do with Emily's situation." Ian looked over Keith's shoulder. "Kurt is on the way here with Emily's parents."

Keith twisted around to see what Ian was looking at. Emily was no longer holding Alexander. Now Ian's little girl Lily was sat on her lap and pointing towards Keith.

"I should warn you, on the way over here Lily asked if your girlfriend was here." Ian grinned.

"Jesus, Fuck. She's not…. We're not…. I don't fucking know what we are. All I know right now is some crackpot is obsessed with her. Bro, I can't let the fucking bastard get near her." Keith kept his voice low enough for only Ian to hear.

"Just so you know, we're here for that reason. You were there for me when Sandy was in danger. I've got your back, bro. All of us got your back, but it is dad's birthday, and we've put off the baptism until Alexander's god-father can be there too." Ian clapped his hand on Keith's shoulder and gave it a squeeze.

"Thanks, bro. I'd be honored to be the little man's godfather, and thanks for delaying it."

Keith didn't doubt between his brothers and the guys that work for him, Emily would be safe. At least from danger. Being safe from his family was another story.

Keith squeezed his way out of the kitchen and made his way to his room. After a quick shower, he walked out of the ensuite wrapping a towel around his waist, Emily came into the bedroom and closed the door behind her. She turned and pressed her back against the door.

"Are you hiding?" He chuckled when she sighed.

"Maybe." She smiled, and her eyes traveled down his body. "Or maybe I knew you'd be in here naked."

"I'm not naked, but I can be." He grabbed the edge of the towel as if he was going to yank it off.

"You do realize there are about a million people outside this room?" Emily hitched her thumb over the shoulder.

"First of all, there aren't a million people in Newfoundland. So I doubt that number is accurate." Keith stalked towards her and braced his hands against the door on both sides of her head.

"I think your family is multiplying out there." Emily slowly slid her hands from his abs up over his chest.

"What do you think we are? Rabbits?" Keith chuckled and kissed his way from her cheek to the crook of her neck.

"Keith," She moaned softly.

"Princess, as much as I would love to lock this door and toss you on that bed, I know my family. The minute they don't see us, they will come looking." Keith sighed when she wrapped her arms around his waist and kissed his chest.

"Lily wanted me to know that she's glad I'm Uncle Keith's girlfriend." Emily peeked up at him under her lashes.

"And what did you say?" Keith teased.

"I told her I wasn't your girlfriend." Emily squeezed her eyes shut.

"Did you say that because you think it's what I'd want you to say, or do you not see this going somewhere?" He needed to know before he could put a label on what they were.

"I said it because I really didn't know how to answer it, but I do want this to go somewhere." Emily cupped his cheek. Keith covered her hand with his and pressed his lips against her palm.

"Me too." Keith stepped back and dropped the towel. "I better get dressed before the search party starts."

"God, I love your ass." Emily sighed when he turned around.

"Leave his ass alone and come out here both of you.." Nick shouted through the bedroom door.

"Stop listening through doors asshole. We'll be right out." Keith replied.

"Well, now I won't be able to face your family." Emily covered her face.

"Trust me, Nick won't say a word." Keith pulled up his jeans and grabbed a shirt out of the closet. "I'll kick his ass if he does."

He couldn't help himself as he pulled her into his arms before they left the room. He brushed his lips against hers, and she sighed.

"I'm pretty sure everyone suspects we're together." She whispered.

"You may be right, and I'm fine with that. Are you?" Keith kissed her lips.

"Absolutely." Emily pressed her hand against his cheek. "I must be because I'm in here with you and there is a huge birthday cake in the kitchen."

"Well, now I feel really special. If you're choosing me over one of Nan's cakes, I must be the luckiest man in the world." He chuckled as he reached around her for the doorknob.

"I feel pretty lucky myself." She kissed his cheek just before she turned and left the room.

An hour later the huge pans of food were scraped clean, and the cake had vanished. Keith's father had recruited the help of all the grandchildren to help him open all the gifts, which ranged from clothes to fishing gear. His dad had a love for fishing that had stemmed from his father.

It made his heart happy that Emily fit in so well with his family. Of course, they treated her like she was one of them.

The house was still full of people, but Kurt was preparing Keith's dining room for everyone to talk. It didn't matter that Kurt had only wanted the family that was members of the N.P.D and N.S.S., Nan had deemed everyone on the team.

Keith walked into his living room to grab a few more chairs to see some of his nieces and nephews dancing around in front of the television. He shook his head and headed for the dining room carrying an armful of folding chairs.

"My television is being tortured by a big purple thing on the screen." Keith chuckled as he leaned the chairs against the wall.

"That would be Barney, and he's become my best friend," Stephanie grinned.

"Yeah, don't be dissing Barney." Marina pointed her finger at him.

"Barney is a gift from the heavens." Sandy sighed.

His three sisters-in-law obviously had found something to keep their kids from driving them crazy. He didn't blame them because his nieces and nephews had a lot of energy.

When Emily's parents arrived, his mother wrangled all the kids into the living room, and between her and his Aunt Alice, they kept the kids out of earshot. The last thing the little ones needed to hear about was explosions and Emily being in danger. The kids had been around more of all this shit than any child should have.

Kurt began to explain the report he'd received from the fire chief. The explosion hadn't been meant to destroy the salon. A small box had been attached below the window. The investigator had found the remnants of what was believed to be a small pipe bomb and traces of gun powder. It was set on a timer made with what looked like a standard alarm clock.

"I think it was meant as a distraction to get to Emily," Kurt said.

"This guy should know by now Emily has security," James said.

"If he doesn't, then he's not the sharpest tool in the shed. Keith's been her shadow for a few weeks." Mike chuckled.

Although Nelson and Lynn seemed comfortable with his family, Emily's dad had started to pace the room. More so when Kurt began the story of what had happened all those years ago. It had to be difficult for him to let everyone hear what he had done, even if it wasn't intentional.

Keith's heart went out to the man, and he actually owed Nelson an apology. He'd been an ass at the hospital, but it had pissed him off to find out that because of what the family had kept hidden, Emily's safety was in jeopardy. It still didn't give Keith the right to be disrespectful. His mother and father would be disappointed.

"There has to be someone that knows the guy's name. There has to be a record somewhere. Especially if the guy was admitted to the hospital." Sandy said.

"You stay out of this. You're on maternity leave. I'll get Smash to check into it." The sudden pain in his shin told Keith that he shouldn't have said that.

"Hope that hurt asshole." Sandy narrowed her eyes at him. "I'm still better than Smash, and I'm going to be the one to do this."

"Jesus, woman. You didn't have to kick me." Keith complained, but Sandy was the best at digging out hidden information, and if it were out there, she'd find it. Not that Smash wasn't good.

"Fer de love a da lord, Nelson. Sit down. Yer makin' me dizzy wit all yer pacin' around de room." Nanny Betty grabbed Nelson by the hand and pulled him into the chair next to her. "Now, so far, Sandy's gonna look on de web net to find dis sleeveen. Wat do we do next?"

Sleeveen was Nanny Betty's way of saying asshole and leave it to her to say what everyone else was thinking.

"Mudder, you won't be doing anything." His father pointed his finger toward Nanny Betty. Would the man never learn?

"Sean, doncha dare try ta tell me wat ta do." Nanny Betty glared at his dad. "I'm still yer mudder."

When he tried to reply a hand reached out and covered his dad's mouth. It seemed Tom knew with Nanny Betty, arguing was futile.

"I'll have to cancel the Sweet Heart Ball," Lynn's soft voice cracked.

"That's probably a good idea," Nelson was quickly at his wife's side.

236

"Mom, you can't do that. The children's hospital depends on that fundraiser." Emily said.

"Emily, we can't take a chance. You'd be in danger." Lynn's eyes filled with tears.

"Then I won't go, and Keith will look after the security." Emily glanced at him for verification, and he nodded. He knew she didn't want to miss the ball. It meant so much to her family, but the thought of her in a crowd made him sick to his stomach. Especially because they had no idea who this guy was. For all they knew, it could be someone the Bradshaw's considered friends.

"If ya want, we can give ya a hand wit tings." Nanny Betty reached out and grabbed Lynn's hand. "It'll save ya some money, and ya can give dat to the hospital too."

"That's a fantastic idea." Lynn smiled at his grandmother. Although, he was pretty sure Lynn and Nelson were not worried about what the ball was going to cost. The only thing that Keith was concerned with was how Emily was going to feel about missing the event.

"I'd like to help too." Pam had been in the corner of the room.

"Won't you be gone back to the mainland?" Cora asked, but her expression was hopeful.

"Mom, I think it's time for me to come home for good." How Pam didn't get shoved through the wall was surprising. Between his cousins and Cora, she was plastered against the wall with all of them hugging her.

"Pammy, we'll celebrate ya comin' home later. Now we got work ta do." Nanny Betty shouted over the excitement. "Is dat all ya got Kurt."

"Mudder, I'm seriously thinking about giving you a job at the station." Kurt chuckled.

"Doncha be so foolish. I got no time fer a job." Nanny Betty waved her hand in the air. "Tryin' ta keep all of ya from getting' killed is a full-time job."

The room erupted into laughter breaking the tension of what they were facing. Leave it to his grandmother to be the comic relief in an otherwise serious situation.

She's one of a kind, Grandda.

Chapter 19

Like hell, she was missing the Ball. Emily wanted everyone to believe she wouldn't be attending. It wasn't that she didn't trust her parents, but nobody knew who the hell this guy was. Her mom and dad could let it slip to the very person doing this without even knowing.

Emily sat back silently and held her mother's hand while she gave Kurt the detailed account of how she was abducted. The room was completely silent as her mother spoke.

"I'd just left the printers next to Nelson's office. I had put in the order for the invitations for the ball. I'd parked my car at the back of the building because as you know the parking in downtown St. John's is awful. It was starting to get dark, and when I opened the car door, someone grabbed me from behind and put something over my mouth." Emily squeezed her mom's trembling hand. "It smelled sweet, and I felt really dizzy."

"Does she have to do this?" Her dad had obviously heard the story, but it still seemed to bother him.

"It's okay, Nel." Her mother's sweet smile appeared to calm him.

"I know this is hard, Lynn but the more we know, the better," Kurt said as John held a box of tissues out to her.

"I don't know what happened after that until I woke up in a room tied to an old creaky bed. I felt him before I saw him. He'd untied one of my hands and shoved the phone into my hand. When I looked at the screen, it had Emily's number on it. I was still woozy, and when I looked up at him, he shoved a piece of paper in front of me. He wanted me to call Emily and have her come meet me." Her mom took a deep, shaky breath and continued to explain how everytime she refused the man would hit her and give her less and less food and water.

"Ya poor girl." Nanny Betty's eyes were filled with unshed tears.

"I don't remember how I got out of there, but I do remember the lovely woman who found me in the parking lot." Lynn sniffed. "She saved my life."

Emily couldn't listen to anymore, she stood up and left the room. Hearing that her mother could have died at the hands of this monster shook her to her core. She couldn't stop the trembling or the anger that was quickly invading her.

"There's a place in hell for a bastard like you," Emily whispered to herself.

"Hell is too good for people like the man that took your mom." Emily turned to the voice. Marina was pouring a cup of tea at the counter.

"True." Emily moved into the kitchen and sat down on one of the stools.

"I'm a firm believer that if people like that don't get what they deserve in this lifetime, they will be in the next." Marina put a steaming cup in front of Emily.

"I don't understand how people can be so cruel," Emily immediately wanted to take the statement back. She'd been told about what Marina had gone through with her late husband's twin brother. He'd killed her husband and taken his place. From what Emily knew the brother was abusive to Marina, and she'd left him thinking something had changed her husband.

"I don't either, but I wouldn't change anything I've gone through. It made me who I am, and I met the love of my life. You want to know something?" Marina rested her arms on the counter.

"What?"

"The O'Connor family are good people." Marina smiled. "and I can say with confidence, the big lug standing in that doorway won't let anything happen to you." Marina glanced over Emily's head and winked.

Emily turned. Keith had his shoulder braced against the doorjamb, and his hands shoved into his front pockets. No matter what he wore, or what he was doing, he always took her breath away and made it easier to breathe at the same time.

"Marina's right. Nobody's going to hurt you." Keith said as he moved in front of her.

"On that note, I'm gonna leave you two alone." Marina winked again and left her alone with Keith.

"I just couldn't listen to what mom went through anymore." Emily dropped her gaze to the floor.

"I don't blame you." Keith put his finger under her chin. "Your mom is a very brave lady."

Keith didn't need to tell her that because Emily had known that her whole life. It was her mother that gave her the advice to stand up to her father and stood by her when Emily made her career choice.

"It just hurts to know that she went through this because of me." Emily swallowed hard.

"This is not on you, Princess." Keith cupped her cheek. "He's disturbed and who knows what made him snap."

"You think it's the guy that my grandfathers paid off, don't you?" Emily had got the impression Kurt believed it.

"I do. We just need to find out who he is." Keith wrapped his arms around her.

When everyone had finally left, Emily felt guilty for feeling so relieved. Especially, since they were there to help her. She wasn't used to being around such a large family. The only ones left were her parents and their ever-present shadow, Rex. Her mother was quiet, and her father was pacing.

"Dad, will you please sit down." Emily groaned.

He turned and gazed at her mother. It was the first time that day she'd seen the bags under her father's eyes. His usually bright gray eyes were dull and bloodshot.

"I'm worried about you, dad. You don't look well." It was evident by the way her mother nodded her head that she felt the same way.

"Don't you worry about me. I'm all right." He grumbled. "I wish I knew who the hell this fucking bastard was."

Her mother gasped, and Emily knew why. Her father never cursed. At least not that she'd ever heard. The situation was changing her dad and not in a good way.

"Nel, watch your language please." Her mother spoke with a soft but firm voice.

"Sorry, honey." He sat next to her and wrapped his arm around her.

"I'm so sad you won't be going to the ball, but I know it's not safe for you." Her mother's eyes filled with tears. "I love having you there."

"I know, mom." She wanted to tell her mother that she was going, but it was better that she didn't. Keith would be the only one to know.

Emily glanced out through the living room doorway. Keith was standing just outside talking quietly with Rex and someone else she couldn't see, but the only one she was really studying was the man that had stolen her heart, and he didn't even know.

He glanced at her, and his sparkling blue eyes met hers. Her stomach did a flip flop but not in a good way. The look on Keith's face told her that the person she couldn't see didn't bring good news.

Now what?

Chapter 20

Just when Keith thought things were under control, someone had to pull the rug out from under him. He glanced into the living room and met Emily's gaze. He hoped his concern wasn't obvious, but something with the way her mouth dropped open said Emily was probably the one person that he couldn't hide his emotions from.

"So from what I could find out, Nelson Bradshaw doesn't know his staff as well as he thinks." Smash had his back braced against the wall, and spoke in hushed tones.

"I've gotten a weird vibe from them since the first day I met them." Rex rubbed his hand over his buzzed hair. "But Bradshaw trusts them. I've been keeping an eye on them when they are around, but I guess I should've been more diligent."

Keith turned away from Emily and glanced between the two men. One or both of the Becker brothers could be involved in all this, and it was possible that one of them could be the guy Emily's aunt had run away with that day. They were the right age, but it was almost comical to think of one of them with long hair and riding a motorcycle. They appeared way too uptight to be such a rebel.

"Just keep Emily's parents safe. We'll deal with these assholes." Keith whispered.

"I just don't understand how them embezzling money, and all this shit with Mrs. Bradshaw have to do with each other," Smash whispered.

"Neither do I." Keith sighed. "Smash you keep digging and check in with Sandy because I know she's doing her own investigating."

"How the hell is she working with a new baby and three other kids?" Smash shook his head.

"Have you met her?" Keith chuckled. "Besides, Sandy thinks the world of Emily, so she wants to help."

"Plus, she thinks she's better than me." Smash chuckled. "She is, but don't tell her I said that."

"I think it's time to head home, Rex," Nelson called from the living room.

"I'm ready whenever you are, sir." Rex stepped around Keith and into the room.

Smash left shortly after Rex and the Bradshaws. Keith found Emily on the couch with her head resting on the back and her eyes closed. Burlap was curled up on her lap. The cat seemed to have a calming effect on Emily as she scratched the kitten's small head.

"So what's the bad news?" Emily sighed without opening her eyes.

"Gas prices are up." Keith sat next to her, and she opened her eyes.

"Keith, I know something's wrong." She turned her head and gazed up into his eyes.

"It's nothing you've got to worry about." Keith cupped her cheek.

"Don't do that." Emily pushed his hand away. "Don't keep things from me, Keith."

"I'm not keeping things from you, Princess." Well, at least not something he was completely sure about.

"Keith, when that wrinkle in between your eyes appears, you're worried." Emily ran her finger down his forehead and in between his eyes.

"You're way too observant." Keith took her hand and kissed the tip of her finger.

"Tell me, please."

"I don't want you saying anything to your dad until we got enough proof and we tell Uncle Kurt." When Emily nodded, he continued. "How well do you know your father's employees?"

"I know most of them but not well. I never worked with dad. Why?"

"How long has Ken and Elliot Becker been working for him?" Keith knew, but he wondered if Emily did.

"As long as I can remember. They are a little weird and to be honest, Ken gives me the creeps." Emily shivered.

"Why?"

"Just the way he glares at Elaine and me. Although, with his squinty eyes, I'm not sure if it's a glare or if he's got gas." Emily giggled.

"Have you ever felt in danger with him?" Keith asked.

"What is with the Spanish Inquisition?" Emily lifted Burlap off her lap and put the kitten next to her. When she straddled his legs, she cupped his face in her hands. "What's going on?"

"Smash found some odd withdrawals from your father's business accounts and amounts matching them deposited into a joint account the brothers have," Keith explained.

"They're stealing from my dad?" Emily pulled her phone from her back pocket, and Keith snatched it out of her hand. "What are you doing? We've got to tell my dad."

"Em, first you can't call your dad and just blurt that out. Smash is meeting with Uncle Kurt and Sandy to figure out what to do." Keith tossed her phone on the couch next to them.

"I guess that makes sense. I don't feel so guilty now." Emily sighed.

"Guilty? Why would you feel guilty?"

"About letting everyone think I'm not going to the Sweet Heart Ball," Emily said.

"You're not." Keith wasn't letting her anywhere near that fundraiser. Especially, since the Beckers would be there.

"Yeah, I am." Emily laughed.

"No, you're not."

Emily jumped from his lap, so fast Keith didn't know what happened. She started to pace back and forth in front of him with her hands fisted at her hips. Something told him if she were a cartoon there would be steam coming out of her ears. When she stopped in front of him again and turned to face him, he would never admit it, but he was a little scared of her.

"I know you're my security, and you were hired by my dad but don't ever think you can tell me where I can or can't go. I'm going to the ball because it's for my little sister. I haven't missed one since mom first started throwing them, and I'm not about to start now. Yes, I told everyone I wasn't going because I wanted it to be a surprise when I show up." Keith stood up because he suddenly felt minuscule next to the enraged woman.

"Em, please," Keith tried to take her hands, but she yanked them away.

"No, Keith," Emily poked her finger into his chest. "I'm going."

"I can't let you do that." He couldn't take a chance with her life. It was his job to keep her safe.

"Are you fucking kidding me? You can't? Let me? I'm not sure what you think, but you don't control me, Mr. O'Connor. I'm…" Her voice trailed off as she looked over his shoulder.

"Sorry I didn't mean to interrupt." Keith turned around. Ben Murphy, otherwise known as Trunk stood in the doorway. He looked rather uncomfortable.

"You're not interrupting, as a matter of fact, you are just in time to take me to my parent's house." Emily pushed by Keith and through the doorway and passed Truck.

"Emily…." Keith growled, but without turning around, she flipped him the bird and disappeared from view.

"Sorry, I just came by to let you know the construction crew will be starting on Emily's shop tomorrow." Truck said.

"Thanks," Keith sighed.

"So, am I taking her to her parents." Truck was obviously trying hard to keep the grin off his face.

"No," Keith grumbled."

"Yes," Emily snapped as she appeared with a bag hung on her shoulder.

"Emily, your father…." Keith began.

"My father hired you to keep me safe because I wouldn't go back to SummerBrook but guess what? Truck here is going to take me to SummerBrook where I'll be safe." Emily's eyes were narrowed, and her face was red.

"Why are you acting like a spoiled child?" Keith wanted to take the words back as soon as they were out. Especially when she stomped towards him and glared up at him.

"Spoiled child? That's how you see all the girls from SummerBrook, including me, isn't it? Trust me I was never spoiled, and nobody ever tells me what to do. Including you." Emily spun around and stomped out of the room. "Let's go, Truck," Emily called out right before Keith heard the slam of his front door.

"What do you want me to do?" Truck asked.

"I'll take her to her parents, but I need you to follow me and stay with Rex. He's there with Nelson, but I've got a feeling he'll need backup with Emily there."

Truck nodded. Keith walked out of the room and grabbed his keys from the hook. When he walked outside Emily was on the deck facing away from him.

"I was starting to think I'd have to walk." Emily snapped as she stomped down the front steps. "I hope your boss didn't give you a hard time."

It seemed the spitfire didn't know it was Keith who'd walked out of the house.

"I'm my own boss, Princess." Keith bit his lip to keep from laughing when Emily stopped and spun around.

"What the hell are you doing?" She spat when he held open the door of his jeep.

"Driving you to your parent's house." Keith motioned with his hand towards the front seat.

"Why can't Truck take me?" Emily looked back at the house. Truck was propped against the post at the top of his deck. Keith could see the amusement on his friend's face.

"Because although I don't tell you what to do, I am his boss and I've given him a job to do." Keith motioned to the front seat again.

"I'll call a cab." Emily slapped her pockets. It seemed in her huff she'd forgotten her phone was on the sofa and Keith had grabbed it when she'd stomped off on her tantrum.

"Not gonna happen, Princess." Keith held up her phone.

"You're such an ass." Emily strode up to him, snatched her cell out of his hand and jumped into the front of the jeep.

"So you keep saying." Keith chuckled as he closed the door and waved to Truck.

When he jumped into the front next to her, she pressed her body up against the door. She seemed not to want any of him touching her, and it cut him like a knife.

Why was she so adamant about going to that fundraiser? Sure, it was in honor of her sister but was it worth her safety? He didn't think so. He'd give her a day or so and she'd call him begging to get her out of SummerBrook. So, he'd drive her to SummerBrook and let her get her little tantrum out of her system. Until then he'd put all his energy into checking out what the Beckers had to do with all of this, and make sure Emily's salon was repaired as soon as possible.

That was going to piss her off too probably. If she knew he'd taken it upon himself to do the repairs she'd probably pop a blood vessel. He'd keep that news to himself until she was ready.

"If you think by driving me you can change my mind you've got another thing coming." Emily broke the silence about ten minutes outside of Hopedale.

"Nope." He checked his blind spot as he changed lanes so he could turn off to the ramp for SummerBrook.

"I can help mom and Elaine get all the preparations done for the Ball." He could feel her stare at him.

"I guess you can." Keith glanced through his rearview mirror to make sure he didn't lose Truck.

"I'm going," Emily grumbled.

"Whatever you say, Princess." Keith turned onto the ramp leading to SummerBrook.

Emily had been adamant about not staying in her hometown when he first met her. It took him being an overbearing ass to get her to return there.

Emily sat back in the seat and crossed her arms over her chest. When he glanced at her, she was staring out the front window with a sexy pout on those full pink lips. His dick twitched. As he turned onto the private road leading to the Bradshaw estate, he pulled over into a clearing and waved Truck on ahead.

"What are you doing?" Emily sat up scanning the tree lined road.

Keith flicked off his seatbelt and slid closer to her. He cupped the back of her head and covered her mouth with his. For less than a second, she struggled against him, but as soon as he gently bit her bottom lip, she groaned into his mouth and threaded her fingers through his hair.

His tongue danced with hers, and she had her hands fisted in his hair tugging lightly. It had his cock hard and seeping. He released her seatbelt, lifted her onto his lap and cupped her round ass without breaking the kiss.

It was a good thing they were on a private road. He'd pulled far enough off the path that even if someone did drive by they wouldn't be able to see what was happening.

With the way she was grinding against his cock, Emily didn't seem to care where they were at that moment. Neither did he. Her hands slid down the front of his shirt and tugged at his belt buckle. The button of his jeans and zipper were quickly opened. When Emily wrapped her warm hand around his throbbing dick, he thought he'd come then and there.

"Fuck, Em." Keith groaned into her mouth.

Emily slid off his lap and at first, he thought she was stopping things, but she knelt on the floor and motioned for him to move over to the passenger side. Keith didn't hesitate and managed to pull his jeans down over his hips in the process.

"You like when I do that?" Emily purred as she ran her tongue from the base of his cock to the tip. Keith couldn't put words together but managed to groan.

"And this?" Emily made a circle around the head and sucked it into her mouth for just a second.

"Oh, Fuck. Yes." Keith pushed his hips forward.

"How about this?" Emily wrapped her lips around the top of his dick and slid her mouth half way down his length as her hand squeezed the base. Once. Twice and then she took him down her throat and pulled him out.

"Jesus," Keith roared, and she repeated her sweet torture again and again. He could feel that tingle in his balls and tried to pull away from her.

"No," Emily growled as she increased the speed of her lips and sucked harder.

"Em, I want to come inside you." Keith panted.

"I want to taste you." She stopped just long enough to say the words and continued to give him the most intense blowjob he'd ever experienced.

"You don't have to do this, baby," Keith growled when her teeth lightly scraped against the tip.

"Come for me," Emily whispered. She flicked her tongue against his balls as she stroked him.

"Em. Fuck. Don't stop." He gasped when her mouth covered the head of his cock again, and before he had a chance to warn her, he gripped the edge of the seat and roared. His seed spilled into her mouth, and he watched as she swallowed every last drop.

Keith wasn't sure how long he'd been sitting there with his eyes closed and his head resting against the back of the seat. He was barely aware of Emily climbing back onto his lap. When she ran her tongue across his lips, he opened his eyes to see that beautiful smile on her sweet mouth.

"That was incredible." She grinned.

"For me, yeah." Keith brushed his lips against hers. "What about you?"

"You don't think I just knelt on the floor and didn't help myself too, do you?"

Keith grabbed her hand and brought it to his lips. He flicked his tongue against her fingers and growled. He could taste her and slowly licked her fingers clean.

"That is so fucking sexy," Keith moaned after he released her fingers from his mouth.

"I'm still going." Emily sat back as if to gauge his reaction.

"Seriously," Keith sighed. "Do you think I did this to change your mind?"

"I hope not because I'm still going to the Ball and I want to spend this week with my mom." Emily ran her hand down his cheek. "Keith, I need to go to this, but it's between you and me. Nobody will know. Not even my family. I'll tell them I'm there to help, but they won't know until I show up."

"Princess, I'll be doing security. I won't be able to concentrate if you're there." He managed to lift his hips and pull his jeans up while she zipped up hers.

"I'll be fine. I'll call an old friend and go with him." Emily said.

"Him?" The thought of her being on the arm of another man made his stomach turn.

"It's okay. I've known him my whole life, and you've met his parents." Emily refastened his belt buckle.

"I have?" Keith didn't remember meeting any of Emily's friends from SummerBrook, let alone their parents.

"Judy and Alf Palmer." Emily ran her finger over his lip.

"You're talking about your ex." Keith could feel the acid bubbling in his stomach. "No fucking way." He lifted her off his lap and slid behind the wheel.

"Excuse me?" Emily snapped.

"Did I stutter? I said no fucking way." Keith started the jeep again and pulled it into drive.

"Fuck you, O'Connor. I'll do what I please, and I'll go with who I want. I trust Mitchell, and I'm calling him when I get to the house." The click of her seatbelt had him stomping his foot on the gas and spinning the wheels as he pulled back onto the road.

"Em, how do you know he won't expect something?" Keith eased off on the gas as the jeep's tires hit the pavement.

"Grow up. Mitchell and I were over a long time ago, and I assure you he wouldn't be interested in me ever again. He might take a liking to you though." Emily laughed when his head snapped to the right to stare at her.

"He's gay?"

"Yes." Emily sighed.

"I still don't like it." Keith turned into the long winding driveway leading up to the Bradshaw house.

"Well I don't like rain and snow, but we still have to deal with it," Emily grumbled when he pulled the jeep in front of the house.

"This isn't a joke, Em." Keith grabbed her hand as she was about to open the door.

"Do you think I don't know that? I'm terrified. This guy could go after my mom again or my sister." Emily squeezed his hand.

"I'm terrified that he'll get you." The lump in his throat threatened to strangle him, but he swallowed it down and stared into her eyes. "I need to keep you safe."

"I'll be okay. I'm not Tessa." She almost whispered the words.

"How do you know about Tessa?" He wondered if she knew everything, including the real reason he'd married his friend.

"Last week you were calling her name in your sleep. I asked Sandy, and don't get mad at her, but she told me everything. She also said your family doesn't know, so your secret is safe with me. Although, I've got no idea why you wouldn't tell them." Emily moved closer to him. "Her death isn't your fault, and from what I know about your family, they'll agree with me."

"I don't know why you were brought into my life, but I'm so fucking glad you were." Keith smiled as she rolled her eyes.

"You're just lucky." Emily giggled when he pulled her against him.

"I am, but I'm really going to miss you. I know you want to be here with your family, but if at some point you want to get out of here, or you feel like you're in danger call me. I'll be here in a flash." Keith brushed his lips against hers.

"I will. I promise." Emily cupped his cheek.

A couple of more kisses and Keith helped her out of his jeep. Truck was on the front step talking to Rex and Cannon. Joel Wiseman, otherwise known as Cannon, was the newest guy to his team. He'd been medically discharged from the Canadian military. Since his sister, Casey was the receptionist at Nightingale's Private Care and Therapy, Keith had met him through his aunt Cora.

"Why do all your guys look like they could bench press a truck?" Emily whispered as they approached the men.

"Cause they can." Keith winked.

He managed to sneak a kiss in before Emily disappeared into the house. He was going to miss her. Hell, he already missed her and it was only ten seconds.

"I see you worked out that little disagreement." Truck chuckled.

"I don't know about that, but I know you guys will keep an eye on her." Keith slapped Truck on the back.

He stayed for a few minutes before heading to his jeep. As he hopped inside, his phone beeped with a text. He pulled it out of his shirt pocket and smiled. The text was from Emily.

Drive safe. I'll miss being in your arms tonight.

Princess, I already miss you.

She texted back the emoticon for blowing a kiss, and he did the same. He sighed and closed his eyes. He was so fucking screwed. He'd fallen in love with her, and it terrified him. He never thought it would ever happen for him and certainly not so fast.

When all of this shit was over, he was going to marry the woman, and the thought surprised him. He never thought he would want to get married again, but he ached to be with Emily and make her his for the rest of his life.

Will she say yes is the question?

Chapter 21

Emily had spent the last two days helping her mother, but she missed Keith more than she ever thought possible. They talked on the phone before she'd go to sleep and send each other texts. Some were cute, and some were hot, but she could never send the one she wanted. The one that said she loved him.

She'd lost count at how many times she'd typed the words and then deleted it without sending it. She was such a coward but then again the first time she told him it should probably be face to face.

"I think we've lost her again." Keith's cousin Isabelle chuckled from across the table.

"Well come on, if I had a dreamy, hot, muscled man to think about, I'd be daydreaming too." Her sister nudged her.

"Ewww, don't use the words dreamy and hot when talking about my cousin." Kristy gagged.

Since the ball was only a couple of days away. Keith's grandmother, true to her word, sent Keith's cousins and sisters-in-law to help with setting up. As usual for the Ball, it was being held at her parent's home, and huge tents had been set up on the back of the house. Her mother had also changed the usual caterer and hired Isabelle's restaurant to provide the food. Isabelle had been ecstatic, and she'd admitted to Emily, a little worried. It was the biggest event she'd ever done.

"Your cousins are very sexy." Marina winked at Emily.

"I think I just threw up in my mouth a little." Kristy groaned.

"I get hot just looking at John." Stephanie gave a deep sigh.

"Are you trying to make me throw up." Kristy gave Stephanie a playful push.

"Would you rather we talk about a certain sexy bald hottie." Sandy laughed from her seat where she was feeding her new baby.

"Oh, what's that Mrs. Bradshaw? You need my help in the house. I'm coming." Kristy hurried toward the open patio doors, but not before she turned and stuck her tongue out at Sandy.

"That was cruel." Emily shook her head. She'd heard that Kristy was head over heels for the huge man that everyone knew as Bull. From what she understood he was keeping her at arm's length, but only he knew why.

For the next couple of hours, the women worked to get everything set up. They teased each other and chatted about the kids. Emily also got to hold little Alexander, and she felt a little tug in her belly when he grabbed her finger.

"It's amazing, isn't it?" Emily peered up as her mother touched the top of the baby's little head.

"It's amazing how something so tiny can demand such attention." Emily smiled as her mother crouched in front of her.

"You were the loudest." Her mother gazed down at the baby.

"Gee, thanks, mom." Emily laughed.

"It only proved how strong you are." Her mother cupped her cheek. "I'm so sorry you've been put in danger."

"Mom, it's not your fault. I'm just glad you're safe." Emily covered her mother's hand with her free hand. It was the perfect time to ask her mother how well she knew the Beckers, but before she could, little Alexander started to squirm.

"Looks like someone is waking up." Her mother stood up.

"Sandy, he's moving." Emily tried not to sound panicked, but she wasn't used to small babies.

"He tends to do that." Sandy chuckled as she lifted the baby from Emily's arms. "Lynn if you don't mind I'm going to head home. Ian is picking the girls up from school and Grace from daycare. I want to be there before they get home."

Kim arrived just as Sandy was leaving. After she had gushed over the baby, she joined in to help. By the time everything was set up all the women were exhausted and headed back to Hopedale.

Her father had himself locked in his office, but Emily figured he was just trying to stay out of the way. It wasn't until she saw Ken Becker coming out of the office that she realized her father wasn't in there alone. A few minutes later Elliot left, and her father exited the room a second later. He looked angry.

"Dad, is something wrong?" Edward appeared behind her.

"Just some business stuff. Nothing for you two to worry about." He shifted on his feet and smiled. No doubt it was forced, but Emily knew her father wasn't going to tell them.

"Did you get everything done?" He asked Emily.

"Yes, mom has the tents closed off now, but I get the feeling she's going to be in there every day checking things." Emily chuckled as her father put his arm around her shoulder.

"I've no doubt. It's good to have you home, honey." He kissed her temple. "Keith says the repairs on your shop are almost done."

"I'm sorry, what?" Emily stared at her father.

"Damn it, I wasn't supposed to say anything. I'm sorry. He wanted it to be a surprise." Her father had been kept in the loop, but for some reason, Keith didn't even tell her what he'd done.

"I'm going to kick his ass," Emily grumbled as she dug into her pocket for her phone.

The phone rang several times before he finally answered and before she had a chance to rip him a new one he started to apologize. Emily glanced towards her brother.

"Don't kick my ass." Keith chuckled.

"It seems I need to kick my brother's first." Emily glared at Edward.

"I just didn't want you to worry about the repairs. I know your insurance won't cover it because they consider it an act of terrorism." He said.

"How did you know that?" Emily had only mentioned it to Kim because she was her business partner. "Nevermind, I think I know the answer to that."

"My foreman is dealing with it, and he gets back to me daily," Keith explained.

"It's not your place. He should be getting back to me and so help me Keith if you don't invoice me for this I will kick your ass." It seemed Keith had hired his own construction company to do the repairs. That wasn't the issue because she'd probably have done that very thing. Her problem was being kept in the dark.

"Kim told me to keep things the same as it was, so there isn't going to be any changes to the place," Keith said.

So it seemed everyone knew about this except her.

"I'm so pissed with you right now. You should've asked me if you could do this. It's my salon, and I make the decisions. Even if Kim told you to go ahead, you still should have checked with me." Emily snapped. "After this Ball is over, I'm coming back to Hopedale, and I'm going back to my salon and apartment." Before he could respond, she ended the call and sent an outraged text to Kim.

She gave her brother and father a piece of her mind and stomped up the stairs to her childhood bedroom. Her phone rang, and Emily was tempted to ignore it, but she pulled it out of her pocket. Her anger subsided a little when she saw the number.

"Hey, Mitchell." Emily closed her bedroom door and flopped down on her bed.

"Hey, I just wanted to make sure we were still on for the Ball?" he asked.

"Yes, of course."

Emily had called him the night she'd arrived at her parent's house. He'd been a little apprehensive at first because he was concerned his parents would think he and Emily were an item. Emily had reassured him that her parents were aware she was involved with someone, or at least they suspected it. Whether they were right or not was irrelevant.

"So your man isn't going to be able to escort you." He asked.

"Right now my man is the last person I want to be my date," Emily grumbled.

"Trouble in paradise?" He chuckled.

"I don't want to get into it, but I'm glad we get to spend some time together. It's been a long while." Emily had not kept in touch with Mitchell too often, which was why she was surprised he said he'd be her escort to the Ball.

"Yes, it'll be fun to catch up." He said.

"Just remember, don't tell anyone that you're going with me." She explained the situation to him, and at first, he thought it was crazy, but he agreed to keep it tight lipped.

"I haven't told a soul." He confirmed.

"But your family knows you're going as well?" Emily wanted to see the look on Judy and Tiffany's faces when they saw her walk in with Mitchell. It was petty, but it bothered her the way they looked down on her. The only one that was nice to her besides Mitchell was the family's staff and Mitchell's dad.

"Yes, and mom asked if I was taking a date." Mitchell laughed. "I told her I was going alone."

"Good, I'm sorry that you had to lie." Emily did feel bad.

"I lie to them every day, Emily. They still think I'm straight." Mitchell's voice sounded strained.

"You need to tell them sooner or later, Mitchell."

268

"I know, and maybe when I find someone I want to spend my life with, I'll have the guts to do it." He sighed.

"You'll find him. Well, I'm going to get some sleep. I'll call you the day of the Ball and let you know where to meet me." Emily hadn't really figured out how she was going to show up at the ball. As far as everyone was concerned, she wasn't attending.

Emily lay down and stared at the glowing stars on her ceiling. She remembered the day her mother put them there. She'd been so excited to go to bed that night to see the glow in the dark stars. They'd calmed her watching them then. She snatched her phone off the nightstand and stared at the screen. He hadn't texted since she hung up on him.

"You had every right to be pissed," Emily whispered to herself, but over the last couple of days that she'd been away from him, it was his smooth deep voice that lulled her to sleep.

She struggled with the thought of calling him, but she was pig headed and tossed her phone back on the nightstand. For what seemed like hours she tossed and turned. Was Keith doing the same?

Chapter 22

Keith should've known she'd be pissed when she found out. He wasn't doing it because he wanted to be in control of her salon. That was the last thing he wanted her to think. She'd been so stressed from everything, and he just wanted to make things easier. Kim had appreciated it at least.

He lay on his back in the bed with Burlap curled up on Emily's pillow. It seemed like the cat missed her too. Since she'd been at her parents, he'd found the ball of fur curled up in Emily's slipper, her sweater and even sleeping on her pillow at night.

It was four in the morning, and sleep had become impossible without Emily. He glanced at the cat and pulled out his phone. He clicked a picture just as the cat popped up her head and attached it to a text.

Don't be mad at Keith. He just wanted to help. I miss you, but Keith misses you more. Love Burlap.

Even if the text didn't get him off the hook with her, she'd probably get a giggle out of it. *Pathetic*. Sending her texts from the fucking cat because he couldn't just come out and tell her he loved her. It was why he wanted to make all her stress and pain disappear.

The next morning he'd spent catching up on email, paying bills, and sending invoices. In between, he frequently checked his phone to see if Emily had read his message. She hadn't, but that was probably because they were up to their ears with preparations.

"Hey, you home, Rusty?" Smash's voice echoed through the house.

"I'm in the office," Keith shouted.

A few seconds later Smash walked in followed by Sandy. Both of them had the same urgent look on their face, but before he got a chance to ask what was going on. His phone rang. Keith glanced at the screen and was disappointed to see it wasn't who he'd hoped.

"Hey, Uncle Kurt," Keith answered as he held up his finger to Sandy and Smash.

"Ken Becker is dead." Kurt sounded pissed.

"What? How?" Keith hit speaker on his phone, so he didn't have to repeat what he was being told to Sandy and Smash.

"Nelson called the brothers into his office yesterday and confronted them about the money. I gave Gage the go ahead to tell Nel about what he'd found." Kurt never called any of the guys by their nicknames.

"They denied it, but when Nel gave them the proof on paper, Ken was pissed and left. Nel said Elliot stayed a few seconds later and swore he had nothing to do with any of the missing money." Kurt continued.

"How did Ken die?" Keith glanced up at Sandy. She had pulled out her phone and was typing something.

"It appears that he hung himself, and Elliot seems to be in the wind." Keith could hear the sound of phones ringing. It meant Kurt was probably at the station.

"Why do I get the feeling you don't think it's suicide?" Smash asked.

"Just something the coroner said. There were two marks on his neck, but only one matched the rope he was hung with. The other mark was deeper and thinner. I'll know more after the autopsy." Kurt sounded rushed.

"You're not telling me everything." Keith knew his uncle well.

"There was a typed letter on the screen of his laptop. He admitted to everything about the money and…." Kurt stopped.

"And what?" Keith sighed.

"The letter apologized for hurting Lynn and damaging Emily's salon," Kurt said.

"You said it was typed?" Sandy asked.

"Yeah," Kurt replied

"That seems legit." Smash's sarcasm wasn't missed.

"We have an all points out for Elliot," Kurt said. "Right now he's a suspect."

"I need to give Rex and Truck a heads up. If Elliot is behind this and he did kill his brother, he could be crazy enough to go after Emily." Keith's heart was pounding in his chest. For all they knew, Elliot could probably be at the Bradshaw estate.

"I've sent A.J. and Nick out there. I gotta run, but I'll keep you in the loop and if they find out anything let me know." Kurt hung up before Keith could respond.

"Well, this just took a complete U-turn." Sandy flopped down in the chair.

"Have you found anything out about the guy Nelson's father paid off," Keith tossed his phone on the desk but not before he checked to see if Emily had read his text. She hadn't.

Sandy handed him a folder and when he opened it he was confused. Inside was a picture of what could be a young Emily and another picture of a man with long dirty hair and an unkempt beard.

"Why do you have a young picture of Emily with this creepy guy?" Keith scanned through the papers under the pictures.

"That's not Emily. That would be Nora Miller, Emily's aunt. The only name they had for this guy was, Wooly. That is the accident report and the statements from Mr. Bradshaw, Mrs. Bradshaw, and that man." Sandy said. "There's nothing about the guy's name, but he took full responsibility. I've got his picture gone to a friend of mine out west. He's going to do an age progression to see if that helps. If you ask me that guy looks nothing like either of the Beckers." Sandy tapped the picture.

"Emily looks just like her aunt." Keith held the picture up in front of him. "If this idiot has snapped, he could think Emily is Nora."

Before he got a chance to send a text to Rex, he received one from Nick. His brother told him things at the Bradshaws were all good. His whole body was wound up tighter than a drum, and his leg was bouncing up and down. He needed to see her. She may be pissed at him, but he didn't care. Keith needed to see with his own eyes that the woman he loved was safe.

As Keith jumped to his feet to go to SummerBrook his phone rang again. Her beautiful face flashed on his screen, and he sighed with relief.

"Emily," He shouted into the phone as he waved Sandy and Smash out of his office.

"Don't yell at me." She snapped.

"Sorry, I've been worried." He eased back in his chair and covered his forehead with his hand.

"I'm fine. Still pissed, but your brother is a pain in the ass and hounded me to call you." She sounded less angry, but he was just happy to hear her voice.

"Thank him for me." Keith chuckled.

"The hell I will, but when he told me what was going on, I had to call. I may want to kill you, but I don't want you to worry."

"Burlap misses you." Keith wondered if she'd even looked at the text.

"That's a pretty smart cat. She can take selfies and text." Emily laughed, and it was the best sound he'd ever heard.

"She wanted me to get in the picture too, but I told her you wouldn't want to see my ugly mug." Keith didn't have to see her to know she was rolling her eyes.

"Yes, because you're so hideous." They didn't speak for a moment, and then he heard her grumble something under her breath.

"What was that, Princess?" Keith laughed.

"You aren't forgiven for overstepping, but I do miss Burlap."

"I'll tell her."

"I hate to admit this, but I miss you too." She admitted.

"I guess I've got a lot of groveling to do when you come back to Hopedale." It was odd for him to say those words, but he would beg her on his hands and knees to forgive him, as long as he didn't lose her.

"Keith O'Connor groveling. That would be a pretty picture." Emily laughed.

"Princess, just promise we can work this out. I didn't mean to make you think I was taking over."

"I know, but you can't do things like this. If we're going to be together, I need us to work together and not keep secrets." Emily sniffed. "I'm in this situation because of things being swept under the rug."

"I know, and again I'm sorry."

"I need to go. Mom, Elaine and I are having a mani and pedi day." She laughed, and Keith pulled the phone away from his ear to tap the FaceTime button. "What the …."

Keith waited until her face appeared on the screen before he spoke.

"What are you doing?" She narrowed her eyes.

"I wanted to see that beautiful face." He smiled.

Her expression softened, but she did roll her eyes. It was as if all Keith's tension drained away when he saw her. That was until his brother's face appeared over her shoulder.

"Hey, bro." Aaron winked.

"I didn't want to see that ugly ass," Keith growled.

"Gee thanks, bro. Love you too." Aaron laughed and stepped away.

"I'll let you go, but call me later, okay?" Keith warned.

"If it gets too late I'll text you." Emily smiled. "I…. " She stopped and glanced behind her. "I'll talk to you soon."

Her face disappeared from the screen, and he blew out a huge breath.

"I love you, Princess," Keith said to the black screen. "I really love you."

Keith stood off to the side of the huge tent in the Bradshaw's yard. It was bad enough he had to be there without Emily, but Nelson invited his whole family. All Keith knew was, being dressed in a fucking monkey suit was not comfortable, and he wanted to make a run for it. The only saving grace was he wasn't alone in his discomfort, his guys looked just as miserable.

Lynn had hired the band his brother's played in. *Rocking The Law* was the name of the band that Aaron, Nick, Mike, and John put together with a couple of friends. The name came from the members either being lawyers or police officers. It was just a hobby for them, but they played at events to raise money for charity. They were also incredibly talented.

Bull had come back to help with security for the event, and with all his brothers close by as well, there were plenty of people to keep an eye on Emily. He scanned the room several times since he'd arrived, but he hadn't spotted her. That bothered him.

For what seemed like the millionth time he tugged on the collar to try and loosen the snug neckline of his shirt. That's when he saw Emily glide into the room wearing a strapless pale pink dress. It clung to each and every one of her ample curves. Suddenly the neckline of the tuxedo wasn't the only part of the stupid suit that was uncomfortable. He was sure his trousers had suddenly become a size too small around the groin.

Keith didn't typically agree with women wearing makeup because he always found the natural look much more attractive. Emily didn't need anything to enhance her beauty. However, the lipstick she wore made him want to stalk over and kiss every last bit of it off. When his cock grew painfully hard, he cursed himself for even thinking about it.

"I thought she wasn't supposed to be here tonight?" Bull whispered next to him.

Keith couldn't take his eyes off her, and although he knew she'd be there, he had to act oblivious to her plan. Whatever it was. He still didn't know how this big idea of hers was going to bring out this guy. He wasn't comfortable with her putting herself out there, but she was stubborn.

"Haven't you figured it out yet? Emily Bradshaw does what she wants and when she wants, regardless of her own safety." It pissed him off that she never listened, but he'd agreed to this.

How stupid am I?

Emily now stood in a tent full of fake people pretending to care about the charity her mother had started all those years ago. The Sweet Heart Ball was Lynn Ann Bradshaw's tribute to her daughter, but Keith was sure she never wanted to turn it into the snob fest it was today.

All the fake people fluttering around as if they cared about the cause. All most of them cared about was showing their snooty asses at one of the biggest parties of the year. To make it worse one of those people could be out to hurt the woman he loved. He sure as hell didn't believe it was Elliot Becker or Ken for that matter.

Elliot still hadn't been found, and something told Keith that they probably wouldn't find him. At least not alive. Nothing pointed to either of the Becker brothers being the man they were looking for. Sandy was still waiting for her friend to get back to her with an age-progressed photo. So until then, they just had to wait.

"So who's the suit that just put his hand on her ass?" Bull growled, but it was nothing compared to the roar that was building inside Keith.

The guy had his hand lower on her back than a gentleman should. This couldn't be Mitchell Palmer because if it was, there was no way the man was gay. If the fucker didn't remove his hand from Emily's ass, Keith would rip the guy's arm off and beat him to death with it.

"I think it's time Ms. Bradshaw and I had a dance." Keith stalked to the side of the room where Emily and the asshole with the hands chatted with another couple. Keith didn't have any idea who they were, and he really didn't give a shit. He was about three strides from her when she turned slowly and smiled.

"Hello, Mr. O'Connor." She grinned, and Mr. Hands pulled her closer to him.

"Ms. Bradshaw, I believe you promised me a dance." Keith held out his hand. He hoped the ass would say something just to give Keith an excuse to throat punch the guy.

"You don't mind, do you, Mitchell?" Keith didn't like the tone of her voice. It was one he'd heard spoiled little rich girls use to get what they wanted. His Emily wasn't like that.

"Umm…. I guess…. it'll be all right." Mitchell said. Although, Keith just wanted to call him an asshole. Keith also didn't like the way the other guy stared at Emily's cleavage. Not that it wasn't on his mind too, but this guy was creepy about it.

"I guess it's time I paid my debt to you, Mr. O'Connor." Emily put her hand in his, and he led her to the other side of the dance floor.

He wanted to get as far away from the assholes as possible. The song had just finished, and when he glanced at John on stage. His brother winked as the music started. *You Had Me From Hello.* How appropriate. The Kenny Chesney song said it all.

"Who's the guy with the hands, Em?" Keith smiled down at her, but his voice was a growl.

"Mitchell. I'm sure I told you who'd be my escort." Emily's tongue darted out to moisten her lips. The action made his cock ache, and he had no doubt she did it on purpose.

"Don't do that!" He snapped as he tried not to squeeze her body tighter against his.

"Do what?" She tipped her head to the side the way she always did when she gazed up at him.

"Just keep your tongue in your mouth. Why is Mitchell touching your ass, I thought he was gay?" Keith glanced over her shoulder. Mitchell had moved and was watching them.

"He is, but his family doesn't know." She whispered. "Keep your voice down."

"Emily, don't play games. Is he gay or did you just tell me that so I wouldn't worry?" Keith's hand slid lower on her back just above her ass. Keith smirked when Emily gasped, and Mitchell narrowed his eyes.

"He's gay, I promise you. It's funny how you didn't want Mitchell to put his hand on my ass, but you seem to think it's fine for you. You also didn't mind my tongue when I was licking your cock."

She whispered, but the sound of the word cock coming out of her mouth had him rock hard.

"That's because you're mine, Em." Keith leaned down and whispered into her ear. "And you didn't seem to mind licking it either." He saw the goosebumps rise on her skin and she shivered.

"I didn't mind," Emily's voice came out breathy.

"Princess, I don't like the way that guy is pawing at you." Keith had to be honest, after all, he was still hired to keep her safe.

"For the love of God, he's my friend and nothing more." Emily snapped and tried to pull out of his arms, but he wasn't having none of it. He'd missed her so much over the last few days that it was heaven to have her pressed against him.

"No way, Princess," Keith growled.

He spun around with her still in his arms and stalked out of the tent pulling her with him. She tried to pull her hand from his grasp, but she couldn't without causing a scene. Keith grinned as he weaved them through the mass of people. No matter how she acted anywhere else, she wasn't about to cause a fuss in front of everyone.

"Let go of me," Emily whispered through gritted teeth. Keith glanced back at her. She smiled at people as they squeezed by.

Keith didn't let her go until they were on the other side of the estate. Nobody was permitted in the part of the house where all the bedrooms were. When he stopped, she slammed against his back.

Keith had to grab her around the waist to keep her from toppling over on the stilettos she was wearing.

"You're acting like an overbearing Neanderthal. Just because I'm less than half your size and weight, doesn't mean you can push me around like a god damn rag doll." Emily pressed her fists into his chest as she tried to push away from him.

"And you're acting like I shouldn't be pissed about someone else touching you." She licked her lips again, and he wasn't sure if she did it on purpose or because she was as turned on as he was.

"He didn't yank me off like some people. Now let me go damn it." She pushed at his chest. The next thing he knew she was pressed against the wall, and he had her head cradled in his hands.

"Why the fuck can't I keep my hands off you?" He wasn't really expecting an answer.

"I don't know, but you may want to get that huge bulge in your pants checked out. It seems to be growing bigger by the minute." Emily grinned.

"Fuck, woman." Keith covered her plump lips with his, and she sighed. Strawberry. The fucking lipstick tasted like fucking strawberries, and that sent him completely out of control. He plunged his tongue into her mouth, as his hands moved down her back to the swell of her round ass. He pulled her against his erection and her arms snaked around his neck. Her fingers threaded into his hair and she tugged on it. She knew what that did to him.

"We can't do this here." She panted as he nipped his way down the side of her neck.

"Where?" He growled when she pulled his hair again.

She kissed him hard on the mouth and reached behind her to take his hand. As much as he wanted to take her right then and there, he really wanted to be somewhere they wouldn't get interrupted. The sight of another man's hand on her made him need to remind her who she belonged to. As bad as that seemed, he didn't give a fuck. Nobody was going to touch her but him.

She led him up a set of stairs in the back of the house. He followed and enjoyed the view of her sweet ass sway in front of his eyes. The staircase seemed to go on forever.

"Where the fuck are you taking me?" Keith grumbled.

"We're almost there, grumpy ass." Emily giggled.

At the top of the longest staircase, he'd ever climbed was a door that led into a huge bedroom. It was clean and bright with windows completely around the room. In the center was a king-sized bed covered with a dark purple comforter.

"Are we in Rapunzel's tower?" Keith walked into the room and turned around taking in the entire view.

"Well, you said I was a princess." Emily smiled as she turned and locked the door, then slowly backed him towards the huge bed.

"This is your bedroom?" Keith didn't stop her.

"Uh huh." She nodded and licked her lips.

"And you live in that little apartment in Hopedale? Why?" Keith had to admit he wasn't one for the finer things in life. He liked to keep things simple, but the room was fantastic and had a full view of the entire town of SummerBrook.

"Because there's this hot guy who lives there and I like to seduce him." She pushed him back until his legs hit the edge of the bed.

"Baby, he likes to be seduced." Keith ran his index finger down the side of her neck. "He's just not sure if he deserves you."

"Keith, don't say things like that. You deserve to be happy, and I don't know if I'm the one to do that, but I want to try." When she cupped his cheek in her hand, he covered it with his own and closed his eyes. Her touch calmed him like nobody else.

"Emily, I missed you so much." He sat on the bed and pulled her between his legs as she helped him out of his jacket and tie. Her eyes never left his as he lowered the zipper at the back of her dress. He dragged the dress down her body and took his fill of the creamy, soft skin. She'd unbuttoned his shirt, and it actually hurt to stop touching her so she could remove the damn thing.

"Keith, stand up," Emily whispered as she stepped back from him. For a moment, he took in the vision in front of him. With her dress pooled at her feet, she stood in front of him in nothing but a pink strapless bra and a sheer pair of pink panties. She was also wearing pink stilettos, and his cock felt like it was going to burst through the zipper at the sight of her.

"You can leave on the shoes, but as fucking sexy, as you look in that bra and panties I want them gone." Keith stood up and reached for her, but she slapped his hands away.

"Hold on a second, Mr. Bossy Pants." She smiled as she kicked the dress away from her feet and reached for the button on his pants. "I want to see if you go commando with everything you wear." Keith grinned.

"I told you I always go commando." Keith gasped when her hand slid inside his trousers and skimmed against the head of his cock.

"It's just so damn sexy." His pants fell down around his ankles, and her hand gripped his shaft. His eyes drifted closed as she slowly worked him. It was fucking heaven to have her hands on him. It hadn't been more than a few days, but it felt like forever.

"Em, I really enjoy the way you do that, but I need to feel my cock inside you." Keith pulled her into his arms and eased her down on the bed. While she made quick work of her bra, he yanked the panties from her. She was about to kick off the shoes, but he grabbed her foot. "No, leave them on."

"Okay, but you are giving me a foot rub after this. These things hurt like a son of a bitch." She smiled when he lowered his body on top of hers. He'd been smart enough to grab the condom out of his pocket and toss it on the bed before he'd lost his trousers.

"I'll rub anything you want, Princess." Keith grabbed the condom used his teeth to tear it open, then he rolled it on without tearing his eyes away from her.

He crawled over her and hovered above her as he lowered his head and ran his tongue across her lips.

"That lipstick tastes like strawberry." He whispered just before he devoured her mouth. His cock was pressed against her warm heat, and he wanted to plunge inside her, but he wanted to go slow. This somehow felt different.

"Keith, I want you inside, now." She gasped against his lips and reached between them and to guide him where she wanted.

"Easy, baby," Keith whispered and ran his thumb across her hard nipple making her gasp when he pinched it.

"Damn it, Keith." She groaned when he pulled the other nipple into his mouth and sucked it hard. Before he knew what happened, she had him right at the entrance of her wetness, and he started to push into her slowly.

"Fuck, you're so damn hot." Keith clenched his teeth together as she raised her hips driving him deeper inside her. "So. Fucking. Hot."

"You feel so good." The heel of her shoe was pressed against his ass, and it was sexy as hell. He pushed deep inside her and dropped his head into the crook of her neck and groaned.

"Fuck... Fuck…. Em, don't move yet. If you do, I'm done."
Keith took a couple of deep breaths to ease the urge to come for just a
few more minutes. "You feel so fucking good around me." He
whispered into her ear when he started to thrust again.

"God, Keith. Don't stop." She panted as he slowly pumped in
and out of her.

The feeling of being so deep inside her was overwhelming, his
life was never going to be the same. He'd never felt such a deep
connection with anyone. Keith raised his head to gaze down into her
eyes, but he was surprised to see them wet with tears.

"I'm sorry, did I hurt you?" Keith stopped moving as he wiped
the tear from her face.

"You didn't hurt me, but you've got the power to break my
heart because Keith…." She closed her eyes and swallowed.

"Em?" If she only knew the power she had over him.

"Keith, I'm in love with you, and I know it's crazy fast but…"
He stopped her with his finger against her lips.

"Princess, the truth is…." Keith looked deep into her eyes. "I
fell in love with you the first time you told me to fuck off."

She laughed, and the vibration made her squeeze around him,
and he pushed in deeper.

"I love you, Emily. You're mine. All mine." With those words,
he covered her mouth with his and pumped into her with everything he

had. The heels of her shoes dug into his ass as she grabbed fists full of his hair and screamed into his mouth. She closed around him, and it was all he needed. His body vibrated as he poured inside her.

When her body went limp underneath him, he rolled her over on top of him. He was still inside her, and she wiggled for a moment, and he heard two thuds on the carpet.

"That's almost like another orgasm." She sighed and kissed his chest.

"Well if that was like an orgasm then I did everything wrong." Keith chuckled. She raised her head and rested her chin on her hands that were folded.

"You did everything right, but you have no idea how good it is to take off shoes like that."

"Then why wear them?" Keith wondered why women would wear something that gave them discomfort. She raised her eyebrow and grinned.

"I'm laying on top of you, naked, and you have to ask why women wear shoes like that. Do you not remember saying they were hot?" She smiled.

"I'm sorry they hurt, but they are hot as hell." He rolled her onto her back and kissed her lips. When he raised his head, she smiled. "I meant what I said, Em, I love you."

"I love you too, Keith. Just don't break my heart, okay." She looked so vulnerable at that moment.

"You're mine, Princess, and if you want me, I'm all yours." Keith touched her cheek.

Chapter 23

Emily giggled as she tried to fix her hair with Keith kissing her neck. They were both fully clothed again, but as soon as she put the shoes back on, he wasn't able to keep his hands off her.

"As much as I'd love to stay in this room all night with you, we can't." Emily turned into his arms.

"It's the fucking shoes." He groaned.

"Well, if you let me fix myself, and let us get back to the party, I'll wear them when we get back to your place." Emily wiggled her eyebrows, and he grinned.

"Deal, but I'm just gonna wait outside the room." He groaned. "I can't stay in here and not want to toss you on that bed again."

"Dear Lord, the shoes have created a monster." Emily laughed.

"Hey, Princess," Keith said as he opened the door.

"Yeah?" Emily glanced at him.

"I fucking love you." He winked.

"I love you too." He closed the door behind him, and she sighed.

Emily loved him more than she'd ever thought she could love anyone. It was why it was even more important to get the man who hurt her mother to show himself. As terrified as she was, it had to end. She couldn't start a life with Keith if she weren't free to live.

They walked back into the tent with Keith holding tightly to her hand. Emily searched the room for her friend. Mitchell had been uncomfortable with the glares Keith was giving him. At one point, he'd told Emily, Keith looked like he was about ready to kill him.

Of course, Emily did enjoy seeing Keith squirm, but it wasn't fair to Mitchell. Her friend had agreed to help her bring out the stalker, not get death glares from Keith. She needed to introduce them properly and make sure Keith understood that Mitchell was only a dear friend who wanted to help.

"What are you looking for?" Keith asked.

"Mitchell," Emily replied.

"What the hell for?" Keith grumbled.

"Because we owe him an apology for vanishing, and I want him to meet you without thinking you're going to kill him." Emily spotted Mitchell off to the left talking to his parents. *Great*! She didn't mind Alfred, but she wasn't in the mood for Judy's nasty attitude.

"Do we have to do this now? The ice queen is shooting daggers at me." Keith nodded his head towards Judy.

"Fuck her, I'm going to talk to Mitchell and say hi to Alf." Emily wasn't afraid of any of the snobs in SummerBrook. Probably because she'd dealt with them her whole life. She never let any of them get to her anymore.

"Hey, Em." Mitchell glanced at Keith.

"Sorry we took off like that, but we needed to get some things straightened out. Mitchell Palmer this is Keith O'Connor." Mitchell held out his hand to Keith, and it took Emily giving Keith's hand a squeeze before he took her friend's hand.

Stubborn ass.

"Nice to meet you, Mitchell." Keith smiled.

"I'm glad you two worked things out." Mitchell was being genuine, and Emily knew it.

"Me too." Keith gazed down and smiled.

"We never got properly introduced, I'm Alf Palmer, Mitchell's father and this is my wife, Judy." Alf smiled at Keith as they shook hands.

"I've had the pleasure of meeting your wife at the hospital. It's good to see you again Mrs. Palmer." Keith was being so polite, but Emily wanted to burst into laughter when Judy's mouth dropped open. She quickly snapped it shut again and gave what was supposed to be a smile. At least Emily thought it was a smile. It looked somewhere between a snarl and a grin.

"This is my daughter Tiffany and her fiancé Woodrow Manchester." Alfred motioned to Tiffany and the much older man she was hanging all over.

Emily had been chatting with them when Keith pulled her onto the dance floor. The guy would be a good one around Penny. He didn't seem to be able to look above the chest area. He gave Emily the creeps, and she had no idea what Tiffany saw in a man that looked old enough to be her father.

"It's nice to meet all of you, but if you don't mind, I'd like to make up for missing most of the dancing with my princess here." Keith nodded, and Emily thanked him in her mind for getting them away from the Palmers. Well except Mitchell. She glanced back at him as she walked away. He looked lost.

"Okay, everyone. We're going to speed things up a little, and I want to see everyone dancing." Nick's voice echoed through the tent. "This is a new song release by *Aaron Goodvin* called *Lonely Drum*. It's only fitting we get A.J. to get us all in a dancing mood."

"Oh, I love this song." Emily started to pull Keith onto the floor, but he shook his head.

"Don't do fast dances, Princess." He chuckled as he pulled her back against him.

294

"Oh, but you are. So, get over yourself and move that ass." Emily tugged and dragged on his hand until they were in the middle of the dance floor. She was sure if he really were against dancing she wouldn't be able to budge him. The man was a brick wall, but damn didn't he look hot in a tux.

It didn't take Keith long before he started to get into the song. She expected the typical man dance of moving feet back and forth and barely moving arms, but she was pleasantly surprised. Keith O'Connor knew how to move that body.

Emily eyed her mother and father dancing as well and almost fell on the floor when her dad tried to copy what Keith was doing. Her mother never married her father for his dance moves that was for sure.

She had to admit it was probably the best music they'd ever had at one of the Sweet Heart Balls. Even her sister and brother were busting out their moves with their dates.

Emily scanned the crowd while she enjoyed herself. Of course, Judy stood off to the side glaring at everyone as if they were committing murder. She was alone, so it seemed like the rest of her family were enjoying themselves, but Emily could only see Mitchell.

"Oh, my God, Emily this band is incredible." Ginger Dwyer twirled by with her date.

"They really are." That was Cinnamon which was really surprising. Emily hadn't seen the girl since she left the salon in a huff, but to Emily's shock and amazement, Cinnamon hadn't said anything to anyone. At least not that Emily had been told.

"They're Keith's brothers and some friends," Emily yelled over the music.

"Awesome," Ginger shouted as she and her sister danced away.

The song ended, and according to Aaron, they were slowing things down again. Not that Emily minded because Keith grabbed her hips and pulled her into him. She wrapped her arms around his neck and gazed up at him.

A thought crossed her mind as he smiled down at her. Keith had sung to her a few times, and he had an amazing voice. She found it odd that he wasn't on stage with his brothers.

"Why don't you sing with them? Or James and Ian?" Emily asked.

"Not my thing. James doesn't like to be in front of crowds. He actually hurled on stage in high school during some talent show, and Ian's too shy. Not that they can't sing."

"Poor James." Emily giggled.

"Plus, I only sing for you and my grandmother," Keith whispered into her ear.

"I love when you sing to me." Emily wrapped her arms around his neck and swayed with him. She wanted to spend the rest of her life with this man. She honestly couldn't see her life without him in it.

"Princess, I want to ask you something." Keith touched her cheek.

"Anything."

Before he had a chance to say a word, the room went black. There were three loud pops as if fireworks had been shot off. Her mother hadn't mentioned anything about fireworks. Emily looked up and then laughed at herself. How the hell were they supposed to see them inside a tent?

When she pulled her hands away from Keith, they were wet and sticky. Keith seemed to be putting most of his weight on her.

"Keith, what are you doing? You're going to knock me down." Emily shouted. The only thing she could hear were screams and crying, but she couldn't understand why people were screaming.

The lights flickered and came on again, but as if everything was happening in slow motion Emily watched Keith fall to his knees. When she looked down her pink dress was covered with something red and wet.

"Emily...." Keith gasped.

"Keith, what's wrong?" Emily screamed and fell to her knees as he fell to his side.

"Emily, get down." She barely heard Bull speaking with everyone screaming.

"What's wrong with him?" She hadn't seen Ian at first, but he was next to Keith with Sean pressing a cloth against Keith's chest.

"Honey, I need you to go with Bull," Sean spoke soft, but she knew it wasn't a request.

"No, what's wrong with Keith?" Emily pulled away from Bull and grabbed Keith's hand.

"Em,... Go..... Bull." Keith was gasping for air.

"What the fuck is wrong with him?" Emily yelled.

"Emily, he's been shot. Bull needs to get you out of here." John crouched in front of her. She couldn't completely understand what Keith's brother was telling her.

"Shot?" Emily stared down on the floor where Keith was gasping and staring back at her. His eyes were wide, and there was blood in the corner of his mouth. His chest was rising up and down way too fast.

"Em..." Keith gasped and coughed.

"No....no...." She shook her head. When Bull tried to pull her away again, she swung at him.

"Emily, please come with me," Bull begged.

"I'm staying with him. Go get everyone out of here." Emily clung to Keith's hand and rubbed her thumb across his knuckles. Minutes later the loud clang of a siren pulled into the driveway. She was so tired of hearing sirens.

Emily ran into the hospital behind the paramedics. Her dress was soaked in blood, and the metallic smell was sickening. She didn't care. They had to save him.

"Emily!" His voice was tight and barely audible.

"I'm here, Keith." She stood at the foot of his bed as the emergency team cut off his clothes.

She'd watched them in the ambulance as they hooked Keith up to an I.V. The paramedics made her sit in front but she had sat with her back to the front of the ambulance.

Now he was in the emergency room with half a dozen people running around him. They kept telling her to stay back so they could work on him but it was so hard when he was calling out to her.

"I want to marry you now." He rasped.

"Honey, don't worry about that now." Emily sobbed.

"Now. Emily. I need to marry you now." Keith cringed as the doctor turned him onto his side. She heard the doctor say there wasn't an exit wound and her knees shook. It meant the bullet was still inside him.

"Mr. O'Connor, we've got to get you to surgery." The doctor said as Keith was rolled back.

"Not ... Ugh... before I marry... ah .. that beautiful woman." Keith's teeth were clenched as he reached for her. Emily sobbed and couldn't answer. She could only hear the way Keith was gasping for air.

"What the fuck happened?" Emily felt a large hand on her shoulder. Dr. Cramer stood behind her.

"Got… shot… asshole." He was trying to make a joke. Really? Had he completely lost his mind?

"Who shot him." Adam turned Emily to face him.

"I... I ... d... d... on't know. I don't even know what happened. It happened so fast." John appeared out of nowhere and pulled her into his arms. Emily took a quick glance around. All his brothers were just outside the room, and their expressions spoke volumes.

"I… need… marry… her now." Keith stammered and roared as the doctor pressed something against his chest.

"What the fuck are you talking about?" Ian stood at the side of the bed. Emily hadn't even seen Ian enter the room. Of course, her eyes barely moved from Keith.

"We don't have time for this conversation, and all of you can't be in here. He needs surgery." The Doctor didn't seem to know what family he was dealing with. "We're taking him to the O.R."

"The hell you are," Keith grunted. "Nobody's taking me anywhere until I marry her."

"Come on Keith, you need surgery." Ian tried to reason, but Keith reached out and grabbed Ian by the front of his shirt.

"You get Father Wallace here. Now." Keith pulled Ian down. "I don't want to die without being married to her, bro." Ian didn't hesitate and ran out of the room. There was no way he said the word die, Keith wasn't going to leave her.

"Keith, stop being a stubborn ass." Emily sobbed and grabbed his hand. "The doctors are going to fix you. You're not going to die."

"Princess, please I need to be married to you. Even if it's just saying the words." Tears ran down the side of his face. "I'll die a happy man.

"You're not going to die. Keith, please don't say that." Tears streamed down her cheeks as he gasped. "I love you so much. I can't lose you. Not when I finally found you."

"I love you more than life itself, but I need to marry you now." The emergency team was moving the gurney out of the room, and he clung to her hand. "Where are you taking me?" Keith gasped.

"Surgery." The nurse said as they pushed him down the hallway. It broke her heart the way his expression turned to complete panic.

"No!" He roared. "Father Wallace."

Ian stood in the hallway with the parish priest. Keith reached out and grabbed the priest. Emily had no idea how Ian got him there so fast.

"Now. Father, please."

"My son we can do this after you're well." The priest said.

"Father, please now," Keith whispered.

It was the strangest sight to anyone walking by. A priest at the foot of a gurney of a bleeding man and a woman covered in his blood. Nurses were surrounding them with tears in their eyes.

"It won't be legal, Keith." Father Wallace warned.

"I just want to say the words," Keith's voice sounded weaker.

"He's losing a lot of blood." The doctor snapped.

"Quick Father." Keith grabbed Emily's hand. She was accustomed to his hand being warm and comforting, but when he covered her hand with his, it was cold and clammy.

"I'll make this quick." Father Wallace said. "Do you Keith Gregory O'Connor take Emily Mary Bradshaw to be your wife?"

"I… I.. I .. do." Keith gasped.

"Do you Emily Mary Bradshaw take Keith Gregory O'Connor to be your husband?"

"I do." Emily sobbed.

"I now pronounce you husband and wife. You may kiss the bride." Father Wallace finished. Emily leaned down and pressed her lips to Keith's.

"I love you," Keith whispered and with those words his eyes rolled up into his head.

Someone grabbed her by the arms and pulled her back from the bed, and Keith's hand dropped to his side. Lifeless and cold.

Dear god, was he gone?

"He's crashing." The doctor yelled, and a nurse climbed up on top of the gurney as the rest of the team pushed Keith through the doors of the operating room. Emily's legs lost all their strength, and she fell to her knees as sobs racked her body. She couldn't catch her breath, and her chest hurt. Her hands were pressed against her chest, and she gasped for air.

"She's hyperventilating." Ian's voice seemed so far off, but strong arms picked her up off the floor.

"I can't lose him." She screeched into the shoulder of whoever had picked her up. She did not care who it was. Nothing mattered if she lost Keith.

"My brother's one of the strongest men I know, Emily." Was that James?

"I love him so much and if he dies…." She stopped. James placed her on a bed in one of the hospital rooms.

"Now you listen here, Emily." It was John. "You're not going to lose him, and I'm not going to lose a brother. Do you hear me?" John grabbed her arms and gave her a little shake.

"Calm the fuck down, John." Ian pulled John back from her.

"No. I'm not letting her give up on him. He loves her." Emily saw the tears in John's eyes. Not just John's, but Ian and James as well. They were all so close.

God, I don't pray often, but please watch over him.

Emily had her knees curled up to her chest on the bed. The room was completely silent except for the usual sounds of the emergency department. Well, until she heard a booming voice echo in from the hall.

"Where is my daughter?" Her father.

"Dad," Emily whispered as her father charged into the room with her mom behind him. He wrapped his arms around her, and she clung to him. They didn't always get along, but he was always there when she needed him most.

"Dad, Keith … he... was ... shot…" Her body shuttered as she forced out the words. It still seemed like she was speaking something foreign. Nobody ever got shot in Newfoundland.

"I know, baby girl," Nelson kissed the top of her head.

"Dad, Keith's in surgery." She sobbed into his chest.

"I'll make sure he has the best care," Nelson squeezed her tightly against him, and her mother wrapped her arms around her from behind.

"He's my life, dad." Emily sobbed.

Edward and Elaine showed up a little while later and brought her a change of clothes. Her dress was soaked in blood. Keith's blood. She couldn't even look at the dress when she took it off. She told her sister to throw it away. She didn't want the reminder of what had happened.

She joined Keith's family in the waiting room once she'd cleaned up. It was almost three hours later, and Keith was still in surgery. Nobody seemed to know how it was going and even Ian or his father couldn't find out. The only response they could get was Keith was still in surgery, and they'd send the doctor out as soon as he was done.

She looked around the waiting room. Keith's family filled almost every chair, and the ones that weren't occupied by his family had his friends. Keith's parents sat across from her. Kathleen was wrapped in Sean's arms with her hands folded in front of her. Tom and Nick sat on both sides of Nanny Betty holding her hands. It was the first time she'd seen Nanny Betty so quiet.

John was on the other end of the room with his elbows resting on his knees and his head in his hands. Stephanie was making small circles on his back as she stared off into space. James and Marina were wrapped in each other's arms in the corner of the waiting room with the same somber expression as everyone else. Ian sat with Sandy holding hands and her head on his shoulder.

Kurt and Alice sat next to Keith's parents, and Cora and Brian were next to them. His cousins and friends were scattered around the rest of the room. All of these people waiting to hear that Keith was okay. All of them here because of her family's drama.

"Ian, are all the kids okay?" It was the only thing Emily could think to say.

Keith's nieces and nephews loved him. They'd always been so excited to see him, and he lit up when they were around. They'd be devastated if something happened to him. God, she had to stop thinking that way.

"Doug and Janet have Olivia and the boys. Dad and his girlfriend have our girls and Alex." Sandy answered for Ian. Doug and Janet were Marina and Stephanie's, parents. Emily had never met them, but she knew they spent a lot of time with the O'Connors.

"Why is this taking so bloody long?" Her father grumbled.

"Nel, please don't start." Her mother pleaded.

"No, da man is right," Nanny Betty snapped. "Why aren't dey tellin us anything?"

"I wish I knew, Nan." Ian leaned back in the chair and plowed his hands through his hair.

"You know considering there are two doctors in your family, you think you would be able to get some information," Her father was being an ass. "And how was this bastard able to get on my property without anyone noticing?"

"Now just one minute you self-centered, son of a bitch." Cora stood up with her fists at her sides. "We're allowing you to be here because of Emily. She loves Keith, and we want her here too, but you need to shut your mouth. The only thing you're doing is upsetting your daughter and our family. If you want to stay with us and support your daughter than stay, but for once in your life keep that big mouth of yours closed. This is not the time or the place for this."

"That's my girl!" Nanny Betty nodded with pride.

The shocked expression on her father's face would have been comical if Emily wasn't so terrified. She couldn't remember ever being so scared in her life. She closed her eyes, and for the second time that day, she prayed. God had to be listening. Keith was a good man, and he shouldn't have to be fighting for his life. He spent his entire life watching out for other people. He was selfless, kind and the most wonderful person she'd ever known.

Watch over him.

Emily ran through the events of the night in her head. The lights had gone out before the popping started. She knew now that it was gunshots but how could someone just shoot blindly.

"How did he shoot when it was completely dark?" Emily whispered mostly to herself.

"What do you mean?" Ian hadn't missed her question.

"Remember, the lights went out, and it was pitch black, I thought the popping was fireworks." Emily glanced at Ian.

"He could have had night vision goggles, or he could've just been shooting randomly. Bastard probably didn't care who he shot." Kurt's voice was gruff but cracked at the end of his statement.

"You know everyone is saying he. With everything that has gone on over the last few years, we are aware women can be crazy too." Marina said. "Is it possible this could be a woman?"

"Anything is possible." James sighed.

The only woman Emily could think of was Judy, but there was no way snooty Judy would hold a gun let alone shoot it. Besides, Emily had seen her just before the lights went out.

Thirty minutes later the doctor walked into the room. The look on his face made Emily's body go cold. He didn't look like he was about to give them good news.

"No," Emily whispered, and everything went black.

Chapter 24

Emily opened her eyes and scanned the room. She was in a hospital bed with her mother asleep in the chair next to her. What the hell happened to her? The last thing she remembered was the doctor coming into the room.

Keith.

"Keith. Oh, my God. Keith." Emily screamed and bolted up. The room started to spin, and she grabbed the rails that were on either side of the bed.

"Princess, I'm right here." Emily snapped her head towards the window.

Keith was sat in a chair, and he looked so incredible. The sun must have been shining in through the window because he had the most beautiful light glowing around him. He was dressed differently from his normal jeans and T-shirt, but the white suit looked amazing on him. He looked so happy and peaceful.

"Keith, you're here, and you're okay." Emily choked through the tears flowing down her cheeks.

"I'm perfectly fine, Princess." He stood and seemed to glide to her side, and his voice almost echoed.

"I thought the doctor was going to say you didn't make it." Emily reached out to him, but he didn't touch her.

"Emily, what's wrong. Who are you talking to?" Her mother grabbed her hand and was glancing around the room. It was as if she didn't see Keith.

What the fuck?

"I'm talking to Keith, Mom." Emily glanced at her mother.

"I'm sure he hears you, sweetheart." Her mother wiped a tear from her eye.

"Of course, he does, he's right next to me." Emily snapped. What was wrong with her mother?

"She can't see me, Princess." Keith smiled at her.

"What are you talking about? You're right in front of her." Emily shouted. They were pissing her off with all this foolishness. She had a massive headache, and the room started to spin again.

"I'm only here to say I love you and I'll always be watching over you." Keith touched her cheek. "I'll always be with you." The last of his words faded, and Keith turned so bright she had to shield her eyes. "Until we meet again, Princess." Then he was gone.

"What just happened?" Emily screamed. "Where did he go?" She was frantic.

"Emily, you need to calm down." Her mother's arms wrapped around her.

"Calm down? Are you crazy? He just disappeared." Emily pointed to the now empty spot where Keith had vanished. How was he just gone?

"Honey, he didn't disappear. He died. He's with God now." Her mother cupped Emily's face in her hands.

"Died?" Emily said the word, but she wasn't sure if she understood what was coming out of her mouth.

"He didn't make it through the surgery. Remember the doctor came in to tell everyone and you fainted. You hit your head pretty hard, and you've been out for a few hours." Was she really hearing this? "I'm so sorry, baby. You finally meet the love of your life, and now he's gone."

"No…. no…. no…. he can't be gone." Emily didn't recognize her own voice as she shrieked his name. "Keith…. No…. Keith."

"Emily," Her mother shook her. "Honey, please open your eyes."

She didn't want to open her eyes ever again. Keith was dead, and her life was over. She couldn't live without him, and she didn't want to. She wanted to die with him.

"Emily, for the love of God wake up. You're dreaming." Her mother shouted, and Emily's eyes popped open.

She stared up at her mother and sister. They were bent over her with concern written all over their faces. She glanced around and even though she was in a hospital bed the room looked different. Instead of it being bright white she was surrounded by a curtain. There was no window and no chairs.

"Mom, what happened?" Emily gasped as she tried to calm her racing heart.

"When the doctor came in to tell us about Keith, you fainted and hit your head on one of the chairs." Her mother let out a huge breath. "I'm just relieved you are finally awake."

"It's true... Keith…. He's…" She wasn't dreaming, he actually was gone.

"Yes, it's true." Her mother smiled down at her. Why was the woman smiling? "Keith's in recovery, and he's going to be okay. He was a very lucky man."

"He's not…. dead." Emily hiccupped.

"No. Honey, is that what you were dreaming about?" Her mom took her hand and squeezed it.

Emily tried to catch her breath because she was still trembling from the nightmare. The dream had seemed so real, she could have sworn she felt him touch her cheek. His hand had been warm against her cheek right before he vanished.

"He's fine. He's going to have to be in the hospital for a few days, and he'll have to take it easy for a while, but the doctor said he'd make a full recovery." Elaine handed Emily a tissue.

"I need to see him." Emily sat up, but it was as if the room became a huge merry-go-round and she felt like she was going to be sick. "Why is the room spinning?"

"Because you thought it would be a good idea to crack your head on one of those hard hospital chairs." Sandy laughed. "Not a good idea."

Emily managed to focus her eyes at the foot of her bed. Sandy, Stephanie, and Marina were standing together. They were smiling which meant her dream really was just that. Not that she didn't believe her mother and sister, but these three women knew what it was like to love an O'Connor man.

"I think she broke the chair." Stephanie squeezed Emily's foot.

"At least her head will heal. The chair won't." Marina joked.

"You're all so sympathetic." Emily shook her head and then wished she hadn't when things started to spin again.

"I really should've been a nurse." Sandy laughed.

"Jesus, I'd pity the patient that got you as a nurse." Nick walked behind Marina and Stephanie and draped his arms over their shoulders. "That was a great swan dive you did, Emily. I need you to show me how to do that sometime."

"Thanks a lot, Nick." Emily rolled her eyes, and the motion actually hurt her head. Now that she noticed, it hurt like hell. She reached up and winced when her hand touched the huge goose egg on her forehead.

"That looks painful." Marina cringed.

"Yeah, just a little bit." Emily sighed.

"Keith's awake and not really happy we let you hit the deck." Nick chuckled. "He wants to see you. No, let me rephrase that. He wants to see you right fucking now, but that, of course, is in between him coming in and out of consciousness. It's pretty amusing to watch. He wakes up and starts flipping out and before he gets too riled up he passes out again." Nick laughed. "A.J.'s recording his rants."

"You know if A.J. puts that on Facebook, Keith will kill him, right?" Stephanie giggled.

"Hey, that's on A.J." Nick held up his hands.

"Yeah, more women for you if Keith kills A.J. right?" Emily couldn't help it. She had to get a dig in.

"Hey, I never thought about that, but that's a good plan." Nick winked. "I'm glad you're okay, Emily. I'll let Keith know." With that, he rushed out of the room.

"I really want to see him." Emily sighed, but she didn't want the room spinning again.

"Hang on," Stephanie hurried out of the room and returned a few minutes later. "The hospital will probably have a fit but who cares. Here you go."

Stephanie handed Emily a phone, and when she looked at the screen, A.J. was grinning. He put his finger to his lips and moved around the room.

"He's waking up again," A.J. whispered.

"A.J. what the fuck are you doing?" Keith's voice was hoarse but her eyes filled with tears just hearing it. It was heaven to hear him.

"Looking at a gorgeous lady." A.J. winked and turned the phone so she could see Keith.

The sight of him made her gasp, and she covered her mouth with her hand. He was shirtless and covered to the chest with a sheet, but her eyes immediately focused on the bandage covering his chest. She tried to stop them, but the tears started.

"Princess, don't cry. I'm all right." He reached out to the phone.

"I'll hold it, bro," A.J. said.

"I was so scared." Emily sobbed.

"I'm sorry. Are you okay? They said you hit your head." Keith's eyes started to flutter. He really was out of it.

"I'm fine. I've got a bump, but I'll be okay. Get some rest. I'll see you soon." Emily smiled.

"I…. love... you...Prin…." With that, his eyes closed.

"I love you too," Emily whispered.

"You hurry up and get better, beautiful." Aaron appeared on the screen again. "That big lug needs you to get his ass out of that bed."

"Thanks, A.J." Aaron really was a good guy and cared about his brother a lot even if he did tease him.

"No problem." The screen went black, and Emily handed the phone back to Stephanie.

"Thank you, Stephanie." Emily's eyes felt heavy too.

"Get some rest. He should be more alert in the morning." Marina gave her a quick hug. "I'm sure he'll wake up looking for you."

For the next few hours, Emily drifted in and out of sleep. Her head still hurt but not as bad, and she'd managed to sit up without the room spinning. She'd even walked to the bathroom with her sister behind her to make sure she didn't get dizzy and fall.

The next morning the doctor gave her the all clear, and she was dressed before he'd even had the papers signed to release her. Her father brought her straight to Keith's room. Mostly because she'd refused to go home until she'd seen him.

When Emily walked in, she rolled her eyes. Keith was grumbling about the green jello. When he saw her come in the room, he pushed the food tray to the side and held out his hand. She ran to his bedside and almost jumped onto the bed. She stopped short when she spotted the bandage.

"Are you sore?" Emily smoothed her hands around his face and through his hair. He needed a shave, but otherwise, he looked incredible.

"A little, but your touch is helping way more than what the doctors are giving me." Keith took her hand and kissed her palm. "My wife."

Emily had completely forgotten what had happened before he was rushed into surgery. She knew it wasn't a legal wedding but just the fact he called her his wife made her giddy. Being married to him would be the best thing in the world.

"That wasn't exactly legal." Emily sat next to him on the bed making sure not to jostle him.

"Legal or not, you said I do. That makes you my wife, in here." Keith pulled her hand over his heart. "I fucking love you."

"I thought I lost you." Emily couldn't stop the tears as they ran down her cheeks. She was so tired of crying, but even the thought of losing him had them making an appearance.

"You can't get rid of me that easy, Princess." Keith brushed his thumb against her cheek, and she closed her eyes.

"I'm really fed up with crying." Emily groaned.

"Once we get this bastard, I'll do my best to make sure the only tears you shed are happy ones." Keith pulled her towards him, but she hesitated.

"I don't want to hurt you." She gazed into his eyes.

"It hurts more not to feel your lips against mine," Keith whispered and cupped the back of her head. Emily leaned in and brushed her lips against his being really careful not to put her weight on him.

"I love you." She whispered as she pressed her lips against his again.

The kiss was slow and gentle as his lips moved against hers. His tongue traced the edge of her mouth, and she opened for him. She swirled her tongue against his in a slow, soft kiss. It wasn't like the heated kisses they'd shared before. It was sweet and filled with promises.

"I'm just gonna leave you two alone." Ian chuckled as he left the room.

"You're going to marry me for real, right?" Keith whispered in between kisses.

"Yes," Emily sighed.

"I know it wasn't really conventional and not very romantic, but I couldn't let them take me without you knowing I wanted to be married to you." Keith smoothed his hand across her cheek.

"Is it crazy? I mean it's so fast." Emily cupped her hand over his. They'd known each other less than three months. Was it even possible to feel this strongly about someone in that amount of time? It certainly felt real.

"If it's crazy then who gives a shit. I love you, and I know we're meant to be together." Keith gazed deep into her eyes.

Emily felt it too. Deep down to her core. Keith O'Connor was her one and only. Maybe all of this happened so they could be together but she could do without all the drama and terror.

She also finally knew what it was like to love someone so much it was hard to breathe without them. To want to spend every single day showing them how much they're loved. Her parents had that love, and Emily hoped she and Keith could have a life like her parents. Well with less drama.

Chapter 25

Five fucking days. That's how long it took them to release him from the hospital. It was going to be a while before he could get back to his usual activities but he'd be a hell of a lot more comfortable at home in his own bed. Especially, since Emily was there. He missed holding her in his arms at night and feeling her skin against his.

It was also pissing him off that nobody was giving him any information on the situation with Elliot Becker. Keith still had a hard time believing the man was the one behind everything or that the bastard shot him. For that alone, Keith wanted five minutes alone with the son of a bitch.

"Do you want something to drink?" Emily asked from the doorway of the living room.

"I want you to come over here and sit on my lap." Keith patted his thigh.

"You're not Santa, and I'm getting supper ready. Plus, the foreman is coming here in like five minutes. He said the shop should be ready by the end of the week." Emily had taken over the repairs to her salon. Keith didn't argue.

"That's great, Princess but you can take thirty seconds to come over here." Keith crooked his finger.

"Thirty seconds. No more." Emily pointed her finger at him and eased herself onto his left leg. The bullet had entered through his right side, so he was a little tender there. Emily had kept him at arm's length since he returned home and it was driving him crazy.

"When are you going to let me make love to you again?" Keith didn't like to complain, but he woke up the last two mornings with a hard on and the only thing Emily would do was jack him off or give him a blow job. Not that it wasn't great, but he was desperate to be inside her.

"When you can sit, and stand without cringing?" Emily gave him a quick peck on the lips.

"You're a hard woman," Keith grumbled.

"But you love me." Emily giggled and jumped to her feet.

"Damn right I do," Keith shouted as she left the room.

That was how it went for another couple of days. Stephanie had come by to help Keith with his mobility. He was having a little trouble lifting his right arm because the bullet had torn the muscle in his chest. It nicked his lung too which was why he'd had trouble breathing. The doctors repaired everything, but he needed therapy to get his muscles back to normal.

"You're doing great, Keith." Stephanie encouraged as he pushed the two-pound weight across the table.

"Is this really going to help?" Keith laughed.

"No, I just like making you do stupid things." Stephanie winked. "Yes, it will help. You have to start slow and build up."

Keith trusted Stephanie because she was the one who got John off his ass when he'd been hurt in the car accident. She was patient but tough and damn good at her job.

"Hey," Emily smiled from the doorway.

"Hey, Em." Stephanie was in the process of packing up her things. "He's doing awesome."

"That's great." Something in Emily's voice told him something was bothering her.

"What's up, Princess?" Keith asked.

"Nothing." Emily avoided looking at him which meant she was definitely keeping something from him. He didn't like it.

"Spill it." Keith stood up and stalked towards her.

"I don't want you to worry." Emily sighed.

"Tell me, Emily. No secrets, remember." He reminded her of her own words when he'd kept her salon repairs from her.

"I was just speaking with your uncle." Emily stopped.

"And," Keith motioned her to continue. Stephanie seemed to be holding her breath.

"Elliot Becker wasn't involved in any of this." Emily plopped down on the chair and sighed.

"How do you know that?" Stephanie asked before he could.

"They found his car at the bottom of the cliffs off Signal Hill. Your uncle said he's definitely been there well over a week. It looked like he was dead before he went over and to top it off Ken didn't kill himself. He was murdered." Emily pulled an envelope out of her pocket.

"Well, that's just an awful lot of fucking great news that doesn't help." Keith slapped his hand on the top of the table.

"Kurt said he's on the way to Sandy's because she's getting in touch with that guy doing the age progression photo." Emily touched his arm. "Maybe it will give us the answer we need."

"It better because we're out of suspects." Keith sat in the chair next to her.

"I'm so worried." Emily sighed.

"Princess, we'll get this guy." Keith hated to see her like this.

"Trust me, if anyone can do this, it's the O'Connors and Keith's guys." Stephanie smiled. "I'm going to head out, but I'll be back in a couple of days. Do those exercises twice a day, and when I come back, we'll add another one."

Stephanie hugged Emily and kissed his cheek. Keith waved to her as she drove off, but his only thought was on Emily. There was something else bothering her.

"There's something else, isn't there?" Keith confronted her as soon as he closed the front door.

"Mitchell called me a couple of days after you were shot and said he needed to talk to me. He was supposed to meet me at the hospital, but he never showed up. I've tried calling him, but his phone goes right to voicemail. I talked to his father, and he hasn't heard from him either. His dad sounded really worried. Judy and Tiffany are in New York shopping for Tiffany's wedding, so Alfred is dealing with Mitchell missing all by himself."

"Did you mention it to Uncle Kurt?" Keith couldn't see the connection, but he didn't know Mitchell. Emily did seem really concerned.

"Yes, he said he was going to send someone to Mitchell's house and meet with Alfred to file a missing person report." Emily rested her head on his shoulder.

"Uncle Kurt will let you know if he finds out anything." Keith wrapped his arm around her and pulled her from the chair into his lap. She rested her head on his shoulder.

"I know Mitchell and I had lost touch, but it's not like him to fall off the face of the earth. He's a really responsible guy." Emily wrapped her arms around his neck. "I've got a bad feeling."

"Don't jump the gun, Princess." Keith got those feelings as well, and it wasn't very often they were wrong. "Let's see what Uncle Kurt can find out first."

Emily's salon was completed, and she couldn't wait to reopen. Ada still wasn't quite ready to go back to work, but Keith made sure she was there to celebrate. Nothing had changed once all the women were together. They chatted and teased each other. Of course, they teased him mercilessly.

Sandy had gotten in touch with her friend, but he hadn't had a chance to work on the photo. He'd promised to get it done by the end of the week if not sooner.

The salon was the busiest he'd ever seen it since he met Emily. What made Keith sit up and take notice was when Tiffany's fiancé walked into the shop with a huge bouquet of flowers. He told her they were from the Palmer family. He'd been asked to drop them off to her because he was in Hopedale to talk to Isabelle about catering his and Tiffany's wedding.

It just seemed off somehow. Keith even went as far as to text Isabelle to ask her if she was indeed catering the wedding. He was a little relieved when she said yes, but something about it wasn't right.

Judy and her daughter had returned from New York, and the family had done a television appearance begging for information on Mitchell. Emily's friend was still missing, and Keith was pretty sure it was all connected to whoever was after Emily.

It's why he'd increased security at the Bradshaw's place and made sure Emily was always in his sights when they were away from the compound.

"I need to get a couple of things upstairs," Emily said when she finished with her last client.

"I don't know why you just don't pack what you have left up there." Keith chuckled because as far as he was concerned, Emily was staying with him for good.

"I might just do that but not tonight." Emily blew him a kiss and disappeared into the back.

Penny was the last of the girls to leave, and he locked the door behind her. Emily was still in her apartment, so he helped out by checking all the stations. Keith had noticed both Emily and Kim did it after every closing before her shop was damaged. He assumed it was to make sure all the hair appliances were off.

Keith slouched in the chair behind the reception desk and scrolled through his phone. It was quiet. Until someone started to pound on the front door. Keith jumped to his feet and ran to the door. Smash was there yelling through the door. Keith fumbled with the lock, and when he got it open, Smash ran inside and out to the back of the salon.

"What the fuck, Smash? What are you doing?" Keith hurried after him.

He found his friend in Emily's apartment at the window in her bedroom. The window led to the back alley behind the shop, but it was two stories up. When Keith saw what Smash pulled in through the window his blood ran cold.

"Where's Emily?" Keith shouted as he stuck his head out the window.

"I was checking the footage and went to the live feed. She was climbing down this, but she wasn't alone. Keith someone has her." Smash tossed the rope ladder on the floor of the bedroom.

"How the fuck did he get in here?" Keith pulled out his phone and called Emily's phone. He heard the chime come from the floor behind him.

"I don't know. The construction crew has been here for a while. Unless he found a way to sneak in with them here." Smash plowed his hands through his hair.

"Uncle Kurt, someone has Emily." Keith had picked up Emily's phone and called his uncle.

"What the fuck are you talking about?" Kurt snapped. "How the fuck did someone get by you?"

That was the same question Keith was asking himself. It was happening again. The only difference was if something happened to Emily it would kill him.

In a matter of minutes, Kurt had a team of guys going through Emily's apartment and behind her salon. Keith had heard his uncle screaming at them to make sure they don't miss a thing.

"How could you let this happen?" Keith closed his eyes when he heard Nelson's voice. Only because Keith had been asking himself the same thing.

"How was he supposed to know someone would be brazen enough to get her through the window?" That was Emily's mother surprisingly defending him.

"He's the best, and the best should be prepared for every situation," Nelson shouted.

"Mr. Bradshaw, I know you're pissed but not nearly as much as I am at myself." Keith walked around Emily's parents and punched the side of the building several times. He'd probably broken his hand, but the pain would be nothing compared to losing Emily. He'd kill the bastard that took her if he harmed one hair on her beautiful head.

"Find my daughter." Nelson grabbed his arm and turned Keith around.

"I won't rest until I find her and make sure the fucker pays for even daring to put his hands on her." Keith marched towards his jeep. He ignored his uncle and brothers calling out to him. He had one thing on his mind. Finding Emily.

Sandy was going to get that friend of hers on the phone, and if he had to put his property up for sale to pay the guy, he'd do it, Keith wanted the guy on that picture right away. It was the only thing that could give them something. Keith had a feeling, he knew exactly who the guy was, but he needed to be sure. He'd checked with Isabelle, and his number one suspect had left her restaurant. It gave him plenty of time to come back and snatch Emily.

The guy had been leering at Emily at the party, and when he brought the flowers, he'd stood a little too close to her. It had to be him. Mitchell was probably coming to tell Emily when he disappeared.

Stay strong, Princess. I'll find you.

Chapter 26

Emily lay curled up in the trunk of the car. The guy hadn't spoken a word, but his gun spoke enough for him. Why hadn't she screamed or ran? Keith was just below her. He would have heard her and come running. The guy had a gun that was why. Keith was still recovering from one gunshot, and she didn't want to be responsible for him getting shot again. He might not have been so lucky.

For the hundredth time, the car hit a huge bump, and she got jostled around. Emily cursed under her breath as she tried to get out of the zip ties the man had put on her wrists. She remembered videos online of how to get out of them, but she couldn't get herself into a position to do what she had to.

"Let me out of here you, asshole," Emily shouted, but she wasn't sure he could hear her.

When she ran into her apartment to grab a couple of her old stuffed toys for the cat she almost shit herself. The guy stepped in front of her and pointed the gun at her head. He was wearing a black ski mask and dark sunglasses making it impossible to tell who it was. The only thing he did was grunt and point to the window.

He held on to her as he climbed out onto the ladder and kept the gun pointed directly at her. He made her climb down above him, but he kept a tight grip on her leg. She had no idea what he'd done with the gun because he had to hold the ladder but she was afraid to look.

When they got to the bottom, he pointed to the trunk of a black car, and when she shook her head, he shoved her towards it. Emily looked at the barrel of the gun as she climbed into the trunk but not before he'd wrapped the zip ties around her wrists. He'd already had them looped so when he held it up to her he didn't lower the gun for a moment.

What was she supposed to do? She slipped her hands into the loop, and he yanked it tight. Painfully tight. When he closed the trunk, Emily breathed a sigh of relief. He didn't kill her. At least not yet.

Emily managed to get herself onto her back, but she still didn't have enough room to slam her hands against her legs. It was supposed to break the ties. She hoped for once the internet was right. As soon as she had a chance she was going to try. She'd looked for the trunk release, but that was a bust. He must have ripped it out.

The brakes squealed, and the car came to a stop. The engine shut off and she heard the car door open. Emily held her breath as she heard his feet crunch against the ground. It sounded like loose gravel. Where the hell was she? She was tempted to bring up her feet and kick him in the face as soon as he opened the trunk but he would probably have that gun, and she didn't want to die.

When the trunk opened, and she tried to lift her head to see where they were. He pushed her back and grabbed something behind her head. She relaxed when he pulled back but then he put something over her head, and she felt like she was going to suffocate.

He dragged her out of the trunk, and since he struggled with her, she knew he wasn't strong enough to lift her. That could be useful. When she had her footing, he gripped her arm and pulled her forward. Emily tripped a couple of times, once accidentally and twice on purpose to gauge his reaction. It wasn't a good one. He poked her in the head with the gun and grunted.

The next time she tripped was because he didn't warn her there was a step. This ass was going to get such a throat punch when she got the chance.

"You could've warned me to lift my feet, you dickhead," Emily grumbled as he pulled her up from the step.

Again, he poked her with the gun but harder. She really needed to control what she said. It bothered her that he still hadn't spoken because she was sure she recognized the cologne he was wearing. She couldn't remember the name of it, but it was familiar.

She heard the click of a lock and then the creak of a door opening. She was pushed inside, and then the door was closed. He grabbed her arm and tugged her forward again. The floor had carpet because it was soft as she walked across it.

"Are you going to speak? What do you want?" He grunted but chuckled a little too.

"Okay, I'm sure some girls like the caveman routine, but I'm not a fan," Emily complained.

Another door opened, and Emily made a step forward. This time he stopped her and stepped in front of her. He took her hands with one of his and pulled her foot forward. Emily felt the step and realized he was taking her down a flight of stairs.

"Seriously, can you just take this thing off my head, I'll go down the stairs myself." Emily hoped he was going to leave her alone so she could get the zip ties off. He didn't answer. Just kept helping her down the ten steps.

When they were at the bottom of the stairs, he walked her about fourteen steps and eased her down onto what seemed like a bed. *Fuck.* If this guy tried anything, gun or not, she'd fight like hell to get away.

He removed the bag from her head, and she blinked several times to adjust to the light. He still wore the mask, but she could see his eyes now. They looked familiar.

"Who are you?" He didn't say a word. He reached up and grabbed the top of the ski mask.

"Oh, my God." Emily gasped when she saw his face. "How can it be you?"

"Hi, Nora." He smiled, and for the first time since she met him, it appeared sadistic. "I knew I'd have you back in my life and soon we'll do everything we had planned before your brother-in-law ruined everything. They thought they'd hide you from me forever. I knew the second I saw you that they lied. Now, they will never keep us apart again."

"I'm not Nora, I'm Emily, and you're insane." Emily probably shouldn't have said the last part because his hand connected with her cheek with a stinging slap.

"Don't backtalk me." He growled. "I'm not going to put up with that. Just ask them."

Emily turned to where he pointed, and all the air whooshed out of her lungs. In the corner of the room were four people laying on the floor. They looked dead, and what was worse, she knew them.

Chapter 27

"Don't fucking yell at me," Sandy shouted probably because he kept screaming at her to hurry and get her friend on video conference. "I can't do anything if he doesn't answer."

"Kiddo, you must have some way to get him right away." Keith lowered his voice when baby Alexander made a little cry from the bassinet.

"All I can tell you is I text him then conference him. He usually…." Before she finished a man's face popped up on her screen.

"Sorry, it took so long to answer." The kid said. He looked no more than sixteen years old, but he worked for the R.C.M.P in Ontario.

"It's okay, Lyon. The guy has abducted someone, and we need this A.S.A.P." Sandy said.

"Look, kid. Have you got this done?" Keith didn't have time for introductions.

"I'm guessing this is your very mannerly boss." Lyon was clicking on keys as he spoke.

"Yes, Keith this is Lyon Tu." Sandy glared at Keith.

"I promise when you turn nineteen I'll buy you a drink but right now I need to know if you got the picture done." Keith pushed.

"You would be about four years late on that since I'm 23 but to answer your question, I've just emailed it to Sandy. Good luck." He disappeared from the screen, and Sandy brought up her email.

The picture seemed to take an eternity to open but when it finally did it was as if someone punched Keith in the gut.

"I was wrong." He growled. "How the fuck did I not see this?"

"You know who it is?" Sandy didn't seem to recognize the man on the screen.

"Yes, but he'd be the last person I'd suspect." Keith pulled out his phone.

"Who is it?" Sandy handed Keith the printout of the picture.

"Alfred fucking Palmer." Kurt's growl was deeper and more frightening then Keith had ever heard it.

Without a word, he disappeared from the doorway, and Keith ran after him. Kurt was in the car before Keith got to the bottom of the front steps and he'd barely jumped in the car when Kurt peeled out of Ian and Sandy's driveway.

"How do you know him?" Keith asked.

"I knew him in school, but he was older than us. He kind of disappeared after high school for a while and then about twenty-five years ago I ran into him in town. I never liked him, but I'd heard last year he had a stroke." Kurt took the turn onto the road out of Hopedale.

"He looks pretty good for someone who had a stroke." Keith held onto the bar over the door. Kurt didn't seem to be worried about the speed limit as he hit one-hundred and forty kilometers.

"I've heard things like that can make someone snap, but I never liked the fucker. He always looked down on your dad and me because fadder was a fisherman. The funny thing was we were more well off than he was."

"Where did the name Wooly come from?" Keith asked.

"Who knows? Do you know how to use that radio?" Kurt motioned to the radio on his dash.

"Yeah." Keith grabbed the hand mic from the dash.

"Get as many units out to the Palmers. I don't think he's there, but it's a start." Something told Keith that there was history between Alfred Palmer and his uncle, but right now the only thing Keith wanted was to find Emily.

Hang on we're coming for you, Em.

Chapter 28

Emily gasped at the four bodies. He'd killed his family. The man had completely lost his mind. She couldn't let him take her anywhere, but if she fought him, she'd probably be next.

"Now, Nora I need to go tie up some loose ends, and I'll be back. Don't worry, Honey. I'll be back by morning." He bent to kiss her, and she pulled back.

"Acting so innocent." He grabbed her face in his hand. "It's okay. I know what you like to do." Emily pressed her lips together as he forced his lips against her.

He pushed her back on the bed and turned. How she didn't throw up when his mouth touched her was a miracle, but she didn't have time for that shit. Emily listened for the car to start. She had to make sure he was gone before she got the hell out of there.

A few minutes later she heard the tires spin on the gravel and she jumped up off the bed. She lifted her bound hands over her head and brought them down across her hips. Nothing.

"Fuck," She glanced around the room and tried to keep from looking at the bodies. There had to be something to cut her free. There was nothing but a bed and a couple of bottles of water on the table. Oh, and the four bodies in the corner.

Again, she raised her arms over her head and after a quick prayer brought them down across her hips again with all the strength she had. The plastic snapped.

"Yes." Emily gasped with relief. Keith would be so proud of her.

The first thing she did was run up the steps and try the door at the top. It was locked which she expected, but it was worth a try. She ran back down and looked around the room for a window. Nothing.

As Emily made her way around the room knocking on the wall to see if there was something under the wood she heard a soft moan. Her head snapped to where the bodies were hunched over. She heard it again and sighed. They weren't dead.

Emily ran to where Mitchell was curled on his side. He groaned, and she helped him sit up. His face was black and blue, and his wrists were bound the same way hers had. The only difference, it was cut deep into his skin.

339

She didn't know how she was going to break Mitchell out of his binding, but she needed to check the others first. She crawled over to where Judy lay face down on the floor.

"They're all dead." Mitchell sounded like a frog.

Emily jumped up to grab one of the bottles of water. From the cracked lips and his voice, Mitchell probably hadn't had anything to drink in a while. She ran back to Mitchell and put the bottle to his mouth.

"Drink slow," Emily said. She didn't know if it was right or not but she didn't want him to choke. He sipped greedily every time she tipped the bottle.

"Emily, you need to get out of here." He lifted his hand to push the bottle away.

"I realize that but the door is locked, and I don't see any other way out." Emily scanned the room again.

"He's going to kill me." Mitchell seemed to be in shock. He was so calm.

"Why are you still alive?" Not that she wasn't relieved her friend hadn't been slaughtered by his father.

"He wants me to suffer." Mitchell winced as he tried to sit up straighter.

"Why?" Emily helped him prop up against the wall.

"He knows I'm gay." Mitchell scoffed.

He was quiet for a moment and glanced over where his mother, sister, and his sister's fiancé were laying. Dead. How she wasn't completely losing her mind at that moment, she had no idea.

"He killed mom first," Mitchell whispered. "Said she was keeping him from being with the one woman he wanted."

"Nora," Emily sighed.

"I don't know what happened to him. He had that stroke last year, and suddenly he's a crazy man. I didn't even know he knew your aunt. Hell, I didn't even know you had one." Mitchell pointed to the bottle of water and Emily helped him hold it to his lips.

"It's a long story but Aunt Nora died in a motorcycle accident, and your dad was driving it," Emily explained.

"Dad? Rode a motorcycle?" Mitchell looked as shocked as she was.

"Look, we need to get out of here. Do you even know where we are?" Emily put her arm around his shoulder and tried to help him stand.

"It's the old caretaker's house on the back of the estate. It's been abandoned for years. I think we're in the storage cellar." Mitchell pushed himself with her help to his feet.

"That means there are no windows." Emily groaned. She knew in the old houses around SummerBrook that the storage cellars were built to store food during the winter months and there was only one entrance. There were still a few of them standing around the town.

Mitchell staggered a little but managed to stay upright. That was progress. She helped him over to the bed, and he sat on the edge. She knelt in front of him and examined his wrists. She could probably break the zip ties, but it was probably going to hurt him and cut his wrists even more.

"I need to get these off. You wouldn't have a boy scout knife in your pocket, would you?" Emily gave him a weak smile.

"You know I was never a boy scout." Mitchell groaned when she tried to twist the plastic around to see if she could bite through. She was probably going to break a tooth, but she didn't have a choice. When she bent to put her teeth on the ties, he pulled away.

"What are you doing?" He asked.

"They need to come off, and I've got nothing to cut it with. I'm going to bite through it." Emily reached for his hands.

"Have you ever tried to bite through one of these things?" He asked.

"Sure, Mitchell. I tie myself up with them all the time just so I can bite through them." She didn't mean to be sarcastic, but she was frustrated.

"Fine but at least wipe off the blood." He sighed.

She grabbed the other bottle of water and prepared to pour it over his hands. It would probably sting like hell because it looked red and raw. She started to pour a little water over his wrists slowly. He winced. She didn't want to see her friend in pain, but it was the only way.

"I'm so sorry. I know this hurts but can you pull your hands apart as much as you can so I can get a good hold on the plastic." Emily held up his hands, and he pulled them apart as much as he could. Not that it helped, but at least she wasn't going to bite his wrist.

After several minutes and lots of unladylike words, she managed to nip through the ties. Mitchell took off his shirt, and she cleaned his wrists as much as they could. She ripped the shirt and tied it around his wrists.

"Now what?" He asked.

"We find a way out of here." Emily tried to sound confident, but she had no idea what to do next.

Keith, I need you.

Chapter 29

Keith had jumped out of Kurt's car before it stopped. He winced as he hit the ground running. This wasn't what the doctor meant by taking it easy. The house was already surrounded by police, but nobody had entered the house. Keith started to run for the entrance, but one of the officers stopped him.

"What the fuck? I need to get in there." Keith tried to sidestep, but his uncle bellowed at him.

"Sorry, that guy says he has the house rigged to explode." The officer said.

"Fuck, no." What if Emily was inside? Where the hell was his family?

"Keith, over here." He glanced behind to see a line of men a few feet back. He didn't doubt they'd be there because they were always there for each other. Keith hurried to where they were stood like some sort of amazing wall of strength. His brothers both blood and not.

"What do you want to do?" Nick handed him a Kevlar vest.

"They won't let us inside." Keith shrugged into the vest.

"Whatever you want, bro." James held out Keith's weapon.

"I don't believe she's in there." Mike scanned the treeline around them.

"This is a pretty big estate." Truck said.

"Maybe Sandy can get some sort of aerial view?" Ian was already calling her.

"Tell her to start from the outside and move inwards toward the house." Smash had his laptop on top of the car. "I'll do from the house out."

"Guys, thanks for being here." Keith was so full of emotion that he wasn't sure how he was keeping the tears back.

"You don't need to thank us, bro." Aaron held up his fist. "We always got your back."

"You were there for us, Keith." John grabbed Keith's shoulder. "Now it's our turn to be there for you."

"The Superintendent up there says Alf has been streaming live from the attic." Kurt jogged up to where Keith stood surrounded by everyone.

"Hey, I see something here." Smash waved for Keith to come closer.

"West corner of the property line?" Ian had the phone to his ear.

"Yeah," Smash confirmed.

"Is that a house?" James leaned in closer.

"It's about four kilometers that way." Smash pointed to his left.

Nobody said another word. They all ran to their trucks and headed in the direction of the little structure. Keith prayed it was where he'd find Emily and prayed harder that she wasn't hurt or worse.

Please, Grandda, keep her safe.

The paths to the place were rough, and they bounced over huge dips in the road. It was killing his ribs and chest, but he didn't give a fuck. He glanced at his uncle and Keith finally figured out where he got his teeth clenching. Kurt was about to crack off every one of his teeth.

"There it is." Kurt slammed on the brakes, and the rear of the car spun in a half circle.

"Jesus, Uncle Kurt." Keith held onto the dash to keep from sliding on top of his uncle.

"You, okay?" Kurt asked as they jumped out of his car.

"Yeah," Kurt took off in a run. "Emily, are you here?" He shouted.

"Keith, be careful," John yelled from behind him. "You don't know what's in there."

Keith continued to call Emily's name as he did a slow circle around the crumbling house. Kurt and his brothers were doing the same but she wasn't answering, and he had a knot in his gut. He couldn't be too late. He knew she was still alive. He felt it.

"We really should wait for the bomb squad to go in there first." James sighed but like everyone else he was slowly easing his way closer to the house.

If anything happened to any of these guys, Keith didn't know what he would do but like Aaron said. They were always there for each other. Keith was the first one to get to the door or doorway because there wasn't an actual door. He called out to Emily again, but he didn't hear anything.

Princess, where the fuck are you?

Chapter 30

So, they'd managed to accomplish almost nothing. Mitchell was free and for the most part okay. They were still stuck in a windowless room with a door that wouldn't open. Now what?

Emily was pretty sure she started to imagine things because she could have sworn she heard wheels spinning rocks around. At least that's what it sounded like. It was difficult to hear anything in the fucking dungeon she'd been shoved into.

"I don't want to be here when he gets back." Mitchell stood up. "There has to be a way to get that door opened. This place is so dilapidated we should be able to kick it down."

Emily knew he was just trying to come up with a solution but what was she a freaking ninja. If he wasn't in such bad shape, he probably could, but there was no way she had enough strength to kick down a door.

Emily shoved her hands into her pockets and stopped. She pulled out a handful of bobby pins. What good were they? She was about to shove them back in her pocket when Mitchell grabbed her hand.

"I can pick the lock." He snatched them out of her hand and slowly made his way up the steps to the door.

"Umm…. Where did you learn to pick locks?" She was actually a little surprised to hear he could do it.

"I figured it out when I used to sneak into the wine cellar." Mitchell was poking the pins around inside the lock of the door, but he didn't seem to be getting anywhere. She was about to tell him to forget it when she heard it.

Keith.

She listened harder and waited.

"Emily, if you're here answer me." It was faint, but it was him. It was Keith. He'd found her.

"Mitchell, did you hear that." Emily almost fell back over the stairs when she started to jump.

"Yeah." He stopped poking at the lock and pounded on the door. "We're in here."

"Keith, we're in here," Emily yelled over and over.

"They must be outside." Mitchell stopped banging on the door to listen.

"Emily, are you inside here." Keith's voice was closer.

"In here," Emily shouted, and her voice cracked.

Mitchell kicked the door a few times, and just as he was about to kick it again, she heard Keith on the other side of the door.

"Emily?" It was the best sound she'd ever heard.

"Keith." She pressed her hands against the door and yelled.

"Are you okay?" Keith shouted.

"I'm all right, but Mitchell should see a doctor." She was sobbing.

"There's a padlock on the door. Get as far back from the door as you can. I'm going to shoot the hinge." Keith shouted.

Emily and Mitchell hurried down the stairs and huddled in the corner furthest away from the staircase. She heard several pops before it stopped and the door swung open.

Emily ran to the bottom of the stairs and stopped. Mitchell was still against the wall. She turned to go back to him, but she was suddenly enveloped in two huge arms that felt like a piece of heaven.

"We fucking found you." Keith hugged her so tightly that she was sure he was going to break her ribs.

"I'm okay, but Mitchell isn't good." Emily pulled Keith to where her friend was now sat on the floor.

"Ian, we need you down here. Now."

Emily didn't turn when she heard several sets of boots stomping down over the steps. She was pulled back out of the way while Ian examined Mitchell. Keith kept his arms wrapped tightly around her, and she watched as James checked the others.

"They're all dead," James confirmed what Emily already knew.

"Is he okay?" Keith asked.

"He's pretty beat up. He could have internal injuries. We need to get a bus here." Ian ordered.

"He was okay for a while." Emily didn't understand how he could seem to be fine one minute and then not able to move the next.

"Adrenalin does amazing things, Princess." Keith turned her and guided her up the steps.

"He's going to okay, right?" Emily glanced back at Mitchell.

"He's in good hands now." Keith kept her against him as they ascended the stairs.

They walked outside. The rest of Keith's brothers and the guys that worked for him stood outside like a bunch of angels. She looked up and smiled at Keith. She didn't know where it came from, but there was a boom, and a huge ball of fire flew up into the air behind the trees.

"What the hell was that?" Emily screamed when Keith crouched down taking her with him.

"That would be the end of all this." Kurt was next to them down on one knee staring at the flames.

"What?" She glanced at Keith.

"I'll explain when we get you home." Keith stood up with her. "Let's just say. It's over."

Keith was helping Emily into the truck when Ian and James carried Mitchell out of the building. The ambulance had just pulled up, and the paramedics quickly took over. Emily didn't know what was going to happen to Mitchell now. He had no family now. He was alone. Emily turned into Keith when he slid in beside her, and she clung to him. Her body was trembling so hard she thought it would never stop.

"Why does this happen when all the crazy stuff is over?" She'd noticed it happened when her mother was found and now this.

"It's the adrenalin wearing off. Happens to everyone differently." Keith hugged her tightly into his side, and she closed her eyes. She was safe.

Chapter 31

He lay in the bed next to her and watched her sleep. She'd fallen asleep before they left the Palmer estate and didn't move the entire drive back to Hopedale. The only time she opened her eyes was when Ian lifted her out of the truck to carry her in the house. Neither James or Ian would allow Keith to lift her.

"The last thing you need is to hurt that wound," Ian whispered as he eased Emily down on the bed.

The two brothers were now drinking coffee in his kitchen, but he didn't want to leave Emily's side. He didn't know if he was going to be able to let her out of his sight after this.

He pulled the quilt over her and eased off the bed. As much as he didn't want to leave her side, he had to find out if that bastard Palmer had been in the house when it exploded. He deserved nothing but to go straight to hell.

James and Ian had been joined by Sandy. She was wrapped in Ian's arms, and James was on the phone with Marina. Keith grabbed a cup from the cupboard and poured himself a cup of coffee.

"Emily still sleeping?" Sandy whispered.

"Yeah, she crashed pretty bad." Keith plopped on the stool next to James.

"I'll be home as soon as I can. Give the boys a kiss." James said. "I love you too, Sweetheart."

"Marina checking on Emily?" Keith asked James.

"As well as everyone else." James shoved his phone into his pocket and stared at Keith.

"What?" He glanced between Ian and James.

"You went into the building without even knowing if it was rigged to blow. Keith, you know better than that." James was right.

"I couldn't help it. I just knew she was in there and that's all I could think about." Keith stared down into his cup. "My life wouldn't matter without her."

"We know the feeling, bro but it was a dangerous move," Ian said.

Keith's door opened, and Bull stomped in with Truck. The men looked like they'd been to hell and back. Sandy took on the duty of hostess as she made another pot of coffee.

"I'm assuming the rest are on the way here."

"Yeah, and we should beat the hell out of you for that shit you pulled back there," Bull growled.

"Oh, calm down, Chrome Dome," Sandy grumbled. "He knows it was a dumb thing, but you tell me you wouldn't do the same if it had been Kristy."

"Chrome Dome? Good one." Truck laughed.

"Fuck you, dick." Bull gave Truck a push, but he didn't comment on what Sandy had said. Keith knew his friend well, and if Kristy had been the one in Emily's place, Bull would have run through a burning wall of fire. Even if Kristy didn't know how Bull felt about her, Keith did.

"Seriously, Rusty what were you thinking?" Leave it to Truck to go back to that.

"It's over. Drop it." Kurt stood in the doorway, but Keith had no doubt the man was pissed.

As requested the subject of Keith's disregard for his own life was dropped. The new topic was that the body of Alfred was found in the house or at least pieces of him. They would have to verify it with DNA, but Kurt was pretty sure.

"All these years of being in the medical field and it still baffles me how the human mind can snap." Ian shook his head.

355

"Mitchell said he changed after the stroke." Everyone spun around at the sound of her voice.

"Did these assholes wake you?" Sandy was instantly at Emily's side giving her a hug.

"Maybe." Emily smiled. "I think it was probably waking up in bed and not remembering how I got there."

"You fell asleep in the truck." Keith wrapped her in his arms when she stepped beside him.

"Is there any word on Mitchell?" She looked like she was about to burst into tears.

"I'll see if I can find out." Ian stepped out of the kitchen with his phone to his ear. A few minutes later Ian returned with good news. Mitchell was going to be fine.

It had taken two weeks before Keith was able to keep himself from dropping into *Snippy Gals*. Emily had to threaten him with no sex to get him to stop showing up finally. He didn't think she'd really do it because Emily was insatiable but he wasn't taking any chances.

Keith was plopped down in his grandfather's chair enjoying the warmer weather. It wasn't take off his shirt warm, but it was T-shirt weather. His phone beeped, and a message popped up from Smash. It seemed Keith had a guest.

He stood up as he watched Mitchell hobble up the walkway. The man's father had really done a number on him. Mitchell had several broken ribs, and he was covered from head to toe with cuts and bruises. Keith could not believe that a father could do that to his only son.

"You're looking better." Keith met Mitchell at the bottom of the front step with his hand held out.

"I'm about ready for a marathon." Mitchell chuckled.

"I bet." Keith motioned to the front door, but Mitchell shook his head.

"I won't be staying long. I just wanted to drop by and thank you." Mitchell dropped his head. "And apologize."

"You have nothing to apologize for, bud." Keith didn't blame Mitchell for his father's behavior.

"That's what Emily said when I dropped by her salon to say goodbye." He shuffled from one foot to the other.

"Goodbye? You're leaving?"

"Yeah, I've got some friends in Montreal. I'm going to spend some time with them. Take some time off and get my head together. I'm having a lot of trouble with what happened." Mitchell's eyes filled with tears.

"I'm sure you do. Have you talked to anyone?" Keith knew better than anyone how talking things out could be difficult.

"My friend's partner is going to help me find a doctor when I get up there." Mitchell held out his hand.

"Keep in touch. I'm sure Emily doesn't want to lose contact again." Keith shook Mitchell's hand.

"Yeah, she's already threatened me." Mitchell laughed.

"Take care of yourself." Mitchell nodded as he walked away.

Keith wondered if the man would ever be the same. How someone got through things like that was beyond him? Family was supposed to support and love you. Not hurt and nearly kill you.

That Sunday his family gathered at Jack's Place. The pub his Aunt Alice owned. They were having a private gathering to celebrate Alexander's baptism and Emily's birthday. Keith had a huge surprise for everyone too, but before he sprung it on his family, he needed to be completely honest with them about what happened in Yellowknife.

It was still a miracle how he'd managed to keep it from most of them for so long. It was time they all knew, and then he could do what he'd been itching to do for weeks.

"Everyone, can I have your attention." Keith grabbed the microphone from the stage where his brothers were setting up the equipment for the band.

Everyone turned towards him, and he froze for a moment. Everyone in the place meant the world to him, especially the beautiful auburn haired beauty smiling at him.

"I've got a couple of things I want to say to everyone." Keith cleared his throat. "It's about me and how what happened to Sandy last year was connected to me."

Keith scanned the group of his loved ones as they gave him their full attention. Before he could continue his grandmother walked up next to him and motioned for him to bend down.

"Keithy, if dis is about dat sweet girl ya married and she was murdered by dat crazy sister of hers, we already know." Nanny Betty kissed his cheek and walked away.

Keith stared after her with his mouth hung open. Then he narrowed his eyes and searched for Ian. His brother was the only one that would have opened his mouth, but when Keith located Ian at the bar, Ian was just as surprised the family knew.

"How do they know?" Ian asked him.

"I've got no idea." Keith glanced at Sandy. She was glancing around the room as if she hoped he didn't see her. "Sandy?"

"Yes?" She smiled at him sweetly.

"Did you tell my family about Tessa?" He asked.

"Yes, because it was stupid you didn't tell them so I had a few drinks with the girls one night and I might have let it slip. Nan was there, and well that was the end of that secret." Sandy lifted the baby into Keith's arms and walked away.

"I feel really sorry for you, bro." Keith shook his head. "I'm glad you married her, but you would be the only one to have patience with her."

"Don't I know it." Ian laughed.

Keith gazed down at the little bundle of white squirming in his arms. His godson was about to help him with the big surprise he had for Emily. Keith searched the room for her parents to let them know he was ready.

Keith had talked to them earlier that week and asked them for their blessing. Nelson hadn't seemed the least bit surprised by Keith's request. According to him, Cora had already prepared Emily's parents for the impending engagement. Of course, Cora knew Keith and Emily were going to be together before he'd even met the love of his life.

"Okay, so I guess that makes one more thing." He held up little Alexander so everyone could see his face. "This little man would like Emily to come take him."

Emily wearily walked towards Keith. What she didn't know was he'd put a box in Alexander's little hands. When he eased the baby into her arms, she narrowed her eyes at Keith.

"What are you up to?" She asked.

"Not me, Alex has a present for you." Keith pointed to the black box under his now sleeping nephew's little hands.

Emily carefully removed it from under the baby's hands and stared at the box. Sandy relieved her of the baby, and she opened the box. Inside was a folded piece of paper, and Keith watched her open it.

"Read it out loud," Marina shouted.

"To find your surprise you need to follow the clues." Emily gazed up at him and sighed. "What is all this?"

"You'd have to ask Alex, but I don't think he's going to tell you much." Keith chuckled. Emily rolled her eyes and continued to read.

"Go to the man that first loved you." Emily read. Keith hoped she knew that the answer was her father.

Emily stared at him for a moment and then looked around the room. She moved toward her father, and when she got next to him, her dad gave her another black box. She opened it to find another piece of paper. Keith chuckled when she groaned.

"Are you kidding me?" Emily glared back at him.

"Alex, what are you up to?" Keith looked down at the baby in Sandy's arms.

"Take six steps toward the bar." Emily read the piece of paper. "Turn to the person on your left and receive the next clue."

Keith laughed when she slapped the piece of paper against her father's hand and took the steps she was required to take. As he'd planned Kim was exactly where she should be holding another black box.

"You too? I thought you were my friend?" Emily snatched the box, and Kim laughed.

"You love me." Kim hugged her. "Happy Birthday."

"Go to the bar and receive your next clue from the bartender." Emily again glared at Keith with a cute little grin on her beautiful mouth. He'd planned for Bull to be behind the bar but his friend had to leave town again. So now Aaron was there with that sly grin on his face.

Emily moved to the bar and held out her hand. Aaron shook his head. Keith was about to go over and smack him in the back of the head. His brother was only supposed to give Emily the box.

"A.J.," Emily sighed as she wiggled her fingers.

"Sorry, this clue requires payment." Aaron turned his cheek and tapped his finger against it. Emily glanced back at Keith and giggled. Keith wasn't amused.

"If I must, but it's an awfully high price to pay." Emily leaned over the bar and gave Aaron a quick kiss on the cheek. He held out his hand with the little black box in the middle of it. Emily snatched it and turned towards Keith.

"How many more of these are there?" Emily opened the box and held up the folded piece of paper.

"Guess you'll have to keep going to find out." Keith raised an eyebrow and grinned.

"I'm not liking you very much right now." She unfolded the paper and glanced down at it.

"Walk to the front of the stage and close your eyes." Emily held up the paper. "If you hit me with a pie I will hurt you."

"That isn't going to happen," Keith assured her.

Emily walked slowly to the front of the stage and turned, so she was facing the crowd. She didn't close her eyes as she stared at him.

"Close your eyes, Princess." Keith reminded her.

Marina stepped behind her and put a blindfold over Emily's eyes. It had been her idea. She didn't believe Emily was going to keep her eyes closed long enough for them to pull things off.

"What are we doing? Playing pin the tail on the horse?" Emily laughed as Marina made sure Emily's eyes were fully covered.

When his sister-in-law nodded, everyone scattered to the job they'd been given. John and James brought out a huge birthday cake with Princess written on it in purple icing. Stephanie brought out a tiara and placed it on Emily's head. Emily squeaked when she reached up and touched what was on her head.

The next thing was the huge black box that was brought out for him to climb into. It had taken an entire day driving all over the city to find one big enough for him to crouch down into. He and his brothers had finally gotten a bunch of big boxes and put them together in a way that looked like it was one big one. Kristy and Isabelle had wrapped it covering all the seams. Jess and Pam had managed to find a big ribbon to put on the cover.

The box was set up so when she lifted off the cover the sides fell open, and he would be inside on his knee holding the last black box. One that contained the engagement ring he'd picked out for her. A single tear drop diamond on a delicate gold band. He also had Burlap inside the box in her carrier. It took some major begging for his aunt Alice to allow him to bring Burlap into her pub.

Once Keith was situated and had Burlap in the crook of his arm, John, James Ian, and Mike closed up the sides while Nick placed the cover on top. Keith knelt in the box his heart pounding in his chest. He could hear everyone whispering around him, and he pressed talk on his phone. When Emily opened her eyes, she would see the cake and Jess would hand her a phone with his recording on it.

Grandda wish me luck.

Chapter 32

Emily waited for someone to give her the okay to remove the blindfold. She did like the little tiara that she'd got placed on her head. It had to be Keith's idea of a joke, but she liked it.

"Is he gone?" She heard Marina ask.

"Yes." That was Pam.

"What's going on? Who's gone?" Emily asked.

"Keith but don't worry," Jess assured her. "Now you can take off that blindfold.

Emily pushed the black mask off her eyes and blinked. It really did keep her in the dark. In front of her was a huge cake decorated in her favorite color. Again, it had to be Keith. Princess was scrawled across the cake. She looked to the right of where the cake sat on a table and gasped.

An enormous black box wrapped with a purple ribbon stood in the middle of the room. She was about go see what it was all about

365

when Jess put a phone in Emily's hand. Keith's beautiful smile was on the screen. She hit the play button and held it up.

"Happy Birthday Princess, I hope you're enjoying the hunt for your birthday present. You just have one last thing to open, and then you can have your present. I love you, and when you open that box, you can join me." Emily lifted her head and glanced at Jess.

"Where exactly will I be joining him?" Emily asked.

"I've got no idea. I was just told to give you that." Jess took the phone and stepped back.

"All of you are just mean." Emily slowly moved toward the scary looking box. It wasn't exactly scary, but it was huge, and she couldn't imagine what was inside the thing. "Where the hell am I supposed to start opening this thing?" She walked around it and couldn't see exactly where to start.

"Just lift off the cover." Aaron laughed.

When Emily glanced across the top of the box, she stuck her tongue out at Aaron. It only made him laugh more.

"I swear if something jumps out at me I'm going to kill someone." Emily grabbed the corner of the cover and lifted it. Nothing popped out, so she pushed the cover to the floor. The four sides of the box flopped to the ground, and she heard a small meow.

"Keith?" At first, she wasn't sure what he was doing, but he held out his hand, and she gasped.

"Happy Birthday, Princess." He was on one knee, and she knew exactly what was happening.

"Oh, my God." Emily squealed and covered her mouth with her hands. Burlap mewled again, and Keith chuckled.

"Do you know what she just said?" He asked. Emily couldn't speak and just shook her head. "She wanted me to ask you something." Emily was bouncing up and down as Keith placed Burlap in the carrier next to him.

"Sorry cat, Aunt Alice will kill me if I let you roam around." Keith closed the carrier and turned back to Emily.

"You're lucky I like you, or that cat wouldn't get close to this place," Alice shouted.

"Emily Mary Bradshaw, from the very second I saw you, I knew my life was about to change. You also nearly drove me out of my mind." He took her hand. "I never thought I could find a love like you ever or for it to happen so fast but it did, and the only thing that would make me happier is if you would agree to be my wife."

Keith dropped her hand and pulled the most beautiful ring she'd ever seen from the box. He took her hand again and gazed up into her eyes. His blue eyes sparkled, and she couldn't look away.

"Emily, will you marry me?"

She was nodding long before he'd even finished the question and as soon as he slipped the ring on her finger, she screamed yes. She wrapped her arms around his neck before he could get to his feet. They fell back onto the floor with her on top of him.

"Hey, that stuff has to wait until you go home," Nick shouted.

By the time, Keith had them back up on their feet, Emily was surrounded. She was hugged, kissed and was welcomed into the most amazing family she'd ever had the privilege to meet. She not only fell in love with Keith she'd fallen in love with the huge group and knew for the rest of her life that nothing would be boring.

Epilogue

It was the fourth of his brothers to tie the knot. This one had been quick, but Keith never looked happier, and Emily was glowing. Mike O'Connor grabbed a beer from the bar and twisted off the top. From the way things were going, he'd be the last of the brothers to settle down.

It was almost comical how his family thought he was playing the field. He hadn't had sex for six months and not because he couldn't. He had a couple of women that called him on a regular basis for booty calls. Mike was sick of the meaningless sex. He wanted someone to spend time with. In bed and out.

Maybe it was because he'd been watching his older brothers all settle down. They were all so sickeningly happy. Not that he wasn't glad for them, but it was getting more difficult for him to be around them. Especially, when they'd start on him about how he had to stop running around.

"Bro, we're a dying breed." Aaron nudged him.

"Hey, with the way this is going Mikey here is the next to sail off into the sunset." Nick laughed.

"Maybe I'll just be the cool single bachelor that your women call and complain to." Mike laughed. That was certainly not what he wanted.

"Bachelor maybe but definitely not cool." Isabelle poked him in the chest.

"That's right I'm the cool one." John draped his arm around Isabelle's shoulder.

"Dream on. Your cool factor dropped after you took the plunge, bro." Nick teased.

"Yeah but his sexiness skyrocketed." Stephanie tucked herself under John's arm and kissed his cheek. She and John had found out they were about to have another baby and they were both over the moon.

"Please, don't use sexy in the same sentence with my cousin." Kristy gagged.

Mike was starting to feel like he was smothering as everyone circled around the bar. He stepped back and let out a breath.

"Hey, are you okay?" Stephanie touched his arm.

"Just been busy at work." Mike forced a smile.

"That makes what I'm about to ask really bad." Stephanie pointed to the door leading to the patio.

"What is it?" Mike didn't care how busy he was. When it came to family, he'd be there. Just like they always were for each other.

"John, I need to talk to Mike about that situation." Stephanie kissed John's cheek and linked her arm into Mike's elbow.

It was a beautiful night even though it was a little chilly for the end of August. Mike walked with Stephanie to one of the patio tables outside the country club. They sat down, and Stephanie smiled.

"I've got a friend who may need some advice on a situation." Stephanie folded her hands in front of her.

"Do I know this friend?" Mike asked.

"I don't think so. She's actually the grand-daughter of one of my clients." Stephanie explained. "She's trying to get custody of her friend's daughter."

"It's hard to get a judge to take a child away from their parents unless there's something dangerous." Mike had seen enough of it to know.

"Her friend was the girl murdered last month," Stephanie explained.

"Did her friend have a will or anything to give her custody?" This was a different situation altogether, and chances were child welfare would be the ones to deal with any arrangements for the child.

"No, but she always told Belinda that if anything happened to her, the little girl needed to be kept safe." Stephanie sighed.

"Then Belinda and her husband need to tell child welfare that," Mike said.

"See that's one of the problems. Belinda isn't married."

"That could make things harder."

"But the little girl is deaf, and Belinda knows sign language. She's also a social worker herself." Stephanie sighed. "She's desperate."

"If she's a social worker than she should know how this works," Mike said.

"She does, but John tells me you know sign language too."

"What difference does that make?" Mike didn't know how him being able to sign could help her friend's situation.

"Belinda don't need a lawyer for herself. She needs one for the child." Stephanie took his hands. "They want to place the little girl with the man Belinda thinks killed her friend and the little girl is terrified of him."

"Well, that really changes things." Mike sighed. "I'll see what I can do. Text me her information."

About the Author

What does someone say to describe themselves? You could start with giving what others say about you. Scratch that. It doesn't really matter what others think about you. It matters what you think of yourself. So here we go.

First of all, I'm a wife and mother. I'm also a grandmother. That alone would fulfil any woman's life and to be honest it does. But.....

I'm also a writer. Someone who loves to tell stories of love, suspense, heartache and of course happily ever after. For most of my life, I've written those stories for myself. A type of therapy, I suppose. I love the characters I create. They become part of who I am because there's part of me in them.

So.... Now that you know this about me. I hope when you read my books, you fall in love with them.

You should also know that I'm a Newfoundlander. What is that you ask? Well we're a proud people who live on an island, off the east coast of Canada. Some people believe Canada ends with Nova Scotia. It doesn't. If you keep going east, there is a beautiful island full of amazing people and magnificent scenery. That is where my stories are set because let's face it. The best stories always come from the places you know and love.

If there is anything else you would like to know about me. Ask me!

Coming Soon

O'CONNOR BROTHERS

Book 5

Available October 30, 2017

A friend's death and a brother's confession

He found love, but it could all be ripped away.

O'Connor Brother Series

Book 1, 2 & 3

Available on

Amazon and

Kindle Unlimited.

Also Available

Dangerous Therapy

Book 1

Officer John O'Connor is giving up on life after a terrible accident. His family are at their wits end when he refuses any kind of therapy. The only thing keeping him sane is his dreams of a beautiful woman he pulled in for a traffic violation months before.

Physical Therapist Stephanie Kelly is healing from a broken heart. When she is hired by Nightingale's personal care and physical therapy, she's ecstatic, but she's shocked when her boss asks her to take on a new patient. Shocked because the patient is her boss's nephew and he's not exactly keen on therapy. He's also the cop who's been heating up her dreams.

As Stephanie helps John get back on his feet, they grow closer, but someone is out to hurt Stephanie, or worse. After multiple attempts on her life, John's family tries to figure out who's after the woman he loves and stop them before it's too late.

Dangerous Abduction

Book 2

Widower James O'Connor has been fighting his growing attraction to his brother's sister-in-law for four long years, but when someone breaks into her home, destroying everything she owns, James takes her and her young son into his home. The break-in wasn't random. Marina and her son are in danger, and James swears to protect them, but can he keep them safe?

Marina Kelly dedicates her life to caring for her sweet little boy, Danny. Since she broke free from her abusive husband, she's sworn off men, but when James O'Connor keeps entering her thoughts and her dreams, it takes everything she has to keep her feelings hidden. Now, her sister and parents are out of the province, and she's in danger, Marina has no choice but to accept James's help and try to hide her attraction and growing feelings.

The attraction between them impossible to resist. Only her ex's family secret may tear it all apart. Can Marina and James unravel the family's hidden mystery without losing each other?

Dangerous Secrets

Book 3

Ian O'Connor has everything going for him. He's got the O'Connor drop dead good looks, an incredible body and to top it off he's a doctor. Why wouldn't anyone want the man but none of that was the reason Sandy Churchill was head over heels in love with the man. After he had stood her up for their first official date, she was weary of taking another chance. When she ends up in the hospital because she turned her back on a criminal determined to get away from her, Ian admits that he loves her and wants another chance. A secret from his past throws Sandy into a tailspin, but she has a secret that she's hiding from everyone.

Ian's on cloud nine when he finally takes a leap of faith and tells the woman he's loved for four years how he feels and wants a chance to make up for his screw up. They have two weeks of bliss, but a murder and secrets come back to haunt him. Sandy's reaction tells him there's another reason why she's avoiding him. She's hiding something, but he has no idea what and to make matters worse there's danger coming from her past that could hurt the people he loves the most.

Rhonda Brewer

Keep up to date on all things new.

Follow me on

Facebook

Twitter

Instagram

Sign up for my newsletter and never miss another release!

http://www.rhondabrewerauthor.com/talk-to-me

www.ingramcontent.com/pod-product-compliance
Lightning Source LLC
Chambersburg PA
CBHW060145260626
47160CB00001B/135